never happen to you

true crime junkies

book three

Christy Barritt

chapter
one

HEIDI BILLINGSWORTH STOOD BAREFOOT in the kitchen and stared out the window at the melting tundra surrounding her. Her back ached from where the leather belt had slapped against her as punishment for her disobedience.

She should be used to being disciplined by now.

She tried not to make him mad. To do as he said.

But it seemed as if every day she failed to meet her captor's expectations.

She pressed her cheek against the cool pane of glass, wishing she could turn back time.

If so, she would have made different decisions.

Decisions that would mean she wasn't here right now.

It had to be May. That was when the snow in Alaska began to thaw.

But the melting precipitation wouldn't change the nothingness stretching as far as the eye could see. A lake dipped on one side of the house and a boreal forest on the other.

No roads. No neighbors. No stores.

No hope.

She swallowed hard and ran her finger across the ice-cold glass in front of her. The moisture trickling down the side seemed a reflection of her tears.

Only she didn't cry anymore.

Her tears had dried up a couple of weeks ago. Now, only fear remained.

Once, she'd tried to run. The opportunity had arisen after Master—that's what he demanded she call him, short for Master of the House—had left for work. His snow machine sliced through a narrow path leading away from the house.

The house doors had been unlocked. He didn't keep her wrists or ankles bound—she couldn't cook and clean for him if he did that. Only at night when she crawled into the twin bed beside his did he cuff her hand to the bed.

Lucy and Ricky beds. That was how she thought of them. On a table between the beds was an old picture of an elderly woman.

Heidi had asked Master about it once. He'd said the woman was his grandmother, the greatest woman he'd ever known.

Master insisted Heidi wear the dresses he'd laid out for her. That she keep his home spotless. Prepare meals to his exact specifications. That she don a frilly white apron when in the kitchen.

And for some reason he called her Anna. She didn't know why. She didn't dare ask.

His whole house was a throwback to the fifties. Everything looked mid-century and well-preserved. Master even listened to music from the fifties on a record player he'd set up in the corner. Patsy Kline. The Flamingos. The Drifters.

Then there was the picture he'd taken of himself with Heidi—a portrait that looked as if it had been arranged in a professional studio with a dark brown background and a vignette around the edges.

He'd placed the photo over the fireplace mantel.

It looked straight from times past with its vintage filter.

The two of them smiled beside each other as if they were a couple.

He'd set up a camera and posed the photo himself.

To the average observer, it might look like this was their home.

But it wasn't.

Despite the snow outside, Heidi had decided one day that leaving was better than staying and living out some kind of sick fantasy with this psycho who wanted her to rub his feet every night.

Quite the change from her old life, one where she'd wanted for nothing. She ran a travel website just for fun, as a way of passing time.

She'd considered it one of the advantages to marrying into money.

One of the only advantages, for that matter.

That day, she'd started on the snow machine path. Then she'd heard him coming, zipping through the snow toward her.

She'd detoured through the spruce-tree-dotted forest instead.

She'd seen no other signs of life besides him since she'd been taken.

But if he was coming, that meant she didn't have much time.

Thirty minutes into her escape, she realized she truly was in the middle of nowhere.

By that point, she'd lost her sense of direction. Had been unsure which way to run in order to eventually find safety.

Then the biting cold began to nibble at her.

She'd been barefoot when she left.

She was always barefoot.

She had no idea where the shoes she'd been wearing when he'd abducted her were. Master kept his closet locked, so she couldn't take his.

All on purpose.

Maybe just for this very reason.

The man's intelligent green eyes showed he was smart and calculated. There weren't many things he hadn't thought through.

Almost as if he were an expert at mind games.

Heidi had forced herself to keep moving through the forest. Convinced herself that anything was better than going back to that house—that prison. Not that she knew which direction would lead her back, even if she chose to go.

But as night had fallen and her feet had gone numb, she'd sunk to the ground against a spruce tree. Exhausted, she'd pulled her knees to her chest and fought despair—and the dropping temperatures.

Then footsteps had crunched in the snow behind her.

Heidi had known it was him.

Master had found her.

She didn't even have the energy to run from him.

Master hadn't said much.

As he'd paused by her, he wrapped a blanket around her shoulders and led her back to the house. The last fifteen minutes she was so weak he had to carry her.

Once they were back, he'd set her by the fireplace in the living room. He'd calmly told her if she ever tried that again, he'd set the dogs loose, and they wouldn't be as gentle as he was.

Then he'd disciplined her. That was what he called it.

He'd forced her to turn around.

Then he'd taken his belt off, and the lashing had begun.

Nothing he did seemed to be sexually motivated. No, it was like he wanted to relive those TV shows from the fifties.

Heidi remembered hearing once that men in the past had spanked their wives for disobeying them.

So that was what he did.

She was always fully clothed—thankfully.

But it hurt so much. The strikes were getting harder, coming more frequently.

Sometimes, she could hardly sit down afterward.

Something wasn't right with the man.

If only she'd seen it earlier. If only she'd run from him when he first approached her.

Heidi hadn't tried to run again after that one attempt to escape.

She needed a new plan. She couldn't be trapped here forever. Was anyone even looking for her? How would they find her out in this vast unknown?

She didn't know.

But she missed her old life. Missed her husband. Missed her coffee with praline syrup and a splash of cream. Missed her cat, Pipa.

Even though Braden, her husband, claimed to hate her cat, he would take care of the feline until Heidi returned. She was sure of it.

But would Heidi ever return?

She and Braden's relationship had been strained. Was he even looking for her? Maybe he was glad she was gone.

Problem solved.

A knot lodged in her throat.

If she got out of here, it would only be by her own doing.

That meant she needed to somehow get her hands on Master's snow machine keys.

He gave her the freedom to roam the house.

He went to work almost every day, but he didn't have a set schedule for when he left or returned. She had no idea what he did for a living. She only knew he left the house wearing a snowsuit. But when he returned home, he smelled like oil.

Right now, he was in the shower. Heidi heard the water running through the pipes in the house.

It struck her that they were in the middle of nowhere, but he had running water and electricity.

Did that mean they weren't as far away from civilization as she thought? Or were there ways of getting water out to places like this? Maybe he had some kind of well water system.

She had no idea.

As she continued to stare out the window, despair clawed at her, threatening to claim her sensibilities.

How long could she live like this?

She glanced across the living room, and her gaze stopped on the desk in the corner.

She'd been eyeing it ever since she arrived, but she hadn't been brave enough to investigate.

Master had warned her to stay away. Told her the desk was off limits.

Yet he left it there, easy to access.

What was so special about it?

Heidi didn't know.

But maybe she should find out.

Maybe there was a gun in one of the drawers. Maybe she could force him to take her back to civilization. Or maybe there were keys to one of the snow machines, and she could use it to escape.

Then she remembered the dogs.

At least twelve of them were outside. They each had their own little house in a large pen where they were tethered at a six-foot radius.

Master had trained them to hunt. She'd watched one time as Master had let them loose and they'd gone after an arctic hare.

As soon as they'd reached the animal, they'd been vicious.

If Master gave them the command, the canines would be vicious with her as well. She flinched as she imagined their teeth digging into her flesh.

She loved dogs. Didn't want to think they would hurt her.

But with the wrong owner, they could.

That meant if she left again, she couldn't get caught. She needed a better plan.

Still hearing the water running, she paced to the desk.

Her lungs froze as she stared at it.

If she wanted to snoop, she needed to do it now.

After another moment of hesitation, she snapped from her fear.

She reached toward the left side of the desk and jerked open the top drawer.

The space held nothing except some paper clips, notepads, and other office supplies—nothing she needed.

The next one contained blank paper, probably for the printer. Again, not useful.

In the final one, the one at the bottom, rested a rectangular metal box.

Heidi stared at it, feeling like this could be exactly what she'd been searching for.

She sat in the desk chair and pulled the container into her lap.

After a moment of hesitation, she pressed the latch.

The top released.

What would she find inside?

A weapon? Money? Drugs?

She wasn't sure.

But this felt somehow significant.

With trembling hands, she nudged the top and stared inside.

A scream caught in her throat as the contents filled her gaze.

Hair.

Human hair.

Locks lined the inside, ponytails that had been severed and remained bundled in their ties.

At least five of them were stretched in rows inside the box—all different colors and hair types.

Did these belong to . . . women who'd been here before her?

Where were these women now?

Had they . . . died?

Heidi's head began to spin.

A footstep sounded behind her.

She sucked in a breath and twirled around.

Master stood there.

She hadn't even heard the water cut off.

He'd pulled on some high-waisted khakis and a white undershirt. His hair was still dripping, and moisture covered his face.

He glared at her, the look in his eyes pure evil.

"Please . . . I didn't mean to." Heidi quickly shut the box and stood.

Panic flooded through her. She should have been more on guard.

How could she not have heard him?

"I told you not to touch the desk." He stomped closer and jerked the container from her hands so quickly that the jagged metal corner sliced her skin.

Blood dripped from her arm.

But Master didn't notice—or care.

Instead, he glowered at her again, his hands clenched at his side.

She backed up and hit the desk.

There was nowhere else to go.

She was trapped.

She dragged her gaze up to his.

"What am I supposed to do with you now?" he

muttered with a shake of his head. "Such a shame. I'd hoped you would be different than the others."

Heidi went still as she tried not to picture what he might do next.

"I'm going to have to punish you for being a bad girl . . . again."

chapter
two

"I'M TELLING YOU, I looked the killer dead in the eye. You think it will never happen to you. But it can. And it might."

Charlotte Schmidt's words hung in the air, sending a chill through everyone sitting at the table around her.

Andi Slade and the rest of the Arctic Circle Murder Club had gathered to hear Charlotte's story.

Charlotte had been listening to their podcast when she heard what they were investigating. She'd contacted Mariella Boucher, their fearless leader, and the two of them had set up this interview.

Currently, they met in a conference room inside the Grayling Lodge in Fairbanks, Alaska. The team had met here last month and enjoyed the quirky hotel so much that they'd decided to come back.

The space was small but insulated. A murder board stood behind them and a round table occupied the center of the room. The table was filled with sound equipment. Lighting shone around them.

The scent of apple pie floated in from somewhere at the hotel, making the whole place feel homier than it really was.

Charlotte Schmidt claimed she'd almost been abducted off the Dalton Highway, and she'd come forward to talk to them on *The Round Table* podcast about her experience.

Andi observed the woman a moment.

Charlotte was probably close to thirty with dark hair that fell in ringlet curls halfway down her back. Her brown eyes were wide and her lips full.

With her shifting gaze and jerky movements, she appeared nervous.

But that was understandable considering the circumstances.

A serial killer had almost grabbed her.

Yes, serial killer.

No bodies had been discovered yet. But murder was the only explanation that made sense since so many women had disappeared.

"We really appreciate you coming here to meet with us." Andi's arms rested on the table, her hands laced in front of her.

She was the designated interviewer right now. When too many people asked questions, it was confusing for listeners. So she'd lead right now, and Mariella would add narration when they put the podcast episode together.

The other members of her team sat around her. To her left was Duke "GI Joe" McAllister, then Mariella "Barbie" Boucher, and her twin brother Matthew "Data" Boucher. To her right was Ranger "Outback" Garrett and then Simmy "Honey" Samuels.

Duke had officially been named her copilot. That was what Mariella had called him.

"I'm glad to be here." Charlotte rubbed her thumbs together as her hands rested on the table.

The woman was definitely nervous.

"You contacted us here on *The Round Table* podcast because you believe you were almost one of the Missing Women of Dalton Highway," Andi continued. "Could you tell us what happened?"

Charlotte nodded, still rubbing her thumbs together as if her memories were a physical stain she tried to erase. "Sometimes when I think about it, the whole experience seems surreal. But I'm also inclined to think it really was him, the same man who took those other women."

Andi stole a glance at Duke. She knew this wouldn't be easy for him to hear since his fiancée, Celeste, was one of those missing women. But he sat at rapt attention, listening to this woman's every word.

His barely there beard was clean and neat. His dark hair that had a touch of curl had been brushed away from his face. His broad shoulders appeared tight beneath his beige Henley.

"Why don't you just start at the beginning?" Andi said.

She felt like she was a lawyer again, cross-examining a witness in the courtroom. Sometimes, she missed those days. She reminded herself not to mourn over the past, however. Instead, she pushed away a rush of nerves.

She didn't want to mess this up. Not for her own sake, but for the entire team's.

"What were you doing on the Dalton Highway?" she pressed.

"I was hitchhiking." Charlotte frowned as soon as the words left her lips. "I know it doesn't sound wise. But at the time it seemed like an adventure. I had friends who'd done something similar, and they were all okay. I figured I would be fine too. Back then, I still thought most people out there were good."

Something about her statement caused Andi's heart to twist.

Nothing was sadder than losing the little optimism you had about the world around you. Andi had been there before. She knew what it was like. At one time, she'd thought she could conquer the world. Be a change maker.

Losing hope was a terrible thing.

"How long ago was this again?" Duke glanced at Charlotte, his head still lowered and his body tense.

"Two years." She touched the ends of her hair as if nervous.

Andi reached under the table and gently squeezed Duke's knee. It wasn't an intimate gesture. Instead, the motion was a reminder for him to keep his cool.

If what this woman was telling them was true, that

meant if she'd come forward to report what had happened two years ago then Duke's fiancée may not have vanished.

Andi knew Charlotte's story had to be a lot for Duke to stomach.

But getting upset right now would *not* help the situation.

Charlotte went on to explain that after finishing trade school, she'd flown from Anchorage to Fairbanks for one last adventure before going to work full time. The first half of the trip to the Arctic Ocean had gone seamlessly. She'd gotten rides to various campgrounds where she'd stayed overnight until she finally reached her destination.

"Then I started back home, and that was when things went south." Charlotte drew in a shaky breath. "A man in a red truck pulled over and offered me a ride."

Red truck? Andi stored that information away.

"This guy seemed pretty friendly, so I said yes," Charlotte said.

"Can you describe him for us?" Duke narrowed his eyes as he waited for her answer.

Charlotte released a long breath. "I hate to say it because it seems so cliché, but he was a little nondescript. He had light-brown hair and hazel eyes, I think. I didn't look closely enough to see if they were blue or green. Probably somewhere in between. He had a small double chin, a squarish face, and he was in his mid-thirties."

"Any accent?" Duke asked.

"Nothing distinguishable. He did have a thin scar than ran along his jaw right here." Charlotte drew her fingers across the left side of her face. "And he wore a shirt with the name Blackwater Contracting."

Blackwater Contracting? Andi had heard of them before.

They were one of the companies working the oil fields up in Prudhoe Bay.

She cleared her throat and continued. "So you got in the truck with him, and you took off going toward Fairbanks. What next?"

"It started off with some friendly chitchat. The man wasn't overly talkative, nor was he really quiet." Charlotte's eyes clouded as if she was getting to the hard part. "Then he asked me if I was traveling alone."

"What did you tell him?" Andi asked.

"I knew better than to say yes. So I told him I had some friends in the area I was meeting up with later. He started asking more questions that made me uneasy. I felt like he was trying to fish for information to see if anyone would miss me."

Charlotte paused and wiped away the moisture beneath her eyes.

As they gave her a moment to collect herself, Simmy—the nurturer of the group—murmured gentle reassurances.

Finally, Charlotte started again. "The truth is, there wasn't really anyone to miss me. I mean, I had a few friends, but they weren't the worrying, attached type. However, I didn't want *that guy* to know that. Even though I didn't tell him, I got a strange sense he knew anyway, like he could read me."

A shudder rippled through Andi.

The situation Charlotte had found herself in wasn't good. Andi wasn't going to judge her for being alone on that road and hitchhiking—all decisions Andi didn't think were wise. But Andi had made choices people didn't think were wise either.

She knew what it was like to be on that side of the firing squad. She tried to listen to Charlotte right now with an open mind, especially since this woman might have the answers they needed to track down the person who may have abducted at least seven women.

"What did you do when you realized you might not be safe?" Duke asked. "And how did you get away?"

"I knew there was a campground coming up in a few miles. I asked him to stop and let me out there." Tears brimmed in Charlotte's eyes, and she quickly wiped them away again. "He told me that was no place for a single woman to stay."

"Creepy . . ." Andi muttered with a shudder.

"I know. It sounded sinister, but I wondered if I was just being paranoid."

"You should always trust your gut in these situations," Ranger told her, a fatherly tone to his voice. The mountain man/survivalist had lots of wisdom hiding behind his gruff appearance.

Charlotte glanced at her hands, a forlorn look in her eyes. "You're right. But when you're in the situation, it's hard to remember that. Only once you're out does it become clear. Does that even make sense?"

"It makes perfect sense," Andi reassured her. "So . . . did this guy drop you off?"

Charlotte bent forward as if she carried an invisible weight. "No. He drove right past the campground without even slowing down. I was like, what are you doing? We're passing our stop. But he got weirdly quiet and didn't say anything, almost like he didn't hear me. He just kept driving."

"How did you get away?" Andi could only imagine the terror Charlotte must have felt.

"I knew I couldn't keep going anywhere with him or I'd probably end up dead. So I did the only thing I knew to do. I opened the door to his truck, threw myself onto the road, and rolled into the brush beside it."

Andi held her breath as she waited to hear what happened next. "And?"

More tears brimmed in Charlotte's eyes. "He slammed on the brakes and pulled over. I tried to get to my feet so I could run away before he could get to me. But I hurt all over. I knew I probably wouldn't be fast enough. But I had to try."

"And then?" Duke's full attention remained on Charlotte as the woman continued.

Before she could answer, a commotion sounded outside the room.

They paused from recording as the noise got louder and louder.

Andi glanced at Duke. They were both expecting the worst.

Maybe even expecting danger.

As if in response, the door suddenly burst open.

Andi braced herself for whoever was on the other side.

three

ANDI ROSE from her seat and rushed toward the door, the rest of the gang following behind her.

A man stood at the door and muttered apologies before darting away.

It was as if he'd fallen or been pushed into the door.

What was going on?

What she saw in the lobby of the hotel was nothing short of a circus.

A man walked through the hotel doors, a swarm of reporters following him.

"Who in the world is that?" Andi muttered.

Mariella appeared behind her, the scent of her flowery perfume floating toward Andi. "That would be Braden Billingsworth."

Andi cut a sharp glance at Mariella. "Heidi's husband? The newest missing woman?"

Mariella nodded, but she didn't exactly look happy

about something. "That's him. I didn't know he was staying here."

"This could be a good thing, right?" Andi asked. "Maybe we can interview him."

"I've tried to, and he wants nothing to do with us. In fact, he spoke of us in rather unflattering terms." Mariella pressed her lips together in a frown.

"Why would he do that?" Andi murmured. "It's not like we have any history with him."

"I have no idea. I told him that we would like to help. That that's our goal. But either he didn't believe me, or he doesn't have any faith in us." Mariella shrugged before sweeping her blonde hair away from her shoulders and into a knot at the back of her head. "Either way, he's not going to talk to us."

Andi watched the man again as he paused in the lobby to give a statement. Did that mean there was an update?

Everyone, including Charlotte, gathered in the doorway to listen.

The man turned toward the mob of media around him. "I'm sorry that you people have come all this way for nothing. We thought we had a lead, but we do not. My wife is still out there, and she's still missing. I implore anyone who has any answers to come forward. We've set up an account with a reward of $100,000 to anyone who can offer us information leading to finding Heidi."

Reporters started to ask him more questions, but Braden held up his hand. "No comment."

Then he wandered down the hallway, leaving the reporters on their own.

Strange, Andi couldn't help but muse.

Why all the sudden media attention?

The team around her seemed to echo her sentiments.

"The media hasn't given this case a lick of attention since it started over four years ago," Duke said. "I find it strange that they're focusing on it so much now."

"Maybe it has something to do with the reward," Mariella offered. "Maybe it has something to do with the fact that the Billingsworth family is worth millions."

"Maybe," Duke muttered.

As Andi watched the man disappear, she realized that there was something about the guy she didn't like.

What sense did that make?

Maybe none. She had no reason not to like him.

Mariella cleared her throat. "We should probably all get back to the interview. Sorry to interrupt you, Charlotte."

"It's no problem. But I don't have a ton of time."

No, she didn't. She had to fly back to Anchorage today.

As they headed back to the table, Andi's phone buzzed.

She glanced at the screen and saw she had a notification from her bank. According to the message, she had overdrawn her account.

How was that possible? She had all her savings in that account, and she was using it to pay her bills right now.

Her heart thrummed harder.

Someone was coming after her.

Had been in her apartment.

Had followed her.

Had tried to run her off the road even.

Was this just another tactic by this person to ruin her life?

There was a good chance that was the case.

But she didn't have time to look into this now.

She would finish this interview first.

They all took their seats again, and Matthew sat at the computer, monitoring the production of the interview. He continually ran his hand through his blond hair, leaving it spiky and messy on top.

After they were all settled, Andi started again. "So you were telling us that you jumped out of the truck where your potential abductor was, and you rolled on the ground on the side of the road. What happened then?"

"Then a semi-truck appeared on the road," Charlotte said. "The man heard it coming and paused. Looked at me. Looked back at the semi. The next moment, he ran back to his truck and sped away. That semi is the only reason I'm alive right now. I'm convinced of it."

"I'm glad that driver came along when he did," Andi said. "Did he pick you up?"

Charlotte nodded. "I was terrified to get in another truck with a stranger. I didn't want to flag him down. But I felt at that point like I had no choice. I knew I wouldn't survive out there on my own. My ankle hurt too badly."

"What next?" Andi asked.

"I asked the driver to take me to the next town, and he did. When I got there, I called a friend to pick me up. I was pretty shaken, but I knew I was lucky to be alive."

"Why didn't you call the police?" Duke shifted in his seat, but his gaze never left Charlotte.

Andi heard the tension simmering in his voice. She knew what he was probably thinking right now. If Charlotte had come forward earlier . . . it could have changed everything.

Celeste might still be in his life right now.

chapter
four

"I COULDN'T CALL the police because at one point, this guy's jacket shifted, and . . ." Charlotte paused and swallowed hard. "I thought for sure I saw a law enforcement badge there."

Andi's heart beat harder. "What?"

"What kind of law enforcement badge?" Duke rushed, some of his agitation disappearing in favor of curiosity.

Charlotte shook her head, shrugging as she did so. "I wish I knew. I couldn't see it very well. I figured if he was a cop, he was dirty. That's one more reason I didn't report what happened. Besides, even if I talked to one of this guy's colleagues, I had nothing concrete. The man didn't hurt me. I figured the cops would chastise me for being stupid and hitchhiking. I just wanted to forget the whole thing."

Andi let that thought settle a moment. If what Charlotte said was true, this guy could be a state trooper. A park ranger. A North Slope police officer.

"At that point, had you heard about the Missing Women of Dalton Highway?" Duke continued to push.

"I hadn't." Charlotte shrugged and gently fluffed her curls with her manicured fingers. "When I heard your podcast, it got me thinking about what happened. Then I heard another woman went missing. That's when I knew I needed to come forward."

"Is there anything else you can remember?" Ranger ran a hand over his beard, looking awfully Rasputin like. "Did you get a license plate number?"

"No. I remember trying to look at the plate, but it was covered in dirt or something. I couldn't tell what it was." She frowned apologetically. "I'm sorry. I wish I could have, especially now that I know another woman is missing."

A month ago, travel website editor Heidi Billingsworth had been taken. She'd set out alone to research and take some pictures of the highway for an upcoming feature, and she'd never been seen again.

Just as before, there were no answers. It was as if she'd vanished off the face of the earth.

And if someone wanted to vanish—or wanted to make someone else vanish—off the face of the earth, Alaska was a good place to do that.

"I know other women have gone missing since this happened to me." Charlotte's voice sounded soft as more tears filled her eyes. She looked at the camera in front of her and shook her head as if to make an earnest plea. "And I'm really sorry about that. I . . . I had no idea I could have helped prevent it."

Just in time, they finished talking to Charlotte and recording her interview.

She needed to get back home to Anchorage so she could work at the hair salon she helped manage. She'd promised to give her statement to the police and to see if the police might allow her to work with a sketch artist to make a composite of the man who'd picked her up.

Duke knew that doing a sketch wouldn't be Charlotte's call—it would be the PD's. But he hoped the cops saw the value in her doing so. He'd already put in a call to Logan Gibson, a state trooper in the area. Gibson was trying to arrange things with his colleagues down south.

As part of the agreement for Charlotte coming here to talk to them, the team had used money they'd made from podcast sponsorships to fly her up. She'd arrived in Fairbanks around lunchtime, and her flight back to Anchorage left at six, which meant she needed to catch the hotel shuttle to the airport soon.

Andi and Simmy walked with the woman toward the front door, gently patting her back while thanking her, and then said goodbye.

As Duke watched, his thoughts still brewed, unable to settle.

Why hadn't Charlotte come forward earlier?

Everything might be different if she'd made that phone call.

The agony of the past two years might have been erased.

If that badge had been real, wouldn't the man have mentioned his official job title? And if it had been fake . . . then he'd probably used it to trick women into trusting him.

Andi headed back toward him, studying his expression as she stepped closer. Duke knew exactly what she was thinking. The woman knew him well enough to sense his emotions over their talk with Charlotte.

He looked away, not willing to go there right now. It took all his energy to keep himself in check. In his experience, emotions only got in the way and made things more difficult.

Everyone filed back into the conference room, taking their seats.

They had a lot to discuss.

"So . . . what do you all think?" Mariella glanced around the table.

She was the youngest, perkiest, and most optimistic of the group. Doing this podcast had been her idea, and her social media savviness was the only reason their efforts had been as successful as they were.

So many complications existed for this whole situation.

Still, Duke had promised to give this venture a chance, so here he was.

Andi leaned back in her seat and crossed her arms. Even though she was petite, her ice-blue shirt and black leather jacket formed a formidable picture—especially when coupled with her white-blonde hair and the air of confidence around her.

Duke had been fascinated with her since the moment they met.

"The possible police badge thing shook me up," Andi said.

"Me too." Simmy rubbed her arms.

"Think about it, though." Mariella tapped her bubblegum-pink nails on the table. "A police officer could hide in plain sight. After all, state troopers travel that highway quite a bit."

"It doesn't even have to be a state trooper," Andi reminded them. "It could be a park ranger or even someone from one of the boroughs around here that have their own police force."

"True . . ." Mariella frowned. "It's something to think about. Any other thoughts?"

"I've got to be honest here." Andi crossed her arms. "I think Charlotte is still hiding something."

Duke's eyebrows shot up. He hadn't been expecting her to say that. "You do?"

He hadn't left with that feeling. But Andi, a former attorney, had good gut instincts.

Duke usually did too.

Had he been so distracted with the information Charlotte shared that he'd missed something?

The thought of losing some of his sharpness left him feeling uneasy.

It had been a year and a half since Duke had given up his job as an official investigator with the Army CID—Criminal Investigation Division—in order to become a tour guide. He'd only taken the new position because it gave him ample opportunities to travel up to the Arctic Circle and search for Celeste.

However, all his efforts may have been in vain.

There was a good possibility Celeste hadn't been abducted, but that she'd left on her own freewill and hidden from him.

Which still made no sense. If Celeste wanted to leave him, she could have. Duke wasn't the violent type. Sure, he would have been devastated and upset. He would have begged her to talk things out. He would have wanted an explanation.

But Duke couldn't conjure any reason why Celeste might stage her whole disappearance in order to get away from him.

Unless he was blind to his own biases.

That very possibility had haunted him for the past month.

Was there something so awful about him that Celeste had felt more comfortable arranging this whole disappearing ruse than she did talking to him?

Duke hadn't told anyone his thoughts. He couldn't.

Instead, the questions circled in his head, causing him to lose sleep and all peace of mind. To lose his edge. He'd even forgotten a couple of things on two of his tours lately, and he'd had to give partial refunds. First, he'd left all the snacks he normally provided back at the office. Then he'd forgotten to make reservations on the charter plane that would take the group up to Gates of the Arctic. They'd ended up leaving two hours late.

He didn't like to operate that way.

"Why do you feel like she's hiding something?" Simmy studied Andi.

Duke snapped back to the conversation.

Andi shrugged, that coolly collected look in her gaze. "I can't pinpoint it. I just feel like there's something more to her story, but I'm not sure what it could be."

"If what she said was true, then at least we have something to go on." Ranger's intense gaze met everyone's in the group. "We know what this guy might look like and what he drove."

"His truck sounds an awful lot like Bobby's." Duke's words cut through the air until everyone went silent.

Bobby Lad, also known as William Ladak, was the man who'd been corresponding with a woman who was using Celeste's image online. The woman very well could be Celeste. They didn't know.

Duke's heart thrummed in his ears as he waited to hear their reaction to his statement.

chapter
five

DUKE ALREADY KNEW Andi was thinking the same thing, even though she hadn't said anything yet. He'd seen the realization on her face as soon as that truck had been described.

"Wait . . . do you think Bobby could be the guy behind these disappearances?" Mariella stared at him, her bottom lip dropping open. "As far as we know, he's a professor and not a cop. And did he have a scar on his jaw?"

Duke shrugged. "I didn't notice a scar, but I wasn't looking for one either. But I've had a lot of time to think. I'm still just trying to put the pieces together, and the idea that Bobby might be involved is one of my theories. I didn't think it was valid until I heard the description of that truck, and it matched. Really, if you think about it, the description of the driver could also match—except for maybe the scar."

Bobby/William was a philosophy professor who'd worked in Fairbanks until he disappeared about a month ago.

Duke had wondered if maybe Bobby was keeping Celeste hostage.

But if that was the case, then who was the woman he'd seen driving away from the house? She'd been by herself. If Celeste was being held hostage, why would she have the freedom to come and go as she pleased?

So much about this entire situation didn't make any sense.

Duke glanced at Andi and wondered about her thoughts on the matter.

He'd thought of her often during the past weeks. A few times, he'd considered calling her or texting to see if she wanted to get together.

But he'd known that was a bad idea. He had feelings for her, feelings he shouldn't have when considering his fiancée was still out there. Until he had answers about Celeste, Duke had no business looking at anyone else, no matter how tempting the idea might be.

The best thing was to put as much space as possible between the two of them.

Duke had prayed fervently before coming to their meeting this weekend. Then he'd decided the safest—and smartest—thing to do was to leave the walls he'd expertly constructed around his heart in place.

When he was around Andi . . . he felt more human.

Happier than he'd been in the past couple of years. Like he had someone to confide in. A friend.

He hadn't realized how much he missed feeling connected.

But he had to put the kibosh on those thoughts before they got out of control.

"So let me get this straight." Andi shifted in her seat, eyeing him carefully. "Last time we spoke, you felt as if Celeste might have faked her disappearance to run off with this Bobby guy, correct?"

"Yes, and that's still the predominant theory in my mind." He shifted his thoughts back to the facts at hand.

Her gaze softened. "But in the meantime, you've also come up with a theory that maybe Bobby was holding Celeste captive and, when he discovered someone was onto what he was doing, he took her and fled, correct?"

Hearing the idea aloud made it sound crazy. He nodded anyway. "It's a theory."

"What about those messages I found that Celeste/Ella and Bobby/William exchanged?" Matthew pushed his glasses up as he waited for their answer.

Matthew had uncovered secret online profiles that showed Celeste and Bobby had been talking before she disappeared. The messages also indicated they had an ongoing romantic relationship.

"I thought about that as well," Duke admitted. "Those messages could still be true. Celeste could have thought she was meeting this Bobby guy only to have him abduct her."

"But if she was truly abducted, why would he take her to live in Fairbanks?" Mariella's expression tightened. "And to a neighborhood? You said you saw him leave for work one time, right? So he just left her at home by herself?"

"There *are* mind-control tactics that could be employed," Andi pointed out, her voice gentle. "It's not out of the question that someone could abduct another person and keep them in a home in the heart of the city, and they wouldn't try to escape on their own. I've seen stranger things."

Duke glanced at Andi, and she clamped her mouth shut.

He was the only one who knew Andi used to be an attorney. That she'd only come to Alaska to track down a former client who was responsible for the death of several innocent people. If she wasn't careful, she'd give away those details of her past.

Andi had encouraged Duke to tell everyone the truth about his past and his connection with Celeste. Yet she wasn't willing to reveal her most of her own background.

It was like the pot calling the kettle black, as the saying went.

Then again, Duke had a feeling that everyone in this group had secrets of their own.

He glanced around the table, waiting for someone to take the lead. They *did* have a lot to talk about. Now they needed to figure out exactly where to start.

They had the rest of the day today, all day Saturday and Sunday, and most of the day Monday. It was all the time they could take off from their jobs as they tried to get this crazy podcast off the ground.

The podcast itself wasn't crazy. The team was trying to do good. To help people.

But this group of armchair detectives might have gotten in over their heads.

Duke had his doubts from the beginning. He'd even tried to quit once. But he'd come back and promised to give it a chance.

He had a feeling this weekend would prove whether they were all cut out to do this or not.

Andi watched as Mariella shifted in her seat at the round table.

Their fearless leader had something else on her mind, didn't she? Something that made her nervous.

Andi waited for Mariella to speak, her anticipation growing with every second.

A moment later, Mariella cleared her throat and turned to address the group. "There are two more things I want to mention. The first is that with the disappearance of Heidi Billingsworth, this case is finally getting some media attention, as we saw when her husband came into the hotel followed by the media. Heidi's family is working hard to make sure people know she's missing, and they're spreading awareness. That's a good thing."

"How does that affect us?" Ranger narrowed his eyes, ever the analytical one. "You said earlier Braden Billingsworth had declined an interview with us."

Mariella sucked in a slow, hesitant breath. "That's true. He did refuse."

A knot formed between Simmy's eyes, and she crossed her arms, her oversized sweater pulled over her hands in a cozy fashion.

"Why would he refuse? I'd think he would want all the attention he could get."

"Apparently, this guy's father has plenty of money, and they're pouring resources into the case," Mariella explained. "He probably thinks he has all the bases covered."

"Why do I get the impression that you think that's a bad thing?" Ranger narrowed his eyes even more as he continued to study Mariella.

Andi thought she knew that answer.

It was because Mariella wanted to be the one to break this case.

Matthew probably already knew about this because he was quiet.

"It's not a bad thing," Mariella insisted, sounding overly sincere. "I just wanted you all to be aware of the circumstances. And the other thing . . . I'm sorry I didn't have time to run this past you all first, but it all came up rather suddenly, and I had to give an answer. Unfortunately, I didn't have the opportunity to consult with everyone."

Andi tried to push away her impatience, but the fact that Mariella was hemming and hawing only showed how nervous she was.

"What's going on, Mariella?" Ranger stared at her, the tight line of his lips showing he was growing impatient also.

She pushed a strand of blonde hair behind her ear and offered a tight smile. "We're all having dinner tonight with Alpine Grist."

"Who in the world is Alpine Grist?" Duke raised his shoulders and narrowed his eyes in confusion.

Mariella lifted her hand as if to slow everyone's thoughts. "Wait . . . I'm getting to that. Just a couple of days ago I was contacted by someone about a sponsorship —a *major* sponsorship—for our podcast. Like the kind of sponsorship where we wouldn't have to worry about money and we could all pretty much quit our jobs if that's what we wanted to do."

Andi continued to listen, intrigued as to where Mariella might be going with this.

"Alpine actually funded Charlotte to travel here. He paid for the flight and all the other expenses. He's agreed to cover the cost in our investigations. His financial support would take *a lot* of pressure off of us."

"Is that really what we want?" Duke narrowed his eyes skeptically. "If someone is *that* invested in us, then we're going to be in his pockets. He's going to be calling the shots."

Mariella wagged her head back and forth. "No, he's not going to do that. He's totally altruistic about this."

Andi wanted to believe that, but she knew talk could be cheap. People usually had some kind of motive, even if they didn't realize it themselves.

"I just looked this guy up." Ranger stared at his phone. "He was named as a suspect in a fraud investigation. He had his friends invest in a company he had no intention of getting off the ground."

"That's only one side of the story." Mariella shook her head, emotion flaming to life in her eyes. "Alpine had every intention of making a go of a new tech idea he had, but the idea fell through. He explained it all to me."

"I'm not sure if this guy is someone we can trust," Ranger continued.

Mariella glanced around the table again. "Can we all just go meet him for dinner? I meant to bring this up at the beginning, but I got distracted with Charlotte being here, and . . . I have to admit I was a little bit nervous. I figured you all might have some mixed feelings on it, and I didn't want a replay of what happened last month."

At their previous meeting, the team had nearly disbanded after an argument and some clashing personalities. But they'd pulled themselves back together and realized they were stronger together than apart.

"Who is this guy?" Andi's voice contained an edge of caution as her discernment kicked into high gear. "I've never heard of him. But it sounds like he has a lot of money—and maybe a lot of trouble."

"Alpine made his fortune in the tech world, but then he sold his business for mega bucks," Matthew explained, clearly knowledgeable about the subject. "However, he still gets royalties on some of his products."

Matthew sounded enamored with the man.

"He sounds an awful lot like Alfonso." Duke narrowed his eyes as if equally as skeptical.

Alfonso Dominic owned this hotel and had more money than he knew what to do with. It was the reason the place was so quirky and eccentric. The elaborate decor fit Alfonso to a T. The man liked wearing bowties, used a cane, and even had a monocle.

Alfonso had liked their team so much that he'd offered to let them use the hotel whenever they wanted as long as they didn't paint the establishment in a negative light.

Mariella waited for everyone's response.

Finally, Andi cleared her throat. "I'm willing to give it a shot. No harm can come from meeting this guy for dinner, right?"

She hoped she didn't regret those words.

"Right," Mariella said almost too quickly.

Slowly, the rest of the group agreed to meet also.

Mariella stood. "Perfect. Because it's time to go. Sorry there's no time to freshen up. The good news is that he's staying about twenty minutes from here."

"I'll drive." Duke let out a subtle sigh—as if he wasn't

entirely sure about this outing—before grabbing his car keys from his pocket. "We can all fit in my SUV."

They were all riding together . . .

Andi wasn't sure why disappointment pressed on her at the realization.

She supposed she'd been looking for a moment she and Duke could talk alone. She wanted to know the thoughts running through his head. How the past month of his life had gone. If he had any updates on Celeste.

Because Andi was sure Duke was still looking into his fiancée's disappearance.

But it appeared they'd have to save that conversation until later.

For now, they all grabbed their jackets and tugged them on. The high today was in the fifties, but as the sun continued to drop, so would the temperature—into the thirties.

They had a lot to do, and Andi wasn't sure this dinner meeting should be at the top of their list.

As they stepped into the lobby, Andi's gaze went to a man seated in a leather chair there. He held a newspaper as if he was reading an article . . . but she could have been certain he was watching them.

Her back muscles tightened.

Who was he?

At first glance, the man wasn't familiar.

And no one else seemed to notice the guy.

Was she being paranoid?

As if to answer her question, a woman stepped from

the bathroom just then and joined him. He kissed her cheek, and the two headed up the stairs.

Andi released her breath.

Maybe she *was* paranoid.

But considering the fact someone had recently hired a hitman to kill her, could anyone blame her for the reaction?

DUKE THOUGHT both this dinner and the potential business deal had terrible idea written all over them.

While money could solve a lot of problems, it could also create them. People with the most money often felt like they should have the most control. That was true in business, in marriage, in social circles.

Was that really what they wanted for this podcast? For someone to control them? Because that was *exactly* where this venture could lead.

Duke wasn't looking to make a profit off their podcast. These true crime investigations were something he did in his free time as a means of using his investigative skills and hopefully figuring out what happened to Celeste. Plus, he'd found some camaraderie within the group, which he could appreciate.

Mariella and Matthew made their income solely off social media. Duke was nearly certain Mariella still brought in cash from some of her old social media channels, where she used to be a superstar in the world of beauty influencing. She knew the ins and outs of the business better than anyone.

He understood why this might make sense to the twins, but for everyone else? He wasn't so sure. Especially if this Alpine guy had been accused of fraud.

That instantly made Duke want to keep him at arm's length.

They all climbed into Duke's SUV, Mariella sitting next to him and rattling off the directions.

They headed away from Fairbanks toward the outskirts of town. As they traveled, Duke glanced in the rearview mirror.

Although he hadn't spotted anyone behind them, he'd sensed someone following him recently. Not only that, but two weeks ago all four of his tires had been slashed. Another time, the office building he ran his tour company out of had been vandalized with graffiti.

He couldn't specifically pin anything on Bobby.

But Duke was keenly aware that danger could be closing in.

If he was in danger, those around him would be too.

He didn't like the thought of that.

They traveled a few miles beyond Fairbanks. Snow still piled on the edges of the road, the mounds dirty from passing vehicles. Duke looked forward toward the summer, when most of the snow was gone and green could emerge for a while.

The in-between seasons weren't the prettiest.

However, he wasn't looking forward to the mosquitoes, which would soon swarm this town come June and July.

Several minutes later, he pulled down a long gravel driveway and up to a large house located on a sparkling lake. It had a Tudor countryside look to it with its white walls and brown trim.

Since it was only six, it was still daylight and they'd get to enjoy the view.

"Nice place," Duke muttered as he stared out the windshield.

Mariella stared also. "Alpine doesn't live here. He's just renting the house while he's in town. He's not actually from Alaska."

"Where *is* he from?" Andi still sounded cautious, like she thought this meeting was a bad idea.

"LA, of course."

Of course . . . Duke thought, resisting an eye roll. Wasn't *everyone* of importance from LA?

He didn't really think that. But Mariella had a bit of a Malibu Barbie vibe at times. She was all about image, having a presence, and making a name for herself. Yet he'd seen that she was more than the superficial woman most people thought she was. She was smart and caring.

They were all so different, but he hoped they could use that fact to their benefit.

That was just one more reason to be cautious.

They climbed from his SUV, a vehicle dinged from all

his trips up the Dalton Highway. It looked out of place at such an extravagant estate.

Mariella took the lead and charged toward the front door.

Before she even rang the bell the door opened, and a man in his late twenties stood there.

The butler? That was Duke's first thought as he observed the man's crisp, tailored suit. His styled red hair, receding hairline, and predominant ears added to the man's formal appearance.

Then a grin split the guy's face, and he held out his arms in a welcoming manner. "Mariella Boucher. It is so good to finally meet you in person."

Mariella gave the man a hug, in a split-second transforming into her bubbly public personality. "It's *so* good to meet you too, Alpine."

So this was the man himself . . .

Duke hadn't expected Alpine to be so young. For someone his age to have such massive wealth was almost stunning. In the wrong hands, that kind of money could ruin someone.

Alpine turned to the rest of the group.

"Welcome, welcome." He clasped his hands together in front of him. "If it isn't the infamous armchair crimefighters! I love your podcast so much. Like, for real. I love it. I'm Alpine Grist, and it's my pleasure to welcome you to my humble, albeit temporary, home. Please, come inside. Dinner is ready, and I'm sure you all must be hungry."

A housekeeper assisted them as they placed their coats into a closet. Duke glanced behind the woman and saw two other men standing near exterior doors.

Security?

That was definitely the look they had.

Interesting . . .

Before Duke could observe the area, the group was ushered into a massive dining room overlooking the beautiful lake. The place smelled clean—like linen—but that scent was mixed with something savory and homey.

For a moment, Duke wondered if this was how royalty felt.

Nearly as soon as they were seated, king crab legs with ramekins full of herbed butter were served.

Now he *definitely* felt like royalty.

Although still cautious, the foodie side of Duke appreciated the meal.

Was food his Achille's heel?

As they started to eat, Alpine spoke from the head of the table. "I know we don't have much time, and I'm sure you're all wondering why I'd want to invest so heavily in a podcast that's so new. So I'll cut right to the chase. The truth is, I'm fascinated with true crime. I don't want to see the guilty walking free. You know what I mean?"

They all nodded.

But Duke's gaze went to the men standing guard in the distance.

There was more to this guy's story. He was certain of it.

Otherwise, why would he have two security guards with him?

"If I can do something to help the victims, then I'm all in favor." Alpine took a crab leg with both of his hands and gingerly broke it in half.

The sound of the leg cracking filled the room, and somehow seemed ominous—almost as if he delighted in tearing the sea creature apart.

"I know police departments are stretched to the max," Alpine continued. "It's not that officers are doing poor jobs. It's just that they don't have enough people and resources, especially here in Alaska. So when I heard your podcast, I was instantly interested."

"We're honored you noticed us," Mariella said as she gently pulled some meat from her crab leg using a seafood fork.

Kiss-up.

"I flew here this weekend just so I could meet you," Alpine continued. "If I'm going to be a part of this, I figured you'd want to get to know me and maybe ask me some questions. Then I'd love to chat about the terms and conditions for the agreement. But I really think that this," he pointed to each of them then back to himself, "could be a beautiful partnership."

Terms and conditions? Duke had never been a fan of fine print.

If a partnership was really what this ended up being, Duke would be shocked.

For now, he kept his assessment quiet. He should

reserve his judgment, but life experience reared its head right now.

"Do you have any questions for me?" Alpine glanced at each of them around the table. "People like to say that I'm the richest person they've never heard of." He let out a self-deprecating laugh. "But let's just say that Mark Zuckerberg and I are golf buddies."

"Do you work a regular job?" Ranger asked as he cracked another crab leg.

"I'm very fortunate in that I don't have to work so I can pick and choose the projects I want to focus on. I've started a couple of charities, which keep me busy. But I'm always looking for good causes to invest in. I think you guys are an *excellent* cause."

"What about the fraud case you're linked with?" Ranger continued.

Alpine's eyebrows flickered up in surprise. "You've done some research. Good for you. I'd expect nothing less. I assure you those charges won't stick. They have no proof —because I'm not guilty."

"What happened?" Ranger asked.

"I attempted a business venture into the world of Artificial Intelligence, but my idea didn't pan out. Investors knew there was a risk. Most of the people involved came to me, wanting to be a part of my project. I had enough money to experiment on my own, but they wanted a piece of the pie—thought they could get rich off it."

Duke supposed the man's explanation made sense . . .

"Are there any strings attached?" Duke's voice cut through the otherwise polite conversation.

Mariella gave him a warning glance, but he ignored it.

Someone had to ask the question. If not Duke, then he was certain Andi would step up to the plate. She'd be just as unapologetic as Duke.

Alpine nodded slowly, almost smugly. "Duke McAllister . . ."

Duke gave him a look. How did the man know his name? They didn't use their actual names on the podcast.

And they hadn't personally introduced themselves to Alpine when they came in.

As if reading his mind, Alpine said, "Sorry—Mariella gave me a rundown on who's in the group."

Duke gave Mariella a look this time. Some people in the group didn't want their real names leaked to the public.

"Wait . . . I'm just looking to enhance our resources so we can help more people." She shrugged as if apologetic.

"Anyway," Alpine continued, ignoring the tension around him—if he noticed at all. "That's an *excellent* question, Duke, and one I'm not offended by in the least. Because the truth is there *is* a string attached."

Duke straightened. He knew it!

He braced himself for what the man would say.

❄

Andi paused from eating the delicious crab legs so she could listen to what Alpine had to say. She was grateful Ranger and Duke had asked the hard questions. These were things they needed to know before jumping into something like this.

Alpine's gaze darkened. "The truth is that someone has been targeting me lately."

"What do you mean by *targeting you*?" Andi asked.

His expression remained placid, absent of its earlier liveliness. "I've been getting some death threats, mostly because of my opposition to the proposal for new oil fields in Alaska. The new drilling the government would like to do would endanger polar bears, along with other wildlife. It's going to eventually kill our planet. I've been vocal about my opposition, and I've made some people mad in the process."

That would explain the two guys working security here at the house.

"So you want us to look into who might be threatening you?" Duke clarified as he wiped his hands.

"It would certainly be nice if you could do that in your free time. I mean, the threats have been going on for a while now, and mostly they seem like a nuisance rather than something I should fear. But I'd still like to know who's behind them so I can know who to look out for."

"Okay . . ." Andi waited for him to say more.

"I may on *occasion* come across a case I ask you guys to look at as well." Alpine shrugged, dramatically inconspicuous as if to soften the reality of what he was actually asking. "I wouldn't force you to do so, of course. But I *would* like for your team to at least consider my suggestions."

The way Alpine worded his statement made it seem as if their involvement would be optional. But was that really the case?

Doubtful.

The guy seemed pretty laid-back. Was he hiding his true self? Was this an elaborate show to win their affection and get them to sign on?

Andi tended to err on the side of caution when it came to things like this.

Judging by the skeptical look in Duke's eyes, he felt the same way.

Before they could talk anymore, the main course was served. Pan-seared salmon, puréed carrots, fingerling potatoes, and some crispy onion strings.

Andi stared at her picturesque plate of food. She had a feeling the small serving would be five-star dining.

If anyone was able to buy their way into Duke's affections—though Andi knew he truly couldn't be bought—food like this was the way to go.

"Please, dig in." Alpine tucked his napkin into his shirt collar and then raised his fork and knife.

Andi cut a small bite of salmon, and the tender fish nearly melted in her mouth. The crispy skin fried on one side added a pleasant texture.

Whoever fixed this meal had done a fantastic job. Andi

was no food critic, but she knew and appreciated good food.

Maybe they could sign on with this guy to provide their meals and nothing else.

What were the chances?

Ha. She knew that answer: slim to none.

She glanced at Duke and saw the surprise flash across his face. He was also enjoying this meal—maybe despite himself since he clearly didn't want to be here.

Alpine continued to ask them questions about the podcast. About what kinds of cases they liked. About how they operated.

Halfway through dinner, the man's phone rang. He excused himself and paced across the room to answer. His voice grew urgent as the conversation drew on.

When the call ended, he turned back to them. "I know the timing of this is awful. But that was one of my charities. Unfortunately, I'm going to have to head back to California tonight. There's a matter I simply must deal with right away. You think you leave competent people in charge." He rolled his eyes. "Is there really such a thing as competent people? I have to ask myself that question entirely too much."

Everyone paused from eating and waited for further instructions.

He seemed to notice and said, "Please, enjoy yourselves. You don't need to leave because I am. Stella will take good care of you."

He gestured to his housekeeper who stood near the kitchen door.

Stella nodded at them and offered a polite smile.

Then Alpine reached into the inside pocket of his suitcoat and pulled out a folded paper. "This lays out the terms and conditions of my sponsorship. Look it over and get back with me. In the meantime, I promise to take care of any expenses you incur this weekend. No strings attached. Now, I'm sorry, but I really do need to go."

Everyone muttered goodbye as he hurried outside. Andi stood and walked toward the window at the back of the room as a new sound filled the air.

A helicopter pad stretched in the distance, a copter parked at the center. Its blades already swung through the air, though no one was inside. The pilot headed toward Alpine as if to escort him.

A moment later, Alpine called a few things to his security guards before stepping outside and rushing toward the chopper.

Right before he reached it, an explosion filled the air throwing both him and the pilot off their feet.

Debris rained over the patio. A window busted near the door. The air around them seemed to change.

Andi sucked in a breath.

What had just happened?

And was Alpine . . . dead?

chapter
seven

DUKE JUMPED to his feet and peered out the window before yelling, "Call 911!"

He pushed past Andi and charged outside, Ranger on his heels.

As soon as his feet hit the patio, a burst of heat from the explosion hit him.

Duke ignored it.

He reached the helipad and spotted someone on the ground.

Alpine.

The explosion had thrown him back several feet.

Duke rushed toward him, his gaze sweeping the man for injuries.

He saw nothing serious.

Meanwhile, Ranger rushed toward the pilot.

The man was talking—a good start.

The two security guards rushed toward them, radios to their mouths. Instead of helping Alpine, they began searching the area—no doubt looking for the culprit behind this.

Duke patted Alpine's cheek. "Alpine, can you hear me?"

A moment later, Alpine's eyes fluttered open.

He let out a moan and tried to sit up.

Duke encouraged him to stay still.

But it was too late.

Alpine spotted the flames, not yet extinguished behind them.

"What . . . happened?" He stared at the carnage of his helicopter.

Duke glanced over his shoulder at the burning aircraft. "That's a good question. Emergency responders are on their way."

The rest of the murder club surrounded them, each of them watching in horror.

"He did this." Alpine's voice hardened.

"Who?" Duke asked.

"The person who's been sending me written threats. And now this? He's escalating."

"I thought you said you weren't really intimidated by him?" Duke asked.

"I wasn't. It felt like the threats were idle. But there's no one else who would have done this. It wasn't an accident. I can feel it in my bones." Alpine's gaze latched onto Duke's. "This is why I need your help."

"Did the person behind this sign his or her name on the threats?" Duke asked.

"Of course not." Alpine lowered his head and closed his eyes, weariness suddenly consuming him. "The threats have been subtle. Anonymous. Smart even."

Duke's jaw hardened.

Was this really what he wanted to do with his time? Was helping this man a good idea? Doing so would take time away from the team's purpose.

They wanted to investigate and solve cold cases.

Yet they kept getting pulled in different directions.

Now Alpine wanted to be a part of their venture.

A man someone was trying to kill.

The group needed to think long and hard before they proceeded. They needed to consider the stakes.

What was more important? Their lives or finding answers?

Andi raised her eyebrows when she saw a familiar figure rush onto the patio, surrounded by EMTs and firefighters.

State Trooper Logan Gibson.

He always seemed to show up when they needed the police. They'd worked with him before—*worked* being a relative term. But Andi liked him.

He was in his thirties with an edginess about him that made Andi wonder if he drove a motorcycle in his after-work hours. Not only that, but when he'd taken off his jacket before, she'd noticed the extensive tattoos on his arms.

He had a bit of a rebellious vibe that made her curious about his life outside of work.

They didn't have the kind of relationship where she felt comfortable asking him those types of questions, however.

He'd been one of the officers Duke had worked with after Celeste went missing.

As the paramedics rushed past Andi toward Alpine and the pilot, Gibson spotted Andi.

An unreadable expression crossed his face.

Irritation? Humor?

May be a mix of both.

"I shouldn't be surprised," he muttered as he paused beside Andi.

"Long time, no see." Andi crossed her arms. "I'm beginning to think you're stalking us."

He raised his eyebrows, his forehead wrinkling before a slight smile feathered across his lips. "Rightfully so."

"So, really," Duke said as he and the rest of the group joined them. "Are you working in Fairbanks still?"

"It looks like I'm in this area for the foreseeable future. Maybe God wants us all to work together."

Andi heard the sarcasm in his voice.

"Wait . . . you may be onto something." Mariella nodded as if she considered that a real option.

Gibson didn't respond. "Quick side note. Since you're all here, I thought I should let you know that I've been assigned as lead investigator for the women who've gone missing along the Dalton Highway."

"What?" His statement caught Andi by surprise.

He nodded. "Now that there's more attention on it, the department has decided to put some resources into finding some answers."

"I'm glad it's been reopened," Duke's voice was absent of emotion.

But Andi knew the truth. He was keeping how he felt close to his vest, not wanting to give anything away.

"I thought you might be." Gibson glanced at the helicopter, clearly shifting his attention back to his real reason for being here. "What happened?"

The group filled him in on what they knew.

His expression grew tighter and tighter with each new detail.

When they finished, Gibson excused himself and walked toward Alpine.

He'd need to get the man's statement. To find out who his enemies were. To flesh out who exactly might have done this.

Andi had a few questions for Alpine herself.

She hated to say it, but they had such limited time. She'd been hesitant about even coming to this dinner at all, not when they had so much work to do. But now they'd probably be here at least an hour or two longer until the police could talk to each of them.

It wasn't necessarily more time wasted—the police needed to catch whoever had done this. But how would they ever solve the mystery of the Missing Women of Dalton Highway with these kinds of setbacks?

They couldn't afford to dillydally any longer.

As the paramedics began to wheel Alpine on the gurney toward an ambulance, Andi quickened her steps and called out to them. "Can I have a moment?"

They glanced at Alpine for his approval. When he nodded, they took several steps back.

Andi moved closer.

"What's going through your mind?" Alpine stared up at her from the gurney, some butterfly bandages lining his hairline and a bruise already forming around his left eye.

She decided to dive in. "If we're going to be working with you—and I haven't looked over that contract yet—there's something I need to know before we can even consider the agreement."

"You're a thinker. I like that. What's your question?"

"Do you have any idea who might be threatening you?"

His gaze met hers, and he nodded, not showing even a hint of hesitation. "I do. It's a man named Victor Goodman."

The blood drained from Andi's face.

Victor Goodman . . . the very man Andi had come to Alaska to find.

If what Alpine was saying was true, Victor would be on everyone's radar. Andi hadn't told the rest of the group about her connection with the man.

Victor was *her* project. Things could get too complicated if everyone else knew. The Murder Club would want to help—and they'd get in the way.

She'd be a fool not to consider these things.

"Why would Victor want you dead?" Her voice trembled as she asked the question, and she chastised herself. The last thing she wanted was to give anything away.

"Because he's heading up a new oil field proposal he's calling Prometheus."

A wave of dizziness washed over Andi.

Prometheus?

She and Duke had followed Victor one night and observed a meeting he attended. That word had been written on a board, but she'd had no idea what it meant.

Now, it appeared she had a better idea.

A new oil field project.

She didn't like the implications swirling in her mind.

chapter
eight

AN HOUR LATER, the team headed back to the hotel.

As Duke drove, the group discussed the evening's events. First, meeting Alpine. Then dinner—and how tasty it was. Then the explosion.

After they'd gone through all those details, they moved on to Alpine's offer and debated both sides of it.

Duke glanced at Andi in the rearview mirror, wondering what she was thinking.

He'd seen her talking to Alpine. When she'd returned to the group, she was noticeably paler and more shaken.

What exactly had that man told her? What had caused that reaction?

Duke didn't dare ask in front of everyone. Whatever their conversation had involved, the subject matter very well could be private. Duke wanted to respect Andi's boundaries.

Instead, he asked, "Has anyone read that contract yet?"

Andi seemed to snap from her thoughts and held it up. "I have it. I haven't looked it over. But I'd like to review it if no one else wants the job."

She said her words carefully, disguising her past career.

No one argued with her vying for the position.

"How do we always find ourselves in the middle of things like that?" Duke asked the group as he gripped the steering wheel. The question had lingered in his mind for a while now. "We seem to have stumbled onto Craig's murder. Then last time we met to talk about a case, three dead bodies were pulled out of the river. Now we're talking to a potential investor who was almost killed right in front of our eyes."

"We do seem to find ourselves in some pickles," Simmy said in that sweet tone she always used.

She'd been relatively quiet tonight. But that wasn't unusual. She wasn't the type who always had to have something to say, and Duke could appreciate that.

"Wait . . . don't you think it's like everything was meant to be?" Mariella asked. "The timing of us meeting. The timing of the murders. The discoveries of the dead bodies. Everything is aligning."

"I'm not so sure." Andi offered no further explanation as to that thought. "Speaking of which, I'm also not really sure we can call ourselves the Arctic Circle Murder Club anymore."

"Why is that?" Mariella craned her head to look at Andi.

"Sure, our first case was in the Arctic Circle," Andi

said. "But now our last two have been in Fairbanks. Am I right?"

"But we *originated* in the Arctic Circle." Mariella's voice sounded animated and convincing. "So I still think the name is fitting. Plus, we're going to be back there sometime. In fact, it wouldn't surprise me if we have to go back to the Arctic Circle again this weekend. That *is* the area where most of these women disappeared."

All the women disappeared along the Dalton Highway. But the road was more than four hundred miles long. The majority of that was in the Arctic Circle, but there was still a stretch from Fairbanks up to the Almost Halfway Trading Post that wasn't quite the Arctic Circle.

It didn't matter what they called themselves. The name was inconsequential.

Duke just wanted answers.

And he wanted to talk to Andi alone. He wanted to hear what was going on in her mind.

But he'd have to wait.

He pulled up to the hotel and, before everyone got out of the car, Mariella turned to them. "Is everyone okay with meeting back in the conference room for a while? I know we're all tired, but we don't have any time to waste."

Duke couldn't agree more.

Before he could answer, someone's phone rang.

Mariella's.

She stared at the screen a moment before frowning and placing it on speaker. "Hello?"

Static filled the air. "Is . . . this . . . round . . . table?"

"You're asking if this is *The Round Table* podcast?" Mariella glanced at the rest of the group, tension in her gaze. "It is. Who is this? You're breaking up."

"I think . . . I think I found . . . a—"

Mariella's eyes widened. "You think you found what?"

"A . . . body . . . of . . . one of the missing . . . women."

Everyone in the vehicle went still.

Had they heard correctly?

"You found a body of one of the missing women?" Mariella asked.

They all waited.

Was that what the man had meant? They'd announced on their podcast that they'd be looking into this. Had asked for tips.

"I . . . I have to go . . ."

"Wait!" Mariella said.

It was too late. Dead air filled the line.

But if the man had found a body . . . whose was it? Where had he discovered it?

They needed to find out.

This could be their best lead yet.

Or it could be a prank.

Duke hoped they could distinguish between the two.

Back in the conference room, seated around the table with warm drinks in their hands, the group waited for Mariella to start.

Andi took a slow sip of her hot chocolate, savoring the warmth as she organized her thoughts.

What would the rest of this weekend hold? So far, they had talked to a potential victim, seen a helicopter explosion, Victor's name had been brought up, and they'd gotten that weird phone call.

And they were just getting started.

The phone call remained on Andi's mind. Who had that been?

They'd tried to call the number back, but it had gone straight to voicemail—voicemail that hadn't been set up yet. Matthew had run the number through his system, but it appeared to be a burner.

There was a chance the caller didn't really know anything. But the possibility also remained that he did.

A body would provide clues. It would provide closure for at least one of the families.

Sure, Andi hoped all the women were still alive. But she knew that was unlikely. She knew the odds with these things.

If anyone was still alive, it would be a miracle.

Mariella cleared her throat before speaking. "I thought I'd let you all know that I looked into the very first victim. A woman named Tatiana Zelensky." She hit a button on her computer, and a projector shined an image on the wall.

An image of Tatiana wearing a beige turtleneck, brown skirt, and knee-high boots.

"Tatiana was twenty-seven when she disappeared."

The picture showed a woman with long, brown hair fixed in braids on either side of her head. Her smile was bright and her eyes hopeful. "This was one of the last pictures taken of her."

"Remind us what she did for a living." Matthew pushed his glasses up, the picture of a young professional with the world in front of him.

Surely, he knew that information. They'd gone over some of these things before, and they'd each even been given homework.

"She was a waitress in Coldfoot, but she moved there from Europe—the Ukraine, to be exact. She had no family in the area. I asked Ranger to look into anyone she may have known in Coldfoot." Mariella turned to Ranger. "Ranger, could you give us an update?"

He shifted as if uncomfortable being in the spotlight before finally nodding. "I talked to a couple of people who used to work with her. But her coworkers didn't have much to say—just that they were shocked when she disappeared. They really gave me nothing else to go on."

"No men in her life?" Andi asked.

Ranger shook his head. "No strange men talked to her in the restaurant or hit on her. She wasn't dating anybody. She mostly just liked to keep to herself. She came here hoping to get a foothold and to try for American citizenship, to start a new life for herself. I'm waiting for a call back from her roommate. She's not in the area anymore, so I had to leave a message on her phone."

Mariella glanced at Simmy. "And you talked to her family via Zoom, correct?"

They all turned toward Simmy.

She nodded almost nervously. "I did. I felt like I was out of my element, but they agreed to speak with me. Their English was broken, but they were nice people who are still very concerned about their daughter."

"Did Tatiana say anything suspicious to them in the days or weeks before she disappeared?" Duke asked.

"No. Apparently, they only spoke about once a month, and Tatiana had only been in the States for two months before she disappeared. That means they really only spoke once, and that was when Tatiana was getting settled. Unfortunately, they weren't able to offer any clues either." Simmy shrugged apologetically.

"Really, when you look at this, there's only one logical conclusion." Andi's jaw was tight as she leaned against the table.

"What's that?" Duke's entire focus shifted as he waited to hear Andi's thoughts.

"I hate to say it but . . . human trafficking. Why else would all of these women disappear? This is a huge problem in today's world."

"You think someone is picking up these victims off the side of the road and taking them somewhere where they're basically sold into human slavery?" Duke clarified.

"It's my best guess." Andi shrugged regretfully. "It's horrible, but it makes sense."

"If what you're saying is true, where would this guy be taking them?" Mariella lifted her pen—the one with a bright pink poof on the end—and twirled it in circles.

Andi hesitated before giving her opinion. "The place that makes the most sense is the oil fields."

Everyone quieted at her words.

"You really think there's human trafficking happening at the oil fields?" Ranger stared at her, a healthy dose of skepticism in his voice. Yet he didn't seem totally closed to the idea either.

"I mean, just think about it." Andi's voice remained unwavering. "People who go up there to work are mostly men who don't see daylight for several months out of the year, and they're working in extremely harsh conditions. It's really the perfect setup for something like this."

"Men are pigs," Mariella muttered.

Andi kept quiet, refusing to agree or disagree. Yes, some men could be. But others weren't.

The trick was being able to distinguish between the two.

"All you need is one person offering their accommodations as some sort of a brothel," Andi said. "And I'm not even saying that the management or leadership would know about this. Or maybe they do, and they're turning a blind eye to what's going on. I'm not sure."

Duke looked at her, his expression unreadable. "If that is true, how would we prove it?"

Andi tapped her pen on the table. "That's the tricky part. They're not going to let us onto those oil fields.

Finding someone willing to talk to us would be nearly impossible. Sure, some of the workers might drive up there. But most are flown in and taken right onto the oil fields. They're practically untouchable."

"Then maybe we should put our thinking caps on," Mariella said. "Maybe there's some way we can figure out if that theory is true. In the meantime, I have an interview set up tomorrow with the family of the second victim, Luna Clark. Then in the afternoon, Ted Sparkman is coming for an interview."

Luna Clark. She'd been twenty when she went missing off the Dalton Highway.

She was an Inupiat from a village on the other side of the state. She'd been dropped off on the highway and never seen again.

"Is the family coming to the hotel?" Duke asked.

"I wanted to surprise you all." Mariella's eyes sparkled. "Her mom invited us to their village, and Alpine has arranged a private charter. We'll leave at eight, and it will take about an hour and a half to fly there. We should be back here by lunchtime so we can continue working."

"We're all going?" Duke clarified.

Mariella nodded, her eyes still dancing. "I thought it might be a good idea. But if anyone needs to stay and do something else, I understand."

Andi was definitely in.

The more people they could talk to about this, the better.

In that regard, Alpine's offer could be very helpful.

But they all needed to weigh the cost.

Because things that seemed too good to be true usually were.

chapter
nine

IT WAS NEARLY midnight by the time Andi and the rest of the gang turned in for the night.

Probably the only reason Mariella had insisted on dismissing them at all was because Simmy had nearly fallen asleep at the table.

They *had* made some progress, however.

They'd put together information sheets and a timeline for each victim. Then they'd added the information to their murder board. They would add more information as the weekend continued.

First victim:
Tatiana Zelensky, 27
5'2", 120 pounds, Caucasian
Waitress in Coldfoot
From the Ukraine
Didn't show up for work

Last seen: 3/3/18

Second victim:

Luna Clark, 20

4'8", 98 pounds, Native American

From Noorvik, Alaska

Dropped off in Coldfoot

Last seen: 4/30/19

Third victim:

Emilia Sparkman, 33

5'7", 135 pounds, Caucasian

Married to Ted, a scientist

Last seen: 7/12/19

Fourth victim:

Kiah Franz, 24

5'5", 142 pounds, mixed ethnicity

Prostitute in Coldfoot

Last seen: 10/2/19

Fifth victim:

Darlene Parks, 28

5'2", 110 pounds, Caucasian

Worked food service in Prudhoe Bay

Heading back there after a week off
Last seen departing from hotel in Fairbanks
Last seen: 4/30/20

Sixth victim:

Angel Washburn
5'8", 130 pounds, Hispanic
Camping off highway
Last seen: 8/15/20

Potential victim:

Charlotte Schmidt, 25
5'3", 113 pounds, part Caucasian, part Native American
Hair stylist in Anchorage
Hitchhiking
Attempted abduction on 4/6/21

Seventh victim:

Celeste Dawson, 30
5'8", 135 pounds, Caucasian
Traveling nurse solo hiking Gates of the Arctic National Park
Last seen: 5/16/21

· · ·

Eighth victim:
   Heidi Billingsworth
   5'1", 122 pounds, Caucasian
   Travel website creator
   Last seen: 4/9/23

By the time they dismissed, all the pictures of the victims had been placed on the murder board, along with their updated information.

Each victim was vastly different—from their backgrounds to their looks to their heritage.

The only thing they seemed to have in common was that they were relatively thin, and they each had long hair—which would be a weird reason for someone to target his victims.

"Can I walk you back to your room?" Duke asked Andi after everyone else had cleared the room.

"Of course." No way would she refuse. She'd been looking for some one-on-one time to speak with him.

Last time they'd stayed at the hotel, Andi and Duke had rooms beside each other. This time, they were right down the hall from each other, which was probably a good thing. Some space was only wise.

"What a day, huh?" The words sounded lame, but Andi needed something safe to talk about.

Duke's steps slowed as they approached her door. "It sure was."

Andi pointed with her thumb behind her. "Listen, do

you want to come inside a minute and catch up? I understand if you're too tired."

Duke stayed quiet a minute before nodding. "Sure, why not?"

The last time she'd invited him into her room, they'd nearly kissed.

Which had been a mistake.

So she understood why he was being cautious.

In the room, Duke sat in a chair near the window while Andi sat on the couch. She pulled her knees to her chest as she tried to unwind. Duke, however, looked stiff and uncertain.

"Anything new with Celeste?" Andi decided to get right to the point.

"I've been trying to find more information on her, but there's been nothing. Bobby/William hasn't been back to work, nor has he shown up on any radar. I even asked some of my old friends with the CID if they could help me investigate him, but there's no indication of where he went."

Andi tucked her legs beneath her. "That whole situation is perplexing, isn't it?"

"You don't have to tell me that." Then Duke's gaze focused solely on her. "Have there been any more incidents between you and Victor?"

Andi's throat tightened. The subject of Victor . . . it was daunting. Victor was untouchable. He hired people to do his dirty work. And he had no conscience.

She shrugged. "I thought I saw someone following me

a couple of times. Once I could have been sure someone had been in my apartment again. But no direct threats."

His gaze darkened. "Someone was in your apartment . . . again? You should have called."

"I didn't want to bother you." The truth was, Andi had thought about calling him.

She'd forced herself not to. She was an independent woman, and she needed to act like it. Coming to depend on someone else would only prove to be a big mistake.

"You wouldn't have been a bother." Duke stared at her as if to drive home his point. "What about that conversation you had with Alpine? I noticed something about you changed after that."

Of *course* he'd noticed. Duke was a little too observant for his own good sometimes.

"This is where it gets weird. I asked him who'd been making threats toward him. If he had any clues. Alpine had one name that instantly came to mind. Victor Goodman."

Duke's eyes widened, and he ran a hand over his face in disbelief. "Really?"

Andi nodded slowly, still in shock herself. "Really. He seemed pretty sure about it. He also mentioned a new oil drill proposal called Prometheus."

"The same word we saw written at that secret meeting."

"Exactly." Andi nodded slowly, giving the information time to sink in.

Duke let out a long breath and glanced in the distance

as if gathering his thoughts. "I don't like the sound of that."

"Neither do I, but maybe this will be our chance to get some answers. Am I right?"

"Is Victor even in town?"

Andi shook her head. "Not that I know of. I've had my doorman friend keeping a lookout for me. Sometimes I wonder if coming to Alaska was a good idea at all. Victor doesn't seem to spend that much time here."

"Maybe it's as Mariella said—we all came here for a purpose."

"Maybe." Andi wasn't quite ready to give in to it that easily.

"What about Charlotte?" Duke studied her. "You said you didn't trust her. Why?"

Andi shrugged. "I can't put my finger on it. I just feel like there's something she's not telling us. I know victims don't always go to the police, but it just seems like she would have. She doesn't strike me as the shrinking violet type. So what happened to make her stay silent?"

"Good question. We may not ever know that answer."

Silence—wrought with tension—suddenly loomed between them.

A romantic relationship was an impossibility right now.

They both knew that.

Andi glanced at Duke, wondering if there was something more they needed to say to each other. She wasn't sure what. But it almost felt as if there was an elephant in the room.

Duke suddenly rushed to his feet, looking ready to run. "You know, I should get going."

Andi stood also, unusually nervous. "Probably a good idea."

"But we'll catch up in the morning."

She nodded quickly. "Sounds like a plan. Good night."

As soon as Duke left the room, disappointment filled Andi until she could think about nothing else. She wanted things between her and Duke to return to the way they had been. When the two of them had at least felt like friends.

But it was better if that didn't happen. If they kept their distance.

There was way too much chemistry between them to risk it.

However, Andi had no doubt this whole weekend would be a challenge.

As Duke turned to head back to his room, he glanced toward the lobby.

A woman whose hair was pulled into a ponytail stared back at him.

The moment their eyes met, she turned and darted away.

Celeste?

His heart lodged in his throat.

Had that been her? It didn't seem possible. Yet it had looked like her.

Duke's thoughts collided inside his head.

Wasting no more time, he darted after her.

If it had been Celeste, she wouldn't walk away this time.

He reached the lobby in time to see the blonde run out the door. She glanced back one more time.

Duke quickened his steps.

But as he burst outside and glanced around, she was nowhere to be seen.

She couldn't have disappeared that easily. So where had she gone?

He scanned the vehicles around him, looking for any sign of her. Any sign of movement. Any sign of life.

Nothing.

On a whim, he headed toward the left. Maybe she'd ducked behind a car.

Duke hadn't been seeing things. A blonde woman had *definitely* been staring at him. Watching him.

Almost as if she'd wanted him to see her . . .

Carefully, he glanced between each of the vehicles, desperate to find her. Desperate for answers.

But so far, nothing.

As he reached the last few vehicles on the row near the corner of the building, a shadow moved behind a truck with an oversized cap on the back.

"Celeste?" Duke called, taking a step closer.

Suddenly, an arm snaked around his neck and something hard pressed into his side.

Duke started to throw his elbow back, to fight.

Until a deep voice said, "I wouldn't do that if I were you. I'm not afraid to use this gun."

Gun.

That was a gun he felt in his rib cage.

Duke went still.

He didn't recognize the voice, he only knew it sounded deep and dead serious.

His heart pulsed in his ears.

His gaze darted back to where he'd first seen the shadow.

Celeste—or whoever the shadow had been—was now disappearing around the corner toward the backside of the building.

Duke wanted to call for her, but he couldn't. Her name caught in his throat.

"You need to drop this," the gunman said.

Duke's muscles tightened even more as the man's breath hit his ear. "Who are you?"

The gunman shoved the weapon harder into Duke's rib cage. He refused to cringe, to give the man that satisfaction. Instead, he remained stiff.

"That's none of your business," the man said.

"I'd say it is."

"You're not doing anyone any favors by pressing this."

"I just want answers."

"You may want to rethink that," the man growled.

What did that mean?

Before Duke could ask more questions, something hard struck him on the side of the head.

Then everything went black around him.

chapter
ten

ANDI STARED at her computer in disbelief.

That alert she'd gotten earlier from her bank . . . her account truly had been over-drafted.

In fact, all the money she'd had in her account—her life savings—was gone.

Every penny of it.

Nausea roiled inside her at the thought.

It had been taken out with two huge transactions, made to a company she'd never heard of—Alyeska Withholdings.

She'd researched the company.

They didn't exist.

This wasn't an accident.

If she had to guess, Victor was behind it.

It was one more way he was trying to teach her a lesson.

Certainly there had to be a way to trace where the money went and who had authorized the transfer.

Something.

She called the bank, and after navigating the automatic system and being cut off twice, she managed to be put on hold.

And she waited. And waited.

After thirty very frustrating minutes, she disconnected and stood.

This was getting her nowhere.

She needed a break and something to drink, and she knew the hotel offered coffee and lemonade all throughout the day and night. There was also a bar that was open until sometime after midnight.

She'd opt for some lemonade.

As she went there and grabbed some, she glanced to the side.

A familiar figure sitting at the bar caught her eye.

Was that Braden Billingsworth?

It was.

He hunched over the bar, four empty glasses in front of him.

The man was definitely three sheets to the wind.

Andi probably shouldn't talk to him.

But there was no better time to find out information than after someone drank truth serum, aka alcohol.

Drawing in a deep breath, she made her way over to him.

She smiled as she sat beside him, lemonade still in hand.

His eyes lit when he saw her. "Well, hello."

Based on the way his words slurred, he was definitely drunk.

"Hello," Andi said. "Mind if I sit here?"

"Be my guest." He glanced at her cup. "You sure I can't buy you something stronger?"

"I'm sure. Thanks." She drew in a breath, trying to appear casual. "So, what brings you here?"

A storm of emotions flashed in his eyes before disappearing. "It's a long story. One I'd rather not talk about."

Interesting . . .

"You from this area?"

"Nope. You?"

"Nope." She could keep things simple also.

But she really wanted to find out more information.

She took a sip of her drink before glancing at him again. "What's there to do in this town? Any ideas?"

His eyebrows flickered up. "I can think of a few things."

Andi heard the suggestion behind his words but ignored it. "Like what?"

"Go back to my room with me, and I'll show you."

She drew in a breath. This man wasn't a grieving husband, was he?

He was a slimeball cheater.

A touch of outrage filled her.

During his interviews, he'd sounded like such a devoted husband.

But that clearly wasn't the case.

"I'm not that type of girl," Andi muttered, starting to rise.

He grabbed her wrist.

Andi froze, not liking the unwelcome touch.

"You sure about that?" He stared at her as if he could see through her clothing.

"Positive." She snatched her hand away.

As she did, she glanced outside and saw someone run across the deck.

Not run as in a casual jog—even though it would be awfully late for that anyway.

But run as if trying to escape.

Braden started to speak again, but she stepped away.

Andi had more important things to think about right now.

Andi stepped out the back door.

Instantly, a cool wind hit her.

She wished she had her coat with her, but she hadn't thought she'd be going outside.

She glanced to the edge of the building where she saw the figure disappear.

She thought the runner had been a woman.

A woman with blonde hair.

She was sure it was probably nothing. But despite that, Andi carefully started to trail behind her.

Maybe she should call Duke. Or Ranger. Anyone.

But it was too late for that.

If she wanted to find out who that woman was, then she needed to act now.

She reached the edge of the building and paused cautiously.

Then she carefully turned, not wanting to be taken by surprise.

No one was there.

But when she looked down, she saw some fresh footsteps in the light layer of snow that must have fallen earlier.

She began following the tracks leading toward the parking lot.

But just as she reached the sidewalk, a car in the distance started.

Headlights glared.

She blinked and shielded her eyes.

The lights were too bright to get a description of the vehicle or a license plate.

The next instant, the vehicle pulled away, quickly merging onto the street in front of the hotel.

That was . . . weird.

What had just happened even?

She started to turn to go back inside when she saw something on the ground in the distance.

Was that a . . . man?

Her heart rate quickened as she stepped toward the figure.

But as she got closer, she realized . . . it was Duke.

Adrenaline surged through her as she rushed toward him and knelt beside him. As she turned him over, he moaned. He reached for his head, and that's when she noticed the bump there.

"Duke . . . are you okay?"

He blinked several times before pulling his eyes fully open.

And then he groaned again and sat up, glancing around. "Where did she go?"

"Where did who go?"

Duke's eyes met hers. "Celeste. I saw her. She was just here."

eleven

I POINTED to the shower the next morning. "Clean this shower with a toothbrush. I want every hint of any mold or mildew gone."

Anna stared at me, tears in her eyes.

Maybe I shouldn't have slapped her earlier.

But she'd deserved it.

I'd told her not to snoop, and she'd done so anyway.

There were consequences for disobedience.

I watched as she got on her hands and knees in her dress.

She sprinkled some Comet powdered cleaner on the grout, sprayed it with water, and then began to scrub.

I was going to watch her.

Nothing brought me more pleasure than watching a woman cook and clean.

My grandmother had said that was a woman's place, what she was created to do.

She said when a household was in order then everything in life would be also.

I'd learned so much from her.

I missed her every day.

But I was grateful to carry on her legacy.

I paused from my thoughts and stepped closer to Anna. "You missed a spot."

I pointed to an area of the grout that was still gray.

"I'll go back and do it again at the end," Anna said.

"I think you should do it now."

"I need to let the cleaner soak on it for a while." She paused from scrubbing and glanced back at me. "The gray isn't coming out."

"That's because you need to scrub harder."

"I scrubbed as hard as I could, and it's still gray."

Anger rose in me. "Are you back talking me?"

Fear filled her gaze. "Of course not. I was just trying to explain—"

"It sounds like you're still back talking me."

Her body went still. "I'm sorry . . . Master. I just wanted you to understand!"

"Stop talking!" The next instant, I pulled my belt from my pants and folded it in my hands.

She needed to be taught more lessons.

Including the fact that I was the king of the household.

My word was the only one that mattered. What I wanted took priority.

"No . . ." She shrank into the corner. "Please. I'll keep scrubbing."

"You had your chance," I growled.

"I promise! I'll s—"

Before she could say anything else, my belt hit her arm.

She yelped, her eyes closing with pain.

"Turn around!" I ordered.

I didn't like to bruise her where anyone could see.

Not that anyone ever saw her.

"But—"

"Turn around! Now!"

She trembled as she stood and turned, bracing her arms against the tile surrounding the shower.

Then I began lashing her with my belt.

Some lessons could only be learned with punishment and discipline.

This was one of them.

With every lash, I felt more and more of the tension releasing from my body.

Some people relieved their tension with a punching bag.

I found my way much more effective.

chapter
twelve

ANDI WAS FIXING herself some coffee near the breakfast buffet the next morning when she spotted Duke step into the dining area.

Her smile faltered as soon as his haggard expression came into view.

He was upset still. Was it about last night? Or had something else happened?

She left her coffee on the table and strode across the room toward him. "Did you see her again? Did something else happen?"

His gaze flickered toward her, surprise in the depths of his eyes. "No."

Andi tilted her head, her Texas accent on the verge of emerging. "Don't lie to me, Duke McAllister."

He let out a long breath and glanced around as if looking for the rest of the group.

Then he took her elbow and steered her toward the back of the dining area. "Let's find somewhere private."

They sat at a corner table just out of sight from the casual observer. The location might buy them a few minutes until the rest of the gang showed up.

Andi turned toward him, giving him her full attention.

Duke sighed and ran a hand over his face. His inner turmoil was obvious—and Andi's heart ached as she observed him.

"It's driving me crazy not knowing if it truly is Celeste I'm seeing." His voice cracked as he said the words.

Andi's lungs loosened. "I can only imagine."

He ran his hand over his face again. "Honestly, I'm not even sure how to proceed from here. All of this is knocking me off my game."

Last night, he'd told her what had happened.

About seeing the woman.

Chasing her.

A man pressing a gun into his side before muttering, "Drop this."

Being knocked out.

Being confused as to whether or not that man had been Bobby.

Andi squeezed his forearm, wishing she could pull him into a hug and tell him everything would be okay. But she could do neither. Given the circumstances, it was better to keep boundaries in place—for the protection of her heart and for the sake of Duke's commitment to Celeste.

"I'm so sorry," Andi murmured instead.

Duke's gaze still didn't fully meet hers. "Me too."

"If you ever need to talk . . ." She scooted closer to him, needing to look into his eyes, to see for herself that he was okay and that he understood her words weren't an empty promise.

"I appreciate that," he murmured.

"Maybe we should have called the police."

"I thought about it, but everything happened in the shadows. It was like every detail had been planned. The cops wouldn't have been able to catch these guys."

Andi opened her mouth to argue, then shut it again. Duke was probably right. That was the way this investigation had gone so far, at least.

"What can I do for you?" She remained close—maybe too close. But she had no desire to move away.

"Nothing." His tortured gaze met hers, unreadable emotions haunting him in the depths of his eyes. "You've done enough. Thank you for listening."

Before they could talk anymore, a gaggle of activity sounded behind her. Andi turned and saw the rest of the gang flood the dining area. There were only thirty minutes until they were supposed to leave for the airport. No doubt everyone wanted to grab some breakfast beforehand.

Andi straightened her shoulders and tried to look casual so no one would ask any questions. Duke did the same.

But it was hard to erase the worry she felt.

Had that woman been Celeste? Who had the man been? And why did they want Duke to back off so badly?

There was clearly more going on here than met the eye.

Andi knew Duke wouldn't have any peace until he had some answers.

Truth was . . . neither would she.

Duke and the gang grabbed some breakfast—corned beef hash was on the menu this morning—before hopping in his SUV.

The airport wasn't far from the hotel, but apprehension about flying embedded itself between his shoulders after what happened last night.

Someone had blown up that helicopter. What if someone had also tampered with the plane they were taking?

Duke didn't voice those concerns out loud. He didn't want to get everyone worried. Yet the possibilities pressed heavy on his mind.

Until they knew why Alpine had been targeted last night, they should assume they might also be in the line of fire. Had it been Victor? Had the man really taken things that far?

Based on what Duke knew about Victor, the answer was a definite yes.

Plus, other people had their own reasons for wanting

their group to disband. What they were doing in trying to solve these crimes didn't come without risk. Killers didn't want to be exposed. Others didn't want their secrets revealed by the group's snooping. Still others didn't want past crimes stirred up. Because maybe they'd be a suspect.

When Duke saw Ranger's brooding expression, Duke couldn't help but wonder if his colleague felt the same.

Duke wanted to give today's investigation everything he had. But he wasn't sure he'd be able to do that.

Because he couldn't stop replaying what happened last night.

"By the way, I heard from Alpine this morning." Mariella's voice cut into his thoughts as she leaned forward and piped in from the back seat.

"How is he?" Andi asked.

"He was released from the hospital, and he's on his way to California. But he said he'd come back up if we needed him for any reason and to let us know what other things he could help us with."

Duke's mood grew darker, although for no discernible reason. He just had trouble trusting that guy.

Instead of saying anything, he gripped the wheel and kept his gaze focused on the road. He didn't want to stir things up—not when he had so many other things on his mind. If Alpine wasn't trustworthy, he would show his stripes soon enough.

Mariella turned to Andi. "Speaking of Alpine, did you read the contract?"

Duke glanced in the rearview mirror at Andi and saw her tight expression.

"I looked over it before I went to bed, and there are a few clauses I want some clarification on," she said. "We don't want this guy to own the rights to our podcast. There's some language within the contract that could be open to interpretation—the last thing we want. Issues like that can go either way in a court of law, so I think some clarity is needed."

Mariella gave her a glance. "Did you used to be a paralegal or something before you were an ice road trucker? Because you sound seriously smart right now."

He glanced at Andi again and saw a flash of red fill her cheeks. But she quickly covered her reaction with a chuckle.

"What can I say?" Andi shoved some hair behind her ear. "I just pick up on things easily."

"It's a good thing you do." Mariella shrugged. "Because when I looked at the contract, I didn't see anything suspicious. I only saw security for our future."

"We should definitely be careful about what we're signing over," Andi said slowly. "And to be honest, I still question this guy's motives. He's pouring a lot of money into what we're doing, and I'm still not sure why."

Andi's thoughts echoed Duke's exactly.

"He just wants to do some good with his fortune." Mariella shrugged again before glancing out the window at the passing landscape. "There's nothing wrong with that."

Duke liked Mariella, but the woman could be naive. She saw the world through rose-colored glasses and was entirely too trusting at times. That made him worry about her.

Even after what happened with the Ice Fairy Killer, Mariella didn't seem deterred or more cautious. She'd been taken captive by the man and had nearly become his next victim. Most people in those situations were different afterward. They were more fearful and paranoid. Mariella seemed surprisingly steady.

Was she really that strong? Or was she just in denial?

Duke hoped it was the former.

They reached the airport, and he pulled into a parking space. He started to get out when Andi cleared her throat.

"While we're all together, I just thought you should know that I ran into Braden last night," she started.

Suddenly, all their attention was on her.

"And?" Mariella asked.

"He hit on me." Andi shrugged, her gaze speaking volumes.

"What?" Mariella's lips parted. "Are you for real? What a jerk!"

"I know," Andi said. "I'm not sure if that's important or not, but I wanted to throw it out there, just in case."

Duke didn't like the thought of that guy hitting on Andi. But he pushed his emotions down.

They had other things to concentrate on right now.

They all clambered out and headed toward the metal building where the pilot waited.

Duke glanced at a plane, a De Havilland Otter, in the distance, one that should hold all six of them. It looked new and well maintained. That should be a good sign.

Still, he had his reservations about flying.

However, driving wasn't a possibility since there were no roads leading into the village. If they wanted to talk to Luna's family, this was the only way to do so.

Maybe today they'd finally make some progress.

Maybe.

But Duke thought that progress seemed more and more unreachable all the time.

chapter
thirteen

ANDI WATCHED as both Duke and Ranger checked out the plane.

They also talked to the pilot. Learned he'd put in more than a thousand flight hours in Alaska alone.

They'd looked at the weather report. Saw they should have clear skies.

She appreciated their thoroughness, especially after what they'd witnessed yesterday. Once the two men gave them the okay, they boarded.

Six seats stretched along the sides, as well as the seat upfront for the pilot.

After buckling up and running through the safety instructions, they were airborne.

Andi had never cared for small planes. She also knew that Alaska was a dangerous place to fly. The mountains easily hid behind clouds, and pilots truly needed to be experienced to safely get from point A to point B.

From what she understood, Noorvik, the village

where they were headed, was an Inupiat Eskimo community with a subsistence lifestyle, which meant they depended on caribou, fish, moose, waterfowl, and berries for survival.

Andi had always been curious about life in these remote villages.

But this wasn't the way she wanted to learn more—not through this tragedy.

She turned in her seat to address everyone, knowing they didn't have time to waste. They needed to use every moment to their advantage.

"Any updates on that phone call we got yesterday?" Andi asked above the hum of the plane's engine.

She couldn't stop thinking about the broken voice on the other line.

What if someone *had* discovered a dead body?

"I've tried to call back several times." Matthew shrugged. "No answer."

"Our only hope is that he'll try to call again," Simmy said.

"We can hope." Andi let out a breath. "What about Heidi Billingsworth? Any updates on her?"

As the woman's name left her lips, an image of the woman filled her mind.

She was pretty in a very natural way with long, dark hair and a scattering of freckles across her cheeks and nose. She had a slim frame and curious eyes.

"I heard her husband and his family on the news again

this morning," Mariella said. "They're pushing hard to find her. But they didn't mention any updates."

"Do you think Gibson would tell us if any new information had been discovered?" Simmy asked.

Duke shook his head. "I doubt it. Not unless the information is public."

Andi agreed with that assessment.

If no one had come forward to talk to the murder club, she had trouble thinking people would come forward to talk to anyone. Although, that reward *could* help.

They chatted about the investigation as they soared through the air.

Andi glanced out the window and saw the beautiful Alaskan landscape around her. The Brooks Mountain range to the north. The tundra below her. The Yukon River as it thawed.

The group continued to talk, some about the case and some about life in general.

Then the plane dipped.

Andi grabbed the arm rests beside her.

Turbulence. That was just turbulence, right?

She could hardly breathe as she waited for them to even out.

But they didn't.

The plane dipped again.

Mariella let out a little scream.

Andi's eyes met Duke's. He didn't look nearly as freaked out as she did.

"It's going to be okay," he murmured.

She wished she felt that confident.

Several minutes passed of steady movement.

Then the plane twisted so abruptly to the left that Andi nearly fell out of her seat and into the aisle. Only the seatbelt held her in place.

Cargo from overhead crashed to the floor. The pilot began talking on the radio. She couldn't make out his words. But they sounded urgent.

What was going on?

Were they going to die?

Duke wished he could reach out and comfort Andi.

He couldn't.

Even if he could, he couldn't.

The plane was shifting too much for him to move. Something had already hit him on the head.

Everyone around him was tense.

"Just give me a minute," the pilot called over his shoulder. "We've hit some turbulence. It's not totally uncommon when we're flying over these mountains. These clouds came out of nowhere."

Clouds and mountains were never a good combination. Duke didn't have to be a pilot to know that.

He waited, praying for their safety.

The plane evened out again.

For how long this time?

He glanced back at Andi and saw she had paled and sweat beaded across her forehead.

She appeared terrified.

They all did.

Duke was used to turbulence. He'd taken plenty of tour groups up in the air. But this was beginning to unnerve him.

Silence stretched in the cabin.

As if everyone was holding their breath.

Maybe they were.

He glanced at Andi once more. She'd squeezed her eyes shut tight.

He wanted to reassure her that this was normal. All part of the Alaskan adventure.

But he didn't think she would necessarily appreciate the words right now.

The minutes ticked by, and finally they approached the runway without any more issues.

The pilot expertly maneuvered the plane into position as if he'd done it a thousand times before. That's probably because he had.

But it wasn't until they were safely on the ground that the group seemed to let out a collective sigh of relief.

Duke stepped off the plane, happy to be on solid ground.

A woman waited for them in a rundown beige truck at the airport.

The "airport" was more of a gravel landing strip than a runway. But Duke knew this village had less than seven hundred people living here year-round. There was no need for large or fancy facilities.

The woman introduced herself as Tootega, the village public safety officer. She was probably in her fifties, with a round face and short black hair. She wore a bright purple jacket and had a stoic air about her.

After introductions had gone around, Tootega piled them all into her truck. Simmy and Ranger sat up front with her on the bench seat, and the rest of the team squeezed into the back. Then she started down the road.

Despite the fact that this was an Eskimo village, the buildings around them were contemporary yet old and not well maintained.

"I'm glad you guys could come," Tootega started, her voice solemn and serious. "I've been looking for answers about Luna's disappearance for years. I'm sure that most of you guys know this, but just in case you don't, indigenous women in Alaska are murdered at nearly ten times the rate of other races."

"That's terrible," Duke murmured. He had heard the statistic before, but seeing the real-life ramifications of such a thing was eye-opening.

"It's a nationwide crisis," Tootega said. "One that seems nearly impossible to battle."

"How many officers do you have here to help you?" Simmy asked.

"It's just me. I'm on call 24-7, and I handle everything on my own. There's no funding to hire more people, and the pay equals out to only twenty dollars an hour. I do a work that's tireless and often thankless. The village is so small that it's nearly impossible not to be altruistic. It's no wonder no one wants this job."

"I can imagine." Andi shook her head, her lips pressed together as if bothered by the statement.

"We don't have police departments out here like you do in the city," Tootega continued. "In fact, one in three Alaskan villages has no police at all. You must imagine what that's like. If we call for help, it can take hours—if not days, depending on the weather—for someone to get here. That's why many crimes go unreported."

Duke had taken it upon himself to become a student of the state of Alaska as part of his job as a tour guide. But he'd yet to make it out to many of these remote Native American villages. The closest he'd come was going up to Utqiagvik on the Arctic Ocean.

Duke's gaze drifted out the window. This village showed a different side of life than in other parts of the state. Something close to gloominess lingered in the air.

Hopelessness. Was that the feeling that saturated the air right now?

Duke couldn't be sure. He didn't want to project his own feelings onto the people living here in this village. Not at all.

But there was still a pervasive emptiness that couldn't be ignored. He'd felt it before when visiting other Indian reservations. The whole thing was a shame, an injustice.

"It's women like Luna and her mother who keep me going," Tootega continued as they drove through the village. "I want to help them. Luna's father is a bit of a brooding man. He was very upset with Luna and told her if she left not to come back."

Tootega gave them a rundown on the village as they traveled. Told them about how the power grid was run off a diesel generator. Told them about how the cars in town were brought in via barge—although, on occasion, the river froze, and people were able to tow vehicles across the ice with their snow machines.

There was a school, a general store, a post office, and even a church.

Finally, she pulled to a stop in front of a house still partially covered in snow. The place was small with gray siding and surrounded by similar homes.

Before they reached the front door, it opened, and a forty-something Inupiat woman stood there. She was thin with bobbed hair, amazing cheek bones, and surprisingly pale skin.

Grief stained her red-rimmed eyes.

Duke understood the emotion all too well.

"Welcome." The woman gripped the door handle as if it were a lifeline. "You're here to talk about my Luna?"

Andi stepped forward and took the lead. "Yes, we are. Thank you for agreeing to meet with us."

"Of course. I'm Elisapee. Come inside."

They all filed into the small house. Posters of eighties rock stars and movies decorated the walls, the kitchen counter was littered with dishes and food, and boxes were piled up along the walls as if the place was too small to have somewhere to properly store things.

That wasn't to mention the fact that it felt surprisingly cold inside. Elisapee didn't seem to mind. In fact, she probably wore four layers.

She motioned for them all to sit on the couch and the folding chairs she'd pulled out. Then she motioned to someone else—a friend perhaps—to bring them something.

A moment later, the woman handed them each spoons and bowls full of steaming liquid.

"Seal soup," she told them. "Please, help yourself."

Seal soup? That was a new one.

It could be worse. It could be muktuk—whale skin and blubber.

When Duke had been doing a tour up in Utqiagvik, he'd been offered a piece. It tasted like fatback that had been soaked in brackish water and then deep fried.

He loved trying new foods, but that hadn't been his favorite.

Tootega nodded at them, indicating it would be impolite for anyone to refuse the soup.

Duke hoped the rest of the team realized that.

He watched as they held the steaming bowls closer to their faces.

In a town like this, for someone to share their food when they had so little meant a big sacrifice.

He took a sip, surprised at how tasty the broth was.

The warm liquid was soothing, seasoned with a few herbs and salt. The seal meat tasted a little gamey but like beef.

Elisapee slipped into a seat across from them and wasted no time getting to the point. Tears welled in her eyes as she said, "I need your help finding my daughter. Please. Sometimes I fear my husband is the one who killed her."

chapter
fourteen

AFTER I'D DISCIPLINED ANNA, I'd carried her into our bedroom and apologized if I'd hurt her.

I handcuffed her to her bed and then brought some hot compresses to put on her back.

It was my way of showing her how much I cared.

She rejected my efforts. Instead, she cried and curled into a ball.

Finally, I'd brought her some soup.

I'd told her she needed to eat every drop if she wanted to leave the room.

Then I closed the door and locked it.

I would give her time to think through what she'd done.

She shouldn't have rejected me.

I cared for her so much.

But an hour had passed, and she hadn't touched the soup. Instead, it grew cold on the nightstand.

Right now, I stood in the hall and watched on the security camera as she cried on the bed.

It wasn't like my Anna to cry. I wanted to comfort her.

But I couldn't.

Teaching her a lesson was more important.

I waited another hour.

Thankfully, I didn't have to go into work.

Finally, she turned in bed and glanced at the soup. Then at the camera.

She knew it was there.

I pressed a button to talk to her. "You need to eat."

"I'm not hungry!"

"Eat anyway."

She drew in a shaky breath and then picked up the bowl. It trembled in her hands.

The chicken noodle wasn't going to taste as good cold. But she shouldn't be wasteful.

She should have eaten when I brought it to her.

A few minutes later, she showed the bowl to the camera. "There. I'm finished."

"There are a few more sips left. Finish all of it."

My grandmother had taught me the importance of eating the sustenance offered to you. *Waste not, want not.* That was what she'd always said.

She took the last few sips and then pointed the bowl at the camera. "There. I did it. What now? Can I come out?"

"You just need to clean yourself up first," I told her. "A woman should always be presentable for her man. I know a lot of women look comfortable with their hair pulled back in a ponytail and wearing sweats with no makeup. But it's a shame really. There's no one more important for a woman to look nice for than her master."

I watched in the camera as a tear rolled down her cheeks.

It would take a while to break her.

But I would.

Then she'd realize she was here to stay. I'd take care of her as long as she listened to my instructions.

And if she didn't . . . then there would be others.

However, I didn't want to go through this process again.

Training your woman was a lot of work.

"I can't clean myself up if I'm handcuffed to the bed."

She had a point.

I stepped inside and unlocked her cuff.

A moment later, Anna disappeared into the bathroom. She walked as if she were sore, as if her back ached.

She could have avoided all of that if she'd just done what I said.

I made sure there was nothing in there that she could harm herself with. Not even a shower curtain. Just some shampoo, conditioner, and soap. A towel and washcloth. A toothbrush and toothpaste.

There were no cameras in there. She deserved some privacy.

I waited until she stepped out, wearing a feminine

dress that modestly showed her curves. It was how a woman should look.

She stared up at me, defiance in her gaze. "There. Are you happy now?"

"I am."

She looked at me with something close to hatred in her eyes.

Ingratitude.

Why were so many women ungrateful?

I worked hard to provide for them. Met their needs. Gave them a warm place to sleep.

It was never enough.

"What would you like for me to do now?" Her voice sounded weak as she asked the question.

Even though she'd splashed water on her face, her skin still appeared red and blotchy. Her eyes remained glazed.

"I need you to put on your best face for me," I said. "A man should feel like the king of his home."

She wiped beneath her cheeks and sucked in a deep breath. "Yes, Master."

"I would like to go sit in my chair. You need to bring me my newspaper and make some dinner. The sandwich I made earlier wasn't as tasty as anything you might make me."

"What would you like this evening?"

"Shepherd's pie. I bought everything that we need. You just need to make it. Follow the recipe I laid out down to the tiniest detail. I expect it to be ready by five. After dinner, I would like for you to rub my feet."

Something rumbled across her expression, but she quickly pulled it back and nodded. "Of course."

I watched as she slipped by me and into the kitchen.

On second thought, maybe she would be my most trainable one yet.

chapter
fifteen

ANDI LEANED CLOSER TO ELISAPEE. "You think
your husband may have killed Luna?"

"Elisapee . . ." Tootega stepped closer, her voice soft
but inquisitive. "Stan is not a good man. However, do you
really think he'd kill his own daughter?"

Elisapee sniffed and nodded. "Yes, I do. I fear he found
her and killed her before she could disgrace the family."

Tootega turned to the group. "As far as we know, he
has an alibi for the time she disappeared. He was seal
hunting."

They turned back to Elisapee, watching for her
response.

Her eyes were glazed, and she waved a hand in the air.
"Maybe."

A couple of moments of silence passed until Mariella
asked about recording. Elisapee agreed. Mariella would be
the only one in the shots, however.

Andi didn't want her face to be in any videos, so she sat to the side of the camera.

After everything happened back in Texas and she'd lost her law license, she didn't want people to know where she'd gone and what she was doing. Partly because it was humiliating to be accused of the things she'd been charged with. Partly because she didn't want to field questions. And partly because there were key people she didn't want to know she was here—which now seemed like a moot point.

Despite all her best efforts, Andi was nearly certain Victor knew she was in Alaska. She was also nearly certain he was behind the attempts on her life. In fact, just last month, she and Duke had seen him meeting with a hitman. Not long after, that very man had tried to run her down in his truck.

Thanks to Duke, he'd been unsuccessful. But the mere fact it had happened had unnerved her.

"Can you tell us about your daughter?" Andi kept her voice low and compassionate as she asked the question.

Elisapee flicked moisture from beneath her eyes before drawing in a deep breath. "She is wonderful. I call her my little moonbeam."

"Why did she leave the village?" Duke asked.

Elisapee pressed her lips together, as if she didn't want to answer. Then she drew in another shaky breath and pulled herself together. "Before she graduated high school, Luna went with a friend to Fairbanks. I warned her not to go, that no good would come of the trip, but she didn't listen. You know how teenagers are. While she was down there, her friend introduced her to the party scene. To alcohol. As you may know, our village is dry—and for good reason."

Andi had heard many villages didn't allow alcohol, but she wasn't sure if the reasoning was religious, cultural, or something else.

"Why is that?" Mariella asked.

"Alcohol has caused problems for many of our people," Tootega explained from her post near the door. "Alaska has one of the highest crime rates of any state, and alcohol only fuels those crimes. When people get drunk, they lose any good sense and do stupid things. Many villages choose to be dry to prevent those problems."

"How do you even police that?" Simmy asked. "I mean, if people want to drink in their homes, how would you know?"

"It is tricky," Tootega explained. "A town can only be dry if there are no roads connecting it to other towns. If someone at the airport gets a package they suspect is alcohol, they report it. Anyone breaking the law can be fined or arrested."

"I didn't think places like that existed anymore," Andi admitted.

"A few villages several years ago decided to allow alcohol back into their community," Tootega continued. "When they did, crime rates went up."

A clearer image of life in the village filled Andi's mind. But she didn't like the picture it formed. Criminals could take advantage of the remoteness. The same help afforded to other communities was nonexistent here as if they were in another country and not the USA.

"Many members of our tribe, when they become of age, decide to leave because of that rule," Tootega continued. "But things rarely turn out for them the way they desire. Oftentimes, they're ill-equipped to find jobs. Alcohol makes them lose their motivation. If you're in Fairbanks or Anchorage, you'll see a lot of homeless people. Many are from our tribal villages. They've moved and are unable to maintain a job or find housing. Yet they are not welcome back in our village either."

"So you're saying that's what Luna did?" Andi shifted as she tried to get into Luna's mindset.

Elisapee exchanged a glance with Tootega before nodding. "She got a plane ride to Coldfoot with a man from the village. He was taking a seasonal job firefighting for the BLM—the Bureau of Land Management. One of her friends said she'd meet Luna there to give her a ride. I found out after the fact that Luna's friend canceled."

"Could I have that friend's name?" Andi asked before taking another sip of her soup.

"Jessika Begay. She lives in Fairbanks."

"Was that the last time you heard from Luna?" Duke seemed to instantly snap back to his days as an investigator. A certain professionalism swept over him, transforming him from tour guide into interrogator. But, in this case, his interrogation was gentle and laced with empathy.

Andi wondered sometimes if he missed those days.

Tears rimmed Elisapee's eyes, and she nodded. "It was. I begged her not to go. I pleaded with her to stay. But she said she had no future here in this village. She gave me a hug and kissed my cheek. Then she left."

"What about the man who flew her to Coldfoot?" Simmy asked. "How can we get in touch with him?"

"Unfortunately, he passed away about six months ago of cancer," Tootega said.

"I'm sorry to hear that," Andi said before scooping up another spoonful of soup. "Before he passed away, did he have any insights to add?"

"He said when he dropped Luna off, he gave her one last chance to change her mind." Elisapee's voice cracked. "Told her he could bring her back home. We like to look out for our own. But Luna wanted to stretch her wings, to be independent."

"Did she get along with everyone here?" Mariella asked.

Elisapee shrugged. "Mostly. I mean, we fought sometimes."

"Something about Luna has always been a little defiant," Tootega said. "She was a bit distant from some of us."

Andi had a feeling there was more Tootega wanted to say. Did that defiance she'd mentioned Luna displaying have something to do with her father?

"Luna refused to come back." Elisapee's voice wavered. "She had her mind made up and wanted to get away from here. So that's what she did. He dropped her off near Coldfoot and left. As far as we know, he was the last one to see her—other than whoever may have taken her."

"You never got any ransom notes or any type of communication from Luna afterward?" Duke set his empty bowl on the table in front of him.

Elisapee swung her head back and forth as if to drive home the definitiveness of her answer. "Nothing. It was like she disappeared off the face of the earth." Her voice cracked, and she began to cry.

Andi struggled to find the words to comfort her. But what could she say?

Because there was no sentiment that would bring Luna back.

An ache formed inside Duke's chest as he listened to Elisapee's story.

He'd largely kept to himself after Celeste disappeared. Maybe he should have reached out more. Done more.

But he'd thought, at the time, he was doing plenty.

Seeing this woman's grief made him realize his pain could be a catalyst to help others. He'd heard it called redemptive suffering before.

He'd just been reading 2 Corinthians a couple of days ago. Chapter 1:3–4 read: The God of all comfort, who comforts us in all our troubles, so that we can comfort those in any trouble with the comfort we ourselves receive from God.

God had been talking to Duke through that passage, hadn't He?

His voice sounded strained as he said, "I'm so sorry to hear about your daughter. My fiancée also went missing along that highway."

At once, something shifted in Elisapee's gaze. "Is that right?"

He nodded. "Her name is Celeste, and I've been searching for her ever since."

She studied his gaze, a touch of desperation and restrained hope there. "Did you ever hear from her?"

"No. I'm like you. I've had no luck finding any answers, and I've been looking for the past two years."

"I'm sorry to hear that." Elisapee reached forward and squeezed his hand. "I know the difficulty your heart has endured, and I'm sorry for that."

The difficulty your heart has endured . . .

That was one way to say it.

The words were also accurate.

Would Duke's heart ever be the same?

He wasn't really sure. Sometimes he thought it would never recover. And living in the in between, in the waiting, had taken a toll on him. He felt as if he couldn't move on until he had some answers.

Lately, he'd been struggling to retain his joy, however.

"Is there anything else you can think to tell us?" Andi implored the woman with her gaze.

Duke wasn't sure if anything this woman had said would help them. But he felt compelled to hear more of her story, to learn more about life out here in the northwest corner of Alaska.

"I wish there was," Tootega interjected as Elisapee tried to pull herself together. "We had a couple of clues come into the village, but none of them panned out."

"What were those clues?" Mariella stirred her soup, probably using the motion to cover the fact it was only half eaten.

"Someone thought they saw Luna once when they were dog sledding about two hours east of here. Said they thought they saw her standing in the tundra with her coat on just staring in the distance."

"But you don't believe that it was really her?" Andi asked.

Elisapee shook her head again. "My friends believe Luna may be dead and her spirit returned to keep an eye on me. I . . . well, I don't know what to think."

Suddenly, the door opened, and a brisk wind filled the room.

They looked over and saw a man standing there.

Based on the veins bulging at his neck and the laser beams coming from his eyes, he was trouble.

Duke braced himself to act.

chapter
sixteen

ELISAPEE STOOD, her hand covering her heart. "Stan. I thought you weren't returning home until tomorrow."

The man breathed heavily as he glared at everyone in the room. "I finished early. Who are these people?"

"They want to help us find Luna," Elisapee's voice trembled. "I invited them."

"We don't speak that name in this house!"

Tootega stood. "Stan . . . they're just trying to help."

"If I wanted help, I would have asked!" He slammed his fist into the table beside him.

Andi wanted to intercede. To jump in and help.

But she sensed this wasn't her place. Tootega seemed to have a handle on the situation.

But Elisapee's obvious fear was unnerving.

"I want answers about our daughter." Elisapee gently touched his arm.

"She's dead to me!" His nostrils flared.

Tootega turned toward them. "I think we should go."

"Are you sure that's a good idea?" Duke's muscles visibly bristled as he turned toward the rest of the group.

"Yes, it is." Tootega nodded toward the door. "This conversation is done."

With one last look at Elisapee, the group thanked her for the soup and then stepped outside.

"Are you sure Elisapee is going to be okay?" Andi turned to Tootega once the door was closed.

"He'll calm down. Elisapee will tell me if he doesn't, and I'll handle it." The way she said the words made it sound as if she dealt with this situation often.

"Why is he so mad?" Mariella asked as they walked toward the truck. "I would think he'd want to find his daughter."

"Our culture is different than yours. She disrespected the family. Stan told Luna if she left, she'd never be welcome back."

Andi listened a moment, afraid she might hear something breaking inside the house or more yelling.

It was all quiet.

They climbed into Tootega's truck, the entire group more somber now.

"There was one other time someone thought they saw Luna," Tootega said as she cranked the engine and the truck roared to life.

Andi listened carefully, desperately wanting to learn anything that would provide them with some answers. Not for her sake, but for the sake of these victims' families and friends who'd been grieving for years.

"One of the young men from our village took a job up in the oil fields," Tootega said as she started down the road. "He could have sworn he saw Luna there when he was riding around with his supervisor. But he rolled down his window and called to her. She didn't answer. Then his supervisor pulled away, and the young man never saw her again afterward."

The oil fields.

Another mention of it.

That couldn't be a coincidence, could it?

How could they get up there to ask the right people some questions?

Andi didn't think they could.

Alpine's connections wouldn't do them any favors since he'd no doubt made enemies up in that area.

Where did that leave them?

They'd use the plane ride back to Fairbanks to talk more, to see what their next step would be.

Duke turned over everything in his mind as they boarded the plane to head back to Fairbanks.

He'd thought before he came here that this trip would yield nothing new. But he'd been wrong.

It was more than the clues Luna's mother had given them.

The connection he'd felt with Elisapee had been healing to his soul.

But he remained confused as to whether or not he should feel grief or anger about Celeste. If someone had hurt her, then definitely grief. But if she'd deceived him . . . how would he move on from that?

It all depended on whether or not Celeste had actually been abducted or if she'd simply run away.

Immediately, his thoughts turned to Stan. The man clearly had anger issues. Tootega said she could handle the situation. But he hated to think of Elisapee living with someone so volatile.

Yet he wasn't part of their culture. How could he really help?

He wasn't sure.

"What do you think we should do now?" Andi's voice cut into his thoughts.

He clicked his seatbelt in place as the pilot told them they were preparing to take off.

Simmy reached into a bag she'd brought with her and handed them each a sack lunch she'd packed before they left.

Duke thanked her and opened his bag and pulled out a turkey on wheat. He hadn't realized how hungry he was until he held the sandwich in his hands and smelled the yeasty bread.

That seal soup hadn't quite done it for him.

"Wait . . . I can't tell you how happy I am to see this!" Mariella practically beamed as she stared at her sandwich. "That seal soup . . . well, all I could think about were the cute little seals in *Happy Feet*—and how I was eating them."

"That was probably a big sacrifice Elisapee made by sharing her food with us," Ranger said.

Outback Ranger had probably eaten much worse. In fact, he'd probably fit right in at the village.

"I know, and I'm not ungrateful." Mariella frowned. "But it wasn't my thing, you know? I didn't even know people could hunt those."

"Only the natives," Ranger explained. "The state also allows them to hunt a certain number of whales every year. I was honored to be able to witness that one year. It was quite the sight—and the undertaking."

"I can only imagine." Mariella frowned again and shivered, as if she hated the thought of Free Willy being a meal. "Moving on to other subjects, I definitely think we should try to talk to Luna's friend Jessika. Especially if she's in Fairbanks."

"I agree," Ranger said. "Although I'm sure the police have talked to her as well as others, it can't hurt to hear her side of the story."

"Maybe we can try to track her down when we get back," Andi said as she peeked between her slices of bread. "What else?"

The plane taxied down the runway.

"I think we need to figure out how to get into the oil fields at Prudhoe Bay," Ranger said before popping a potato chip in his mouth.

"It's nearly impossible." Andi shook her head,

knowing that from experience. "They're locked down tighter than a military base."

"Why is that?" Mariella shrugged as if confused by the situation up there.

The plane bumped and bumped and bumped. Andi gripped the armrest, clearly nervous—especially after their flight here.

"This is your pilot," he said over the speaker. "I'm expecting a much smoother flight back to Fairbanks. So sit back, fasten your seatbelts, and off we go into the wild blue yonder!"

A few minutes later, they were airborne.

Andi seemed to relax and turned back to her sandwich.

"Probably because if the wrong person, aka a terrorist, were to be able to access that area, they could shut down the pipeline and oil production," Duke explained. "Then life as everyone knows it right now would change. It's too risky."

"I guess so . . ." Simmy said.

"People don't realize it, but oil is life," Duke continued. "Oil is to civilization what blood is to a human. I'm not saying that it's right or wrong. I'm not saying there aren't environmental implications to that. But that's just the way it is right now."

"As Alpine mentioned last night, some groups are advocating to start more drilling," Mariella said. "I have mixed feelings on that. I mean, we used gas to fly here. I'd be a hypocrite to say we shouldn't use oil or natural resources. But I just have to wonder if there's not a better way."

"Most people don't like the development that comes with the oil industry," Ranger added. "They opposed the pipeline because of the impact it would have on the area. Yet rules were put in place. It had to be a certain height so migrating animals would fit beneath it. It's monitored every day by a helicopter to make sure there are no leaks."

"Alpine said he opposes this new development," Matthew reminded them. "*Vehemently.*"

"There are definitely two sides to the issue," Duke said. "Let it be noted that Alpine flew in a private plane from California to Alaska and back."

"You have a point." Andi raised her eyebrows and nodded. "But returning to the subject at hand . . . let's say we decided that we should try to get onto the oil fields. What are some ways we could do that?"

"We could just ask," Mariella offered with a shrug.

If Duke could just have a touch of her optimism sometimes . . .

"They'll say no," Duke explained. "Though they do a limited number of tours, those tours won't take us anywhere helpful. We need a good reason to get as close as possible to the offices of this operation."

"What if we explain our podcast?" Mariella continued. "Don't you think they'd want to help?"

"Quite the opposite." Duke shook his head. "They'd definitely say no. Slam the door in our faces. They might even laugh before they slam the door."

Mariella frowned and slumped back into her seat.

"Anyone else have any other ideas?" Andi glanced at each of them, ever the negotiator.

"One of us could apply for a job there," Ranger said.

His suggestion startled Duke. It seemed so drastic, and other than Mariella and Matthew, they all had jobs. Duke didn't see either one of the twins getting their hands dirty.

"They *do* always distribute flyers, asking for workers," Simmy said. "I think I have one hanging in the trading post right now."

"Part of me likes that idea," Duke said. "But even if one of us were to get a job there, I've heard the process often takes months. I'm not sure how helpful it would be, especially when you consider the time commitment that would be involved. Who's going to give up everything to do that?"

Duke's question hung in the air.

Because it was a valid one.

However, Duke couldn't think of any more ideas about how to get onto those oil fields.

Was that where the answers waited?

Or did the answers rest with Jessika?

He didn't know. All they needed was one good lead.

chapter
seventeen

AS A MOMENT OF SILENCE FELL, Andi mentally reviewed everything she knew.

Eight victims had supposedly been taken, including Heidi Billingsworth who had disappeared last month.

None of them had been seen since they disappeared. No one had been found. And there had been no real sightings—unless you counted Luna, who'd possibly been seen in the tundra or in the oil fields. But there was no proof of that.

She supposed one could also include Celeste. No one was sure if that woman really was Celeste or someone imitating her. That was a whole other mystery within itself.

Charlotte had almost been a victim, but she'd gotten away. The man who'd tried to abduct her had been wearing a shirt bearing the name of an oil company.

In fact, more than one clue seemed to point to the oil fields.

If women were being taken there, Andi could think of only one reason that would be happening.

It was the same theory she'd thrown out earlier: human trafficking.

However, it also seemed like there were plenty of women who would freely go up to that area and offer their services. Andi didn't want to be crude, but that was a sad reality. Some women willingly and purposefully made a living from prostitution.

Despite that, human trafficking still existed. Maybe it was the demand. The money that could be made by those in charge. The control people liked to exert over others.

The details made Andi sick to her stomach.

Then there was the Celeste situation. Was she truly a victim here? For that matter, maybe these women weren't all connected. It seemed unlikely, but there still could be other outliers—women who maybe wanted to disappear.

Was Celeste one of those women?

Had that been Celeste in the hotel last night? If it was, why was she still hanging out in Fairbanks? Why would she want to hurt Duke? Why not just leave him alone?

So many things didn't make sense.

A few minutes later, they landed back in Fairbanks, and Andi let out a sigh of relief as she stepped back onto solid ground.

After they disembarked, the group circled around near Duke's SUV.

"What now?" Duke stared at each person as he waited to hear the next plan of action.

"I think that you and Andi should track down Luna's friend and talk to her. You two seem to be the best at that." Mariella glanced at Ranger and narrowed her eyes. "Wait . . . Ranger, you'd probably be good at it too, but we need someone close by to keep an eye on the rest of us."

Ranger grunted in response, not seeming to mind.

"I'm fine with doing that," Andi said. "What will you all do while we do that?"

"We can try to set up appointments with any of the other families. I tried several of them before we met this weekend, and most were unresponsive. I feel like it's mostly because they don't take us seriously, which surprises me since we did solve two murders so far."

"Not everyone keeps up with podcasts," Ranger reminded her.

"That's true," Mariella agreed with a slight frown. "But I'd still like to pursue this avenue and see what people say."

"Let's do it," Duke said.

They climbed into his SUV and made general chitchat as they headed back to the hotel. Once there, Duke dropped everyone but Andi off.

With the rest of the gang heading back inside, Andi climbed into the front seat and pulled her seatbelt on.

"I know this sounds random," Andi started. "But I just thought you should know . . . someone drained my entire bank account."

"What?" He turned toward her, shock in his gaze.

She nodded. "I was hoping it was a fluke. But it wasn't. All my money is gone."

"You think Victor is responsible?"

Her gaze locked with his. "He makes the most sense."

"Yes, he does. What are you going to do?"

"I can try to fight it at the bank, but I'm not sure how much good it will do. I know Victor covered his tracks."

"Can you even live on what you're making cleaning those offices?"

"No, not really. But don't you worry about it. I'll figure out something. I just thought you'd want to know." She shrugged, feeling self-conscious—not a normal emotion for her. She definitely needed to change the subject. "Anyway, I looked up this Jessika woman as you were driving here. I have an address."

Duke put his SUV back into Drive. "Great. Let's go."

Maybe their streak of bad luck would end . . . she could hope, at least.

"Here we are," Andi murmured.

Duke and Andi pulled up in front of a small house that couldn't be more than six hundred square feet.

The place wasn't well-kept on the outside. Parts of the siding were missing or cracked or crooked. Wood covered a window. Five cars parked in a driveway designed for only two.

Duke had been taken by surprise last night in the

parking lot. He didn't intend on letting that happen again.

He was usually much sharper than that.

But the chaos with Celeste continued to mess with his head and put him on edge.

"Stay on guard."

"Definitely," Andi agreed.

As he and Andi climbed from the SUV, memories of their last case filled his mind.

The investigation where they'd discovered Bobby and the woman who looked like Celeste. The investigation where they'd stumbled upon Victor meeting with a hitman.

Wherever they turned, the stakes seemed high and steep. One wrong move could land them not only in hot water, but maybe even in a coffin.

For that reason, part of Duke wished Andi hadn't come with him.

But he trusted her instincts, and she seemed to know how to handle herself.

As they approached the door, music blared from inside and laughter drifted outside. Was someone having a party? At 2:00 p.m. on a Saturday?

Duke knocked at the door, but there was no answer.

No surprise there since no one could probably hear over the music.

He knocked again, louder this time.

Still no answer.

He tried the doorbell, but he had his doubts it was working.

"Let me try." Andi reached for the door and pushed it open.

It was unlocked.

Duke's senses instantly went on alert. What was she thinking?

She could be like a tornado—unstoppable.

"Hello?" she called, waving a hand in the air. "Can anyone hear me?"

The music suddenly stopped. The room went silent. People froze and stared.

Eight people filled the small space.

Then a twentysomething man with a haze of smoke surrounding him broke through the shock. "What are you doing coming into my house like that?"

"We're looking for Jessika," Andi started, her voice unwavering. "It's important."

"Nobody barges into my home." The man stomped toward them, shifting his shoulders with every step in a way clearly meant to intimidate.

Duke braced himself for a fight. But they were outnumbered. Based on the smell in the air and the bottles in these people's hands, everyone here was both high and drunk.

Not a good combination.

"I'm trying to find out information about Jessika's best friend who went missing," Andi explained, still unflinching. "I don't mean any harm."

The man stopped and studied them with suspicion still flickering in his gaze. "You're not cops?"

"Do I look like a cop?" Andi stared up at him, cocking an eyebrow.

"Not really." Then his gaze went to Duke. "What about him?"

"I'm a tour guide." Duke decided to play up that angle of his life. Maybe it would come in handy right now.

The man squinted as if unsure he believed Duke.

Duke braced himself, waiting to see what this guy would do next.

Then a woman pushed through the group toward them. "I'm Jessika. What do you need?"

ANDI HAD to admit she felt slightly self-conscious as she sat on a ratty couch wedged between Duke and another large man who'd introduced himself as Boo Bear.

The whole group had squeezed into the living room, where they all sat together in a tight circle. Beer cans littered every visible surface, along with fast food wrappers, popcorn kernels, and Nerf bullets.

Andi wasn't sure what was thicker: the tension in the air or the smell of pot.

She glanced at Jessika, who sat in a chair across from her. The woman was in her mid-twenties with long, dark hair that had been crimped and then pulled into a side ponytail. Her face was round, making her appear heavier than she really was. Her eyes appeared glazed, probably from the dope she'd been smoking.

"Thank you for agreeing to talk to me," Andi started.

"So you guys are podcasters?" Jessika stared at them, a touch of fascination in her voice.

"That's right," Andi said. "I'm sure you heard about the Ice Fairy Killer here in Fairbanks a month ago."

"I did. It was horrible." She frowned. "More than horrible. I couldn't sleep knowing that guy was out there."

"We helped solve that." Andi was still proud of the work they'd done in that case, proud of the fact that a killer was now off the streets and women were safe—from this guy, at least.

"My friend is being humble," Duke added. "We *did* solve that case."

"That's fascinating." Jessika nodded before shrugging. "But why are you looking into Luna?"

Andi glanced at Duke, waiting for him to take the lead. He did.

"My fiancée also went missing off Dalton Highway two years ago. Since then, I've been obsessed with finding her. More than anything, I want answers."

"For sure." Jessika shifted, her foot kicking a crumpled beer can on the floor. "I still can't believe that Luna is missing. It seems like a nightmare."

"What can you tell us about her?" Andi started. "I heard that you were supposed to meet her up in Coldfoot."

Jessika glanced down in shame. "I was. But my friend got appendicitis, and I had to take her to the hospital. Luna didn't have a phone, so I wasn't able to reach her. I felt terrible about it. I didn't want to leave her stranded up there. But I didn't know what else to do."

"So what *did* you do?" Duke asked.

"I took my friend to the hospital and stayed with her until she was out of surgery and I knew she would be okay. By then it was too late to go anywhere that day. The next morning, I drove up to where Luna and I were supposed to meet. I was hoping she'd be there waiting for me. That maybe she'd found a place to stay overnight and had just assumed we got our days mixed up or something." Her voice dropped. "But she wasn't there."

"Did you stick around to look for her?" Andi asked.

"Yeah, I did. There aren't a lot of places to stop up that way. I didn't even run into that many people. It was frustrating, to say the least. It's not like here in the city where you can ask business owners or people who live in the area if they saw anything. Up there, it's barren. There's nothing."

Andi couldn't argue. Jessika's words were true.

"Did you turn around and go back to Fairbanks?" Andi asked.

Jessika shrugged as regret filled her gaze. "I didn't know what else to do so I just assumed Luna had found another way into town. When she didn't call me by the next day, I really got worried."

"Did you call the police?" Duke asked.

"I did, but they didn't seem that concerned. I mean, they seemed to think Luna had just run away from home and didn't want to be found. I couldn't even argue because the thought had crossed my mind as well."

"It's been almost four years now, and she hasn't been

seen or heard from since then," Duke said. "Is that correct?"

Jessika's eyes filled with tears, and she used the sleeve of her ratty flannel shirt to wipe beneath her eyes. "It is. I keep hoping that one day Luna will pop back into my life and explain it all with a laugh. But that hasn't happened yet."

"Do you have any other theories about what could have happened to her?" Andi shifted her leg, accidentally kicking a beer can beneath it. It clanked across the floor and hit the leg of the coffee table.

Jessika thought about Andi's question a moment before shrugging uncertainly. "There was this guy she liked. His name was Tito. They met when I brought her into town. Part of me wondered if the two of them had run off together because he disappeared around the same time."

Andi perked at her words. "Is that right? You haven't heard from him since then either?"

"Correct."

"You have this guy's last name?" Duke asked.

"Jackson, I think. Tito Jackson." Jessika nodded slowly. "But that's all I can tell you."

"I'm not sure if we know anything more now than we did before or not," Duke muttered as he and Andi climbed back into his SUV.

"It does almost seem like a no-win situation, doesn't it?"

"Absolutely. With communication being so difficult in the Far North and everything so barren, you're pretty much out of luck if you get lost or stuck up there. That's why I like doing the tours. I'd much rather people go up that way with me then try to venture out on their own. At least I have a satellite phone and people I check in with who know when I'm supposed to be where."

"Do you think we should check out this Tito guy?" Andi asked.

"We should search every possible lead." Duke nodded at her phone. "Do you want to do the honors or shall I?"

"Let me see what I can find out." She typed Tito's name into the phone.

As she did that, Duke turned on the radio. A news story blared from speakers.

"Crews are looking for missing travel website creator Heidi Billingsworth," the reporter announced. "They've sent a helicopter out to the area of Dalton Highway where she was last seen. Billingsworth is just one of many women who have disappeared along Alaska's Haul Road in the past several years . . ."

Andi sucked in a breath. "I can't believe how much coverage they're giving Heidi."

"It's about time."

Andi stole a glance at him. "If you don't mind me saying so, I'm surprised you haven't talked to the family and friends of the other victims already. It seems like something you'd do."

"I did try to contact some of them." Memories filled him of those desperate days. Days when he couldn't sleep or eat. When searching for Celeste had become an obsession. "Many of these women didn't have a strong social support system. I ran into dead ends. When I got nowhere, I decided to try to focus simply on Celeste. But there were no leads . . ."

"Did you ever consider going on air and asking for the media's help?"

"I tried. But there was a lot going on in the world at the time she disappeared, a lot of other hot topics to fill the airwaves. No one seemed interested. A couple of stations ran some brief clips about it, but nothing in-depth. Some of my Army buddies tried to help me. The problem was that every lead led nowhere."

"I can only imagine how frustrating that must have been."

"Extremely. You don't think things like that happen in this day and age, right? Stories of missing people fill the news. Only, you don't realize it, but not every missing person gets attention."

"Celeste seems like she would have been perfect for the news. She's pretty, young . . ."

"I wish I could tell you more, but I can't. It perplexed me also. I just had nothing to go on. I wonder if people thought she was looking for a reason to leave, to disappear."

"Refresh my memory: does she have any family?"

"No one she's close to. No siblings, and her parents are both dead."

"I see . . ."

His gaze clouded. "Now she's reappeared—it seems—and I have no idea what to do about it."

Andi cast him a soft smile. "I'm sorry. But here's some good news. I found someone named Tito Jackson online. He lives in Fairbanks, and he just posted on his social media thirty minutes ago. Says he's working at a drugstore about five minutes from here."

Duke's spirits lifted. "That sounds like a good start."

"Then let's go."

chapter
nineteen

IT WAS good to hear Duke open up. He usually kept everything inside him, almost as if he were protective of that information.

Did he think if he shared too many details that others would judge him? Did that scare him?

Andi didn't ask any of those questions. She'd simply be grateful for what he did open up about.

Besides, Andi had no room to talk. She had her own secrets. But her reasons were to protect others—and to protect her investigation.

She had a feeling Duke's was more because he felt like a failure.

She resisted the urge to reach out and touch him.

That wouldn't be a good idea.

Instead, she kept her hands in her lap as they headed down the road. When necessary, she threw out directions.

Finally, they pulled up to a little corner drugstore.

Duke parked, and they climbed out. Andi hoped Tito was still here.

The whole thing felt a little too easy.

But this guy could have some of the answers they needed.

She and Duke stepped inside and glanced around.

A woman worked the register, but she barely acknowledged them as they entered. Two customers milled around near the end of the aisles, shopping baskets in hand.

From the photo Tito had posted, it had appeared he was restocking the shampoo. Andi glanced at the overhead signs then headed in that direction, and Duke followed.

As they reached the aisle, she spotted the man wearing a navy-blue smock and a nametag.

Tito really was here.

The guy was probably forty pounds overweight, with most of the extra pounds in his stomach. He had thick, brown hair and large jowls. But there was still something very boyish about him.

He looked up as they approached and started to smile.

But something about them made him freeze. Perhaps it was the look of determination in their eyes. Or maybe it was the way they walked with purpose.

His eyes widened.

His muscles stiffened.

"Tito?" Duke called.

The next instant, the man dropped the shampoo bottles in his hands and took off in a run.

Duke wasn't going to let this guy get away.

Especially not if he had some answers.

He took off after Tito, dodging past the bottles on the floor.

Tito ran through the back door, into an employees-only area.

Duke followed, muttering apologies to the other employees he passed.

Tito burst through an outside door and into the daylight.

As he did, Duke was only a couple of steps behind him.

He closed the distance and grabbed the back of Tito's smock. "Stop running, Tito!"

The man jerked to a stop.

He froze, and then turned toward Duke as he slowly raised his hands. "I didn't do it."

What was this guy talking about?

Andi caught up with them and paused, barely out of breath. But her shorter legs had made her slower.

"You didn't do what?" Duke stared at Tito, daring him to try to lie.

"Whatever you think I did." Tito shook his head, sweat covering his skin.

"We're here to talk about Luna Clark," Duke said.

Tito's shoulders seemed to soften just slightly. "Oh,

Luna. Not about that fight I had last night with the jerk at Mulligan's?"

"We don't know anything about that." Andi recognized the name of a local bar. "And we don't care."

He studied them, a healthy dose of skepticism in his gaze. "You cops?"

"Nope," Duke said. "We're just looking for Luna."

Tito's shoulders softened even more. "You should have said so."

"You didn't give us a chance," Andi reminded him.

"What do you want to know?" He ran a hand through his hair and straightened his smock.

"We're trying to find Luna," Duke explained. "Her family is worried."

Tito snorted. "Her *family* is worried? Maybe her mom. Her dad couldn't wait for her to leave. It was one less mouth for him to feed."

Duke and Andi exchanged a confused glance.

"What are you talking about?" Andi's words came out as a squeak.

"Luna couldn't stand her father, and her father basically told her to leave. He would sneak alcohol into the village and get drunk. When he did, he was awful to Luna and her mom."

"That's the real reason Luna left?" Duke asked, his thoughts racing toward a conclusion that was both good and bad. Good because it could mean Luna was safe. Bad because they may have been following a lead that led them nowhere.

"Yeah. Of course." Tito shrugged as if the question was stupid.

"Did you hear from her after she left Noorvik?" Andi asked. "We know she got a ride to the highway. But no one has seen her since."

Tito snickered.

Duke's muscles tightened at his reaction.

This was no laughing matter.

What was this guy hiding?

chapter
twenty

ANDI WAITED, hardly able to breathe.

Why did Tito look as if this conversation amused him?

There was nothing funny about the situation with Luna.

Based on Duke's bristled muscles, he was thinking the same thing.

"I just talked to Luna last week." Tito let out another chuckle.

"What?" Andi's mouth nearly dropped open.

Was this guy joking? Because, if he was, it wasn't funny.

"Yeah, why do you look like it's a big deal?" Tito shrugged, appearing earnestly confused.

"Because everyone thinks she was abducted," Duke explained. "They've been looking for her for years."

Tito's smile slipped. "I don't know anything about that. I just know Luna is fine."

Andi tried to hold at bay her impatience. "Where is she?"

"Seattle. She moved there a couple of years ago. She seems to like it."

"The two of you aren't dating?" Andi continued.

"We did for a while, but we were better as friends."

"You never thought to report this?" Duke's voice hardened with agitation.

"Why would I?" Tito's words came out louder than before. "Her dad wanted her gone, so she left. She caught a ride down to Fairbanks, and we hung out for a while. She saved her money, and then went to Seattle. Nothing wrong with that."

"You had no idea people were searching for her?" Andi couldn't contain her surprise.

It was more than surprise.

She was downright dumbfounded.

Tito shrugged again. "No idea. It never came up."

Duke shifted, his gaze growing darker. "The police never talked to you?"

"No, never." Tito glanced back and forth between them. "You guys look super intense."

"We thought Luna was dead," Andi told him. "Her mom thinks she's dead."

"I don't know what to tell you. Luna left. End of story. Do you want proof?" Tito pulled out his phone. "I'll give you proof."

❄

Duke watched as Tito hit several buttons on his phone. A moment later, a woman's voice came from the speakers.

"Tito? What's going on?"

"I have two people here who don't believe you're still alive," he said.

The woman on the other line snorted. "Of course I'm alive. What's this about?"

"They said you disappeared from the highway, and they believe you were abducted." Tito stared at the screen, his expression relaxed and casual.

"Don't be ridiculous. Who would think that?"

Tito eyed Andi and Duke from over the top of his phone. "I don't know who they are exactly. Can you talk to them so I can get back to work? I can't afford to lose another job."

"Sure thing. Put them on. I can set them straight."

Tito turned the phone toward them, and the face of a woman who looked exactly like Luna Clark filled the screen. Her hair was different now—shorter with streaks of purple. Her face was a little fuller.

But it was clearly Luna.

"I hear you're looking for me." She stared at them through the phone.

"Are you Luna Clark?" Duke still sounded cautious.

"Yeah, who else would I be? Blake Lively?" She let out a laugh. "Why do you look so surprised?"

Andi moved closer to Duke so Luna could see her on the screen also. "Because you were reported missing. We're investigating the disappearances of several other women along the Dalton Highway. We thought you were one of them."

Luna shrugged, seemingly unaffected by Andi's words. "Oh . . . I get it. But I'm fine. I wanted to leave home and start a new life. So I did. I couldn't stay in the village anymore."

"You never told your mom this?" Andi asked. "She's been worried sick."

Luna's expression fell. "I wanted to. I did. But then my father would force her to share what she knew. I didn't want him to find me. It was better if I just lost all contact."

"From what I heard, he thinks you're dead," Andi murmured.

"He might say that. But the truth is that he wants me dead. He hates me. He hates me even more for leaving my family behind."

Andi shook her head as she processed Luna's words. "If you haven't seen him since you left, how do you know that?"

"I saw him in Fairbanks looking for me once. That's when I knew I had to get away. He thinks I disrespected the family, and he wants me to pay. That's the way my father has always been. He's just too smart to say things like that out loud. He'd rather people think I'm already dead."

"What about Jessika?" Andi continued. "You didn't tell her that you were alive either?"

Her gaze darkened. "Jessika only thinks about one person—Jessika. Don't believe her story about her friend going to the hospital to have surgery so she couldn't meet me. No, she'd met a new guy, got high with him, and left me stranded up there. I knew I didn't want anything to do with her after that."

"Well . . . I'm glad you're okay," Andi finally said.

"I'm fine. You can tell my mother and maybe even the police. But please don't make this public. I've started a new life—one I'm enjoying. The last thing I want is for my father to find me."

"We'll be discreet," Andi said. "I promise."

Duke and Andi exchanged a look.

Luna Clark wasn't missing after all.

The police had barely searched for her.

And now they'd wasted precious time looking into her disappearance.

ANDI AND DUKE climbed back into his SUV and sat there in stunned silence.

"That was a twist I didn't see coming," Andi finally said as she mentally replayed the conversation.

"Me neither." Duke raked a hand through his hair. "I can't believe the police didn't look into Luna's disappearance any more than they did. They should have found her. Gibson should have been more on top of this."

"I guess we have one answer." Andi was trying to look on the positive side.

"We'll have to let everyone else know—starting with Elisapee and Gibson," Duke let out a slow sigh. "I *am* glad Luna is okay. But I have to wonder how many of these other women might also be okay. Maybe we're chasing answers to a crime that isn't really a crime."

"You're thinking of Celeste, aren't you?" Andi studied him. "It was two years ago this month she disappeared."

"Two years today."

She sucked in a breath. "This is the anniversary of her disappearance? I'm so sorry."

"Don't be sorry. It is what it is."

Andi nodded, knowing there was nothing else to say. He didn't want her to make a big deal out of this.

After a moment, Duke released a long breath. "So far, every lead has brought us answers we haven't anticipated. I have no idea what's going on. I don't know if Celeste is a victim or if she played a part in her own disappearance."

"We'll figure it out," Andi assured him.

He cast her a glance. "Why do you sound so certain about that?"

"I just am." Andi wasn't prone to giving up. It wasn't in her DNA. People had said it was what made her a good lawyer.

They stared at each other a moment, something unspoken passing between them—an understanding, of sorts.

Duke wasn't prone to giving up either.

They would both stick with this until they found what they were looking for.

"I guess we should get back to the hotel," Andi finally said.

"I guess we should. Maybe the others found some answers."

"Let's hope." Andi grabbed her phone. "As you drive, I'll make those calls to Elisapee and Gibson."

A few minutes later, Duke and Andi pulled into the lot in front of the hotel.

As they did, Duke scanned everything around him.

He knew it wasn't likely that the person who'd knocked him out last night would still be around. But it was prudent to look. However, he saw no one. Only parked cars and trucks.

Where had that man and woman gone? How could he figure out exactly who they were?

Duke wasn't sure.

These people didn't want their identities to be known, which made everything more complicated. But Duke wasn't about to give up.

As soon as they walked into the hotel, Mariella greeted them. Based on the excited look in her eyes, she had an update for them.

Anticipation thrummed through Duke's blood.

Maybe they finally had a real lead.

"I have news," Mariella announced.

"So do we," Andi said. "You first."

"You'll never believe this." Mariella's eyes danced. "But I just got a call from Keith Morrison."

"*The* Keith Morrison?" Andi asked. "From *Dateline NBC*?"

"He's the one!" A grin stretched across Mariella's face.

"Why did he call?" Duke asked.

"He heard we'd solved two cases, and now *he* wants to interview *us*." She squealed and did her cheerleader clap. "Can you believe it?"

Duke saw the apprehension wash over Andi's features at the possibility. Her lips went taut, her eyes narrowed, and her shoulders broadened.

She didn't like that idea, did she?

"I don't think that's a good idea." Andi's voice hardened as she shook her head.

Mariella's smile dropped as if Andi had just told her Santa didn't exist. "Why not? This is what we wanted. More recognition and exposure."

"I think we should stay focused on solving these cases." Andi shrugged, unaffected by Mariella's argument.

"Publicity like this would *help* us solve more cases," Mariella continued. "If we put out a plea for answers on national TV, maybe someone will come forward."

"Or a whole lot of people are going to come forward with information that really doesn't mean anything," Andi said. "Then we're going to waste all our time combing through leads that take us nowhere."

Mariella curled up her nose in offense. "I never took you as a pessimist."

"I'm not trying to be a pessimist. I'm just trying to think this through."

Mariella shrugged as if brushing off Andi's words. "Well, I think it's a great opportunity. Someone out there knows *something*. Maybe this will spur them to reach out."

"Then you go, Mariella."

Mariella tilted her head, still staring at Andi. "I don't understand why you want to stay hidden. Are you ashamed of what we're doing?"

Andi nearly blanched. "Not at all. But . . . I guess there are things in my past I prefer to keep in my past. If I go on national TV, I'm going to have to face them."

"If I go on national TV, maybe I can redeem myself from the fiasco I left behind!"

The two women stared at each other.

Mariella had left scandal behind when she fled California. Good publicity would only help her. But any amount of publicity could hurt Andi.

Matthew strode up, clueless about their turbulent interaction. "I just heard back from Ted, the husband of Emilia Sparkman. He's about twenty minutes away."

"That's great." Duke kept his voice even. The tension was so thick right now that one wrong word could send everything around him crashing. "Where does he want to meet?"

"Here." Matthew pointed at the floor. "At the hotel. We're going to need to put together our questions fast."

"Then we should get started." Andi took a step back.

But as Duke glanced from Mariella to Andi, Duke saw strain still in Andi's gaze.

Working as a team wasn't easy, especially when they each had strong personalities.

If they didn't work together, then they'd be working against each other.

And part of their strength was their differences.

How were they going to keep that in the forefront of their minds?

chapter
twenty-two

ANDI CLEARED her throat as they all gathered in the conference room several minutes later. Then she announced, "We found Luna."

Everyone turned to them, their eyes widening with shock.

She knew she needed to tell them before she got too caught up in preparing their interview questions.

"What?" Mariella paused near Matthew's computer and gave Andi a death glare. "Why didn't you tell us?"

Andi resisted a smart answer. She could be mature here. "She's in Seattle. She basically wanted to get away and start a new life."

"Are you sure?" Simmy leaned against the table as if trying to find her balance.

"We talked to her ourselves on a video call," Duke said. "She said another friend picked her up off the highway after Jessika blew her off. The two women didn't talk after that. But Luna is fine."

"So this guy doesn't have eight victims . . ." Mariella rubbed her temples as if she had a headache coming on. "Who else is on our list who shouldn't be?"

No one answered—the question was clearly rhetorical.

"We'll need to give our listeners an update on the podcast." Mariella sucked on her bottom lip a moment. "The good news is that this will make for a great episode, especially if we're the ones breaking the news."

"Luna doesn't want people to know," Andi said. "Only her mom and the police. We can't go live with this."

"But this is the kind of update we need!"

"If the people we're interviewing and trying to help don't trust us, then our podcast is going to be meaningless!" Andi shot back.

"I'd love to talk about this more." Matthew glanced at his smart watch. "But right now, we need to get our thoughts together. Ted should be here any time now."

Matthew was right.

Andi tried to mentally prepare herself for meeting Emilia's husband. But her thoughts were all over the place.

She hated the idea of going on national TV to be interviewed, even if it was by Keith Morrison. She had a feeling other people in the group would feel the same way since they were using nicknames instead of their real identities—other than Mariella and Matthew, who were the face and backbone of all this.

Sometimes Andi wondered if they'd all gotten in over their heads. She certainly felt that way sometimes.

She'd come to Alaska for a very specific purpose, and she'd allowed herself to become distracted. She'd told herself it was just as well since she wasn't making any progress on bringing down Victor, nor did she have very many leads or opportunities to find out the information she needed.

But she had to remember not to let down her guard. Victor was not one to be underestimated.

The rest of the group talked about questions they'd ask Ted, but Andi barely listened.

Someone else would have to take the lead on this interview. She had her mind on too many other things.

As she sat at the table thinking about how difficult it might be to track down her missing money and wondering what else Victor might try to do, her phone buzzed.

Her video doorbell sent her a notification. She'd just installed it a couple of weeks ago after she feared someone had been in her apartment while she was away.

Usually, the notifications were nothing. Neighbors leaving their homes at the apartment building. People walking their dogs. Maintenance men shoveling snow.

But this time, Andi clicked on it to see what was happening.

A woman wearing a baseball cap that shadowed most of her face stood at her door.

The woman stared at the camera, making no move to try to get inside.

Andi straightened her back as she studied the woman.

That was when the realization hit her.

This was Celeste . . . or Ella. Or whoever that woman was.

Andi was certain of it.

"Duke . . ." she said, but she couldn't drag her gaze away from the video screen.

Her pulse quickened as she waited to see what the woman would do.

What was she doing at Andi's apartment? Her showing up there didn't make any sense.

"What is it?" Duke leaned closer.

She showed the image to him.

He sucked in a breath when he realized what he was looking at. "Is that your place?"

"It is."

"What in the . . . ?" He ran a hand over his face as if trying to ward away his frustration.

That was her thought exactly.

Anger burned through Duke as he stared at Celeste's image.

Was this woman mocking him? Crying for help?

Was this Celeste at all?

Without asking permission, he hit a button on the screen that allowed him to speak through the doorbell.

"Celeste?" he called. "Is that you?"

The woman looked up, her eyes startled and wide. She stared at the camera again, her lips parting.

The next instant, she darted away.

Duke had spooked her.

She'd recognized his voice, hadn't she?

He squeezed the phone hard enough to burst.

Why hadn't she talked to him?

Or was there someone else with her? Someone maybe waiting just out of sight?

He had no idea.

One thing was sure: he was tired of these games.

He stood and turned to Andi. "We've got to get to your apartment. Now."

"What's going on?" A knot formed between Mariella's eyes as she glanced back and forth between them.

Duke didn't answer. All he could think about was Celeste showing up at Andi's door.

Maybe this woman had been watching him. She'd clearly known he was staying at the Grayling Lodge.

If that truly had been Celeste, was this her way of making a statement? Of saying she suspected Duke had feelings for another woman?

For that matter, was this entire situation and everything that had happened in the past two years calculated?

The questions and possibilities continued to haunt him.

Andi grabbed his wrist before he rushed from the table. "Duke . . . she's gone. We can leave now, but she won't be there, and we won't catch up."

His gaze burned into Andi's. "What was she doing at your apartment?"

"I have no idea," Andi murmured. "But she didn't go inside. She just paused outside my door."

"She looked right at the video doorbell." His muscles tightened as he remembered what he saw.

Her face had been mostly shadowed, but her gaze had clearly been on the camera. Unfortunately, Duke couldn't tell anything else by the video.

Couldn't see if the woman was bruised or disheveled. Couldn't see any fine details to confirm if it was really Celeste or someone who looked like her.

"She wanted you to know she was there," Duke finished.

Andi couldn't deny his words. "You're right. I don't know what's going on. But, like I said, even if we rush over there right now, we're not going to catch her. She's gone."

Duke knew Andi was right. He fisted his hands, not liking any of this.

"Can someone fill us in?" Ranger tapped his pen on the table.

Andi glanced at Duke, waiting for him to take the lead.

He unfisted his hands and drew in a deep breath as he tried to get his emotions under control.

"Someone who looked an awful lot like Celeste just showed up at the door to Andi's apartment," he told them.

"What?" Simmy sounded nearly breathless as she stared at Duke. "What sense does that make?"

"It doesn't make any sense." Andi kept her voice all-business. "Someone is clearly trying to mess with us right now."

"Is this because we're investigating this case? Or is it something more personal?" Ranger stared at Duke.

"I have no idea."

Before they could talk about it anymore, someone knocked at the door.

They turned to see Ted Sparkman standing there.

This conversation would have to wait till later.

But those images wouldn't leave Duke's thoughts.

chapter
twenty-three

SHE WAS AGITATING ME.

I'd given her chances.

Over and over again.

But she kept messing up.

The shepherd's pie needed salt. The potatoes on top weren't whipped the way they were supposed to be. And she'd used too much paprika.

When she sat across from me to watch me eat my meal first—as it should be—her eyes were glazed and teary again.

I'd asked her to pull herself together.

She nodded, but her eyes remained lackluster.

I was trying to be her knight in shining armor. I'd tried to rescue her from the life she'd once had.

All she had to do in return was to take care of me.

Why was that so hard?

She didn't have anyone else in her life to worry about.

It was just me. Why couldn't she simply follow my commands?

The agitation grew inside me, turning over and over again.

I tried not to show my temper. It wasn't manly.

But I wasn't sure I'd be able to control it much longer.

"You don't like it?" She stared across the table at me.

"You didn't follow the recipe as I told you."

"But I did, Master. I was very careful."

My fist hit the table, and the plates jumped. "Not careful enough!"

She drew back, fear fluttering through her gaze. "I'll do better next time."

But would there be a next time?

Maybe this wasn't panning out the way it should.

"Now it's your turn to eat. You can see what I'm talking about." He shoved the casserole dish toward her.

"But I'm . . . I'm not hungry." She stared at the food.

"Eat anyway." My voice hardened.

"Yes, sir." She nodded and quickly served herself some from the dish at the center of the little table. She took a bite and swallowed.

"Well?" I asked her.

"It's fine to me, but . . . I don't usually eat this."

My fist hit the table again, causing everything to clatter. "It's *not* fine. I told you it wasn't fine. Are you not listening to me?"

"You asked my opinion, so I thought you wanted it."

Rage filled me, and I flew from my chair. In one

motion, I grabbed her shoulders and slammed her against the wall.

"*My* opinion is *your* opinion. Don't you understand that?"

Tears poured from her eyes as she stared at me. "Yes, of course I understand."

"Your job is not to question me. Do you understand?"

She nodded, grasping at my hand as it circled her neck, trying to pry my fingers away. "Yes." Her voice cracked.

As her face began to redden, I realized I was squeezing too hard.

I released her, and she slipped to the floor.

Pathetic.

That's what she was.

"Get up," I told her.

She glared at me once before pushing her hands against the floor and attempting to stand.

But she was clumsy. Taking too long.

Using my foot, I pushed her. She seemed to spill onto the floor, collapsing into a heap of tears again.

I couldn't take the weeping anymore. It was driving me mad.

"Stop crying." Each word came out hard and pointed.

"I *am* trying," she insisted as more tears flew down her cheeks.

"Try harder."

"Yes, Master."

"Now stand up."

She managed to pull herself to her feet. "Clean the

kitchen. When you're done, I'll be in my recliner waiting for you to rub my feet."

She nodded. "Yes, Master."

"Good. I don't want a repeat of what just happened."

"Me neither."

I reached for her and ran my thumb along her cheek. Maybe she was learning after all.

She went still at my touch. Didn't flinch.

Yes, she was learning.

"You're being a good girl now," I murmured. "My lessons have taught you well."

chapter
twenty-four

ANDI DIDN'T THINK she'd be able to concentrate, but Ted was surprisingly compelling.

The man was forty-two years old and a Wisconsin transplant. He'd moved to Alaska to work for the National Science Foundation and study caribou for a year. He and Emilia didn't have any children or any family in the area.

He told them about how his wife had always wanted to drive to the Arctic Ocean. He had planned to go with her, but she didn't want to wait for him to get time off from work. She thought it would be an adventure.

So she took off one morning, determined to get to the sign proclaiming Arctic Circle and take a picture before returning home. It would be a long day, but the drive was doable.

She knew the dangers of the area. Knew that cell phone service was nearly nonexistent.

But she'd made up her mind to do it anyway.

A lot like Celeste had done.

When Emilia didn't return home that evening, Ted became worried. He tried to call her, but it was no surprise when she didn't answer.

He waited a couple of hours, assuming the trip was taking longer than expected.

When Emilia wasn't home by eleven that night, Ted got in his truck and took off to drive the route.

He'd known traveling the Dalton Highway was risky, that the road could be treacherous. At least it was September, and he still had hours of daylight.

But he'd been on edge at that point.

Halfway to the Arctic Circle, on the opposite side of the highway, he spotted Emilia's parked car.

He did a U-turn and pulled behind it. But when he checked out her vehicle, his wife wasn't inside.

In fact, it appeared she'd gotten a flat tire.

So where had she gone? Had she walked somewhere for help? Had someone come past and offered to give her a ride back into town?

Those seemed the most likely theories.

At that point, Ted had still held onto hope. Maybe Emilia was just trying to get to some cell phone service and then she'd call.

He left a note inside the car saying he'd been there and was looking for her. Then he started back to Fairbanks.

He thought for sure by the next morning he'd hear from her.

But he didn't, and that was when he called the police.

That was when the investigation started.

Out of all the women who'd gone missing along the highway, the search for Emilia was one of the most predominant. Ted was a respected scientist in the area, and he had many colleagues behind him.

But he never heard a peep from her. No one had any clues as to where she might be. No trace of her had ever been found.

Ted's story didn't surprise Andi. But it was another tragedy.

Where were these missing women now? Were they still alive?

Did the person behind this abduct these women, keep them for a while, and then murder them? After all, there were various time spans between each disappearance.

Either way, this seemed to be the same story just with different players.

"You decided to stay in this area?" Mariella asked Ted as they wrapped up. "I think you were only supposed to come for a year, correct?"

"That's right." He twisted the wedding ring on his finger. "I did end up staying. In fact, I just got remarried a few months ago."

Andi's eyebrows shot up in surprise.

"Wait . . . aren't you still legally married to Emilia?" A knot formed on Mariella's brow as she asked the question.

"Officially, a person must be missing for five years before they can be declared dead." Ted shifted, sweat spreading across his forehead. "I didn't know what to do, but my gut told me she wasn't coming back. It was a hard decision, but the only way I could get remarried was by divorcing her."

"Really?" Mariella tilted her head, still in obvious shock.

Ted nodded slowly, in a way that made Andi wonder if he'd gotten a lot of flak over his decision.

"Obviously, Emilia wasn't around to contest it." Ted rubbed his jaw and glanced away. "Like I said, it was a hard decision. But I still have life left to live. We're not promised tomorrow, and I was tired of being miserable. Kate makes me happy. That's what Emilia would have wanted."

Andi's gaze slid to Duke, but his expression was unreadable.

However, this conversation had to make him think.

Ted had remarried . . .

The thought circled in Duke's mind.

That meant Ted assumed his wife was dead. That he'd chosen to move on.

Something Duke couldn't bring himself to do.

He and Celeste weren't even legally bound together like two people who were married. But he'd been committed to her. They'd planned their future together.

Duke had held out hope for so long.

Yet with all these new developments with Celeste, he

didn't really know what to think.

When was the right time to let go?

He wasn't sure if he'd ever know that answer.

They thanked Ted, and then Mariella and Ranger walked him to the door.

They rejoined the group a few moments later, and Duke waited for them to evaluate everything the man had said.

"I'm inclined to think the person behind these crimes is either brilliant or lucky." Andi leaned back in her chair and took a sip of coffee. "I mean, he's chosen the perfect location for his crimes—there are so few people out in the Far North to witness anything. But everyone's got to mess up at some point. I just can't believe the police haven't found any footprints or fingerprints or anything to help them."

"It *is* kind of unbelievable." Mariella rubbed her lips together in thought. "How are we going to find answers?"

"I know we talked about this earlier, but I still feel like this all goes back to the oil fields." Ranger crossed his arms as if sealing his opinion. "Maybe if we could figure out a way to get there then we could find out answers."

"Maybe." Mariella shrugged.

"Think about it," Ranger continued, a surprising passion in his voice. "Charlotte said the man who picked her up was wearing a shirt with the oil company name on it. Those fields are our connection point, the place that makes the most sense. The people most frequently using the highway are those traveling to the oil fields."

"We could reach the camps, but we can't reach the high security areas where the pump stations are located," Andi said. "Even when I was driving trucks up there, I was only allowed so far into the facility."

"Where did you stay when you were there?" Mariella asked.

"I stayed at one of the camps where Windswept Transportation made arrangements for us," Andi said. "Truthfully, most likely, that's where any illegal operations would be taking place anyway. You need a badge to get into the important areas of Prudhoe Bay."

"Did someone say Prudhoe Bay?" a new voice entered the conversation.

Duke looked up to see Alfonso standing there.

The man stepped inside the conference room, his eyes bright with curiosity. "I wasn't trying to eavesdrop on your conversation, but I happened to be walking past and overheard."

They must have accidentally left the door cracked.

Mariella pouted before saying, "We have some roadblocks with our new investigation. Big ones. Security clearance ones."

"I can get you into Prudhoe Bay," Alfonso announced.

Duke straightened at the man's words. "How do you propose doing that?"

"My brother runs operations up there. Every once in a while, I send shipments of odds and ends for him and his crew, just for giggles."

Now this guy had Duke's interest. "What kind of shipments?"

"Things they won't get otherwise. I always like to put my own personal touch on them. Once I sent everyone bobblehead dolls that looked like abominable snowmen. Another time I sent them decks of playing cards made with disappearing ink. One of my favorites was the time I sent them nose flutes." He imitated what it would look like to play one and then laughed, obviously amusing himself.

Duke didn't know what to think about that, yet another part of him wasn't surprised. Alfonso was pretty off the wall.

"Do you have anything you plan to send them now?" Andi put her hands on her hips as she waited for his answer.

He shrugged. "I'm sure I could think of something."

"Who do you usually hire to take those up for you?" Duke asked.

"Various transportation companies. But I can have my brother add your names to the list at the gate. They'll let you in. Then my brother can give you a tour."

Andi tilted her head as she observed Alfonso. "You would do that for us?"

Alfonso nodded with gusto. "Absolutely. You all are doing a good thing, and I'd love to help."

Duke glanced at the rest of the team.

This could be the opening they'd been looking for.

chapter
twenty-five

"I CAN SEE it in your eyes," I told Anna as she rubbed my feet. "There's something you want to ask me."

She glanced at me as if uncertain.

And she said nothing.

"I'm giving you permission to ask," I told her, feeling gracious. "Go ahead."

She remained silent another moment before finally asking, "The hair in the box. Who did it belong to?"

"Those who came before you."

Her skin dropped three shades lighter. "There were others?"

"Of course there were others. One day, I'll find the perfect one."

"The perfect one?" She eased from rubbing my feet as if she couldn't do two things at once.

I nodded at her, and she began to rub harder.

"One day I'll find the one who will stay forever. She'll appreciate me. She'll know her place."

"What happened to the women the hair belongs to?"

"It's not important."

"It's important to me." Her voice shook as she said the words.

My gaze locked with hers. "You don't want to know what happened to them."

Anna froze, her eyes glazing as if she might pass out.

"All you have to do is listen," I told her. "That's it. If you do, you can keep your hair. Do you understand?"

Her eyes widened, and she nodded.

"Say it," I growled.

"I . . . I understand."

"Say it louder."

"I understand."

"I understand, who?" I asked her.

"I understand, Master."

I stared at her a moment, wanting to feel satisfied. But I didn't.

This one was taking a long time to break.

"No one is looking for you, you know," I told her.

She looked up at me, startled. "What?"

"Your family doesn't care that you're gone. You weren't important to them."

"That's not true." Her voice trembled again.

"But it is. Let's talk about that other man."

Her eyes lit. "Braden?"

"Yes, Braden. He says he loves you. But he doesn't."

"Why would you say that?" She stared at me, hardly breathing.

A burst of pleasure shot through me. "You and I both know he's unfaithful. He's not a real man. I rescued you from him."

"You think my husband . . . cheated on me?"

I locked gazes with her. "I know he did."

"No, he wouldn't do that. He's a good man."

"He's not a good man!" My voice rose. "And I don't want to ever hear you say that again. Nor do I want to hear you say his name. Understand?"

She swallowed hard. "I understand."

"I understand what?"

"I understand, Master."

It was going to take some more work to break her. But I wasn't giving up yet.

Instead, I grabbed a book from beside my chair.

A Woman's Guide to Making Her Man Happy.

My favorite.

I shoved it at her.

"Read the first chapter," I barked. "Out loud."

She glanced at me uncertainly before taking the book. Her hands shook as she opened it. Then she began reciting the words.

"A woman's place is in the home," she said. "Her goal should be to make her man happy . . ."

I settled back.

Yes, this was my favorite book of all.

I hung onto every word.

Just like my granddad had.

twenty-six

ANDI LEANED back in her chair as she tried to think through the details of Alfonso's proposal.

The hotel owner had left, giving the group a moment alone to hash this out.

Before he'd stepped away, he'd promised to brainstorm what he had on hand to send to his brother, if the murder club chose to accept his invitation.

Andi glanced at the team around her as they stood in the conference room. "This could be our best opportunity to find out answers."

"I agree," Duke said.

"But we still have a lot of things we'd need to work out," Mariella added as she propped her hip against the table.

"We only have a day and a half left here," Andi said. "If we do this, it's going to take the rest of our time together. It takes at least eleven hours to drive up there."

"The good news is that we could talk and work as we

drive," Mariella said. "And it would give us an opportunity to see the locations where some of these women were abducted. Plus, I believe up in Coldfoot is where the next victim disappeared. The one who just happened to be a prostitute. Kiah Franz."

"The other question is what do we do when we get there?" Duke asked. "Even if Alfonso's brother gives us a tour of this place, it's not like this guy is going to show us where a brothel or human trafficking organization might operate. If we ask too many questions, people will get suspicious."

"We can be subtle. Maybe even talk to people and make an inside connection. That's what I tried to do as an ice road trucker." Andi clamped her mouth closed as if realizing she'd said too much.

"Wait . . . why did you want to make connections up in Prudhoe Bay?" Mariella squinted in confusion.

Andi's cheeks reddened. "It's a long story, but I have a bit of history with someone who works there, and I've been trying to find out some information."

Mariella narrowed her eyes and nodded slowly as realizations seemed to click in her mind. "I *knew* there were other reasons for you being here."

Andi licked her lips and remained calm. "It would be suspicious if all of us went up there. Especially if we're supposed to be delivery drivers."

"She's got a point," Duke said.

"Then I think Duke and Andi should go up to Prudhoe Bay and report back to us what they find afterward," Mariella said. "You guys make the most sense. Duke because it's your fiancée who's missing. And Andi because you've driven up that way so many times before."

Andi and Duke exchanged glances before nodding.

"It seems like a crazy idea," Andi said. "But I think we need to grab hold of this opportunity while it's dangling in front of us."

"The rest of us could talk to some people in Coldfoot," Ranger said. "We could take two vehicles. That way Simmy and I could just stay up there instead of coming back down here only to leave again."

"That sounds like a good idea to me," Simmy said. "We should move our operations up north for the remainder of our time together. We've done most of what we can do here."

At just that moment, Andi glanced out the door and saw that man again.

The one she'd seen earlier, the man she'd thought was watching her.

He'd been lingering near the conference room.

Had he been eavesdropping?

She jumped to her feet, her chair hitting the floor behind her.

"Andi?" Duke asked.

"Excuse me a minute." Before anyone could stop her, she charged from the room.

But no one was in the hallway.

She rushed to the lobby, but the man wasn't there either.

Andi scanned the room.

Where had that guy gone?

Who was he? Another hitman? The guy responsible for draining her bank account?

He couldn't have gotten that far away.

She hurried through the space, asking anyone she ran into if they'd seen the man.

No one said they'd spotted him.

It was almost like he was . . . a ghost.

However, Andi didn't believe in ghosts.

And she would figure out who this guy was, if it was the last thing she did.

The gang went next door for dinner and discussed things as they ate.

Duke listened as Andi explained what happened, why she'd run out of the room like she had. But there was clearly more to the story.

He would ask her more later.

First, they ordered their food, including some cheese sticks as an appetizer.

As they waited for the waiter to return with their drinks, Duke scanned the area around them.

His gaze stopped on a man eating at a table across the restaurant.

Something about the man seemed familiar, but Duke wasn't sure what.

He was with another man, and the two seemed to be catching up over some beer.

There was nothing suspicious about that.

So why had the guy caught Duke's attention?

He wasn't sure, but he stored the man's image away in the back of his mind.

Mariella began talking about their plan for tomorrow.

They'd need to leave bright and early—no later than three a.m. Make sure they were gassed up and had food and blankets just in case things went wrong.

By the time they finished that discussion, their food arrived.

As it did, those two men sitting across the restaurant tossed some cash on the table and left.

Neither of them looked back as they did.

Maybe Duke was just reading into things.

Duke lifted a prayer and then took a bite of his elk burger.

As they all started eating, Mariella's phone dinged. She glanced at it before gasping.

Duke braced himself. What now?

"You guys . . . it's Charlotte." Mariella's voice danced. "She did a sketch with the state police down in Anchorage."

"And?" Duke prodded.

"And she sent it to me." Mariella turned her phone so they could see. "This is what he looks like."

Duke stared at the picture.

The sketch showed a man who very much fit the

description Charlotte had shared with them. However, the guy really didn't resemble Bobby Lad after all.

He didn't look like anyone Duke had ever seen.

At least they had an image of the possible perpetrator.

It was something to go on. He was certain Mariella would add it to the murder board.

Duke stared at the sketch again, trying to burn the man's face into his mind.

Then Mariella's phone dinged again.

Her expression dropped this time.

"What is it?" Duke asked.

"It's breaking news. They're reporting that Luna has been located."

"What?" Andi gasped. "How did the news find out about that? We're supposed to be discreet. I *promised* we'd be discreet."

Andi's gaze turned to Mariella as revelation flashed in her gaze.

She thought Mariella had done this, didn't she?

Mariella seemed to pick up on the subtext of the conversation and pointed at herself. "Wait . . . you think *I* did this?"

"We're the only ones who knew." Andi's voice held a sting of accusation.

"Maybe Luna's mom made a statement to the press," Simmy suggested, ever the peacemaker.

Andi shook her head, leaving no doubt she didn't for one minute believe that. "She wouldn't do that. She wants to keep it quiet from her husband, especially considering his temper."

"Well, I didn't do it!" Mariella crossed her arms. "I can't believe you think I'd leak this. I mean, why would I? I wanted *our podcast* to break the news."

"That makes sense. But if you didn't leak it, then who did?" Duke tried to defuse the situation before it exploded.

He wasn't hopeful that his efforts would be successful, however. Not based on the tension in the air.

Mariella raised her chin. "How am I supposed to know?"

"My sister wouldn't do that." Matthew shoved his index finger into the table to drive home his point.

"Someone leaked it." Andi shrugged, making it clear she thought the shoe fit.

"All I know is that it wasn't me." Mariella glared at Andi. "And I can't believe you think that it was."

chapter
twenty-seven

WHILE THE REST of the team worked on the podcast, Duke and Andi went to her apartment. Duke wanted to check things out after seeing that woman who resembled Celeste on the doorbell video.

Besides, it was better if they all split up for a while.

Duke knew both Andi and Mariella could use some space from each other to cool off.

Duke had volunteered to drive, and he and Andi headed down the road.

He'd never been in Andi's apartment before, nor did he know where she lived. But he was curious about her life outside this group. In fact, one time he'd even looked Andi up online. He hadn't been able to resist.

Articles about her past cases had filled search engine results. Images of her as an attorney were prevalent.

Back then, her white-blonde hair had been cut into a neat bob. Her clothes had been professional. The look in her eyes intense.

He had to admit he liked Andi's laid-back look more —even though the woman always had fire in her eyes and appeared ready to defend those who needed it.

Then there were articles about the accusations she'd faced. Articles about her disbarment. Pictures showing a disgraced Andi leaving the courtroom.

He could only imagine the humiliation she'd felt when she'd lost her license to practice law.

And Duke could only imagine the vengeance coursing through her when she'd packed up her life and moved to Alaska.

All of her actions showed just how determined and dedicated she was. Some people might even see it as an obsession.

Not Duke. He knew she only wanted justice.

As they headed down the road, Andi glanced at her phone, appearing as if she was researching something.

Then she grunted.

"What is it?" Duke glanced at her screen, trying to get a clue about what she was thinking.

"This is all weird . . ." She still stared at her phone.

"What's weird?" The suspense was killing him.

"Just out of curiosity, I decided to check out Charlotte online. She did a live interview today with a station down in Anchorage about her attempted abduction."

"She's really decided not to hide her story anymore, it sounds like."

"That's not what's weird. I also checked her social media. Don't ask why. I just have an insatiable curiosity."

"Did she say something strange?" Duke gripped the wheel, keeping his eyes on the road.

He had to be careful because he never knew when trouble might arise again. He'd been on guard for weeks—but now with Andi with him it was like double-trouble.

"She's obsessed with movie star Freddie Dylan."

That wasn't what Duke had expected Andi to say. "What about him?"

"I may be off-base here." Andi shook her head, clearly contemplating her words. "But . . . Freddie Dylan looks a lot like the man Charlotte described as the guy who tried to abduct her."

"What?" Duke's voice rose in surprise.

"I mean, it's really uncanny. They both even have that scar along their jaw that she mentioned."

Duke let out a slow breath. "That has to be a coincidence."

Andi glanced up at him as if trying to read his expression. "Is that really what you think?"

Was it? He tried to think through the possibilities. But nothing made sense.

"Why would she lie to us?" Duke finally asked. "What would she gain by doing so?"

"I have no idea." Andi turned back to the phone and continued to scroll. "I hate to say it but, based on what I'm seeing on her social media, she seems to like attention. She's constantly doing stupid things, calling people out, wearing obnoxious clothes. You name it. The more obnoxious, the more attention she gets."

"So you think she's been scamming us this whole time?" His thoughts raced as he tried to process this new theory.

Andi shrugged. "I can't say for sure. But that's what my gut is telling me."

"If what Charlotte told us is incorrect . . ." Duke's voice trailed. "Then we've been looking in the wrong direction. There is no badge. No Blackwater Contracting connection. No scar on this man's jaw. We've been wasting our valuable time . . . again."

Andi didn't like the idea that they could have been taken for a ride by Charlotte. Nor did Andi know why the woman would even do something like that. What sense did it make?

Then again, she'd seen crazier things as an attorney. Some people were all about drama—and/or money.

A lady had once approached Andi who had wanted to legally change her age so she could be younger. Andi had declined to take the case, but another lawyer in the area had agreed to represent the woman.

Another time a man with split personalities wanted to sue his other personality.

That wasn't to mention the bogus cases people came up with, trying to collect money for the slightest infractions.

Without scruples, a person's integrity could be all kinds of compromised.

Andi had stood up for what was right while being on Victor's defense team.

And he'd ruined her because of it.

Shoving those thoughts aside, she gave the final directions to her apartment, and Duke pulled up to her complex. It was one of the newer buildings located in downtown Fairbanks. The place was nothing fancy or overly beautiful.

But it was a place to sleep at night.

It was Andi's temporary home, paid for each month out of the savings she'd brought with her from Austin. She'd had a decent amount in her account before her career had been destroyed.

But now that money was gone.

Frustration clawed inside her.

Another means of trying to destroy her.

Well, it wasn't going to work.

She didn't know what she'd do to make ends meet. But she wouldn't give up.

She filed a claim with her bank, and she would deal with that when this weekend was finished. Otherwise, it would be all she could think about.

Andi pushed down the shiver that wanted to emerge as she and Duke climbed from the SUV. "This way."

Duke walked beside her toward her door.

For some reason, this wasn't the way she envisioned showing Duke her apartment.

Up until this point, Andi hadn't even realized she *had* imagined how that might play out one day.

Or how much she *hoped* it would play out one day.

But in all of those scenarios, it hadn't happened like this.

Apparently, deep in the recesses of her mind, she'd imagined bringing Duke here. Maybe after a date. Maybe so they could spend more time together.

Her cheeks heated at the thought.

She wasn't one to obsess over a man. She wasn't even interested in dating.

But there was just something about Duke . . .

Did the fact he was unavailable make him even more attractive to her?

Scratch that. Not *more* attractive. But safer.

Maybe Andi felt comfortable liking him for the sole reason that she knew they couldn't have a future.

She'd always had a habit of pulling away from relationships when they got serious. With Duke, that didn't seem like an issue.

But one thing was for sure—she wasn't the cheating type. As long as Celeste was in the picture, Andi would remain a friend.

However, Duke's situation was complicated, to say the least.

She shut down those thoughts as she approached the door. A paper had been wedged near the handle.

Her heart beat harder as she looked at it.

She pulled her sleeve over her hand, just in case there were any prints, and then she carefully unfolded it.

The words scrawled there made her blood grow cold.

Stay out of this.

The message had been handwritten in a sloppy scribble with a thick black marker. The paper looked nondescript, like something anyone could pull from any notebook. No other marks or stains were on it.

She and Duke exchanged a glance.

Duke might see this as a sign they should drop this.

But Andi saw this as a challenge.

twenty-eight

DUKE DIDN'T LIKE the thoughts going through his head—or the danger in the air.

He glanced behind him, making sure no one was watching as they read the note.

Because the woman who'd left this warning clearly wanted them to know she'd been here. She'd looked directly into that video doorbell.

It seemed as if she was playing a game with them.

A game with Duke's heart.

"Come on," Andi murmured. "Let's get inside."

She took his arm and ushered him inside the apartment as if she sensed how risky it was to be outside. Quickly, she closed the door and locked it.

Electricity—or was that danger?—seemed to zap through the air.

Duke cleared his throat and glanced around, desperate to break the tension.

Andi's place was decorated simply without any frills.

The white walls were nearly bare, and the shelves absent of knickknacks. But the apartment was clean and smelled faintly of oranges.

Andi followed his gaze and shrugged as if trying to read his thoughts. "Since I don't plan on staying in Alaska forever, I only bought the essentials when I got here."

That was right . . . she *didn't* plan on staying here forever. That was something Duke needed to keep in mind. With or without Celeste in the equation, it would be better for Duke to keep his distance. He'd be wise to remember that.

But why did he have to remind himself of the fact so often?

"I need to search your apartment—just in case," Duke said.

"Be my guest." Andi extended her arm out.

Cautiously, he began doing a walkthrough. The living room, kitchen, and dining room were clear.

Then he made his way back toward the bedrooms.

The first one was clear.

The bathroom in between was also clear.

But as soon as he walked into the last bedroom—Andi's, if he had to guess—he realized it was noticeably cooler and breezy.

Tension threaded up his spine.

He glanced across the room and saw the window was cracked.

It didn't seem like Andi to leave a window open while

she was gone, especially considering everything that had happened recently.

Before stepping inside any farther, he glanced around the dark space.

Initially, nothing.

He reached for the light switch and flipped it on.

The rest of the room came into view.

A cozy, homemade quilt. A white headboard and matching dresser and nightstand.

It wasn't exactly what he expected Andi's room to look like. It was simple and modest.

But he liked it.

He stepped farther into the space so he could check behind the bed and in the closet.

But as he reached for the closet door, it opened.

A figure wearing all black rushed out and shoved Duke before racing from the room.

The motion threw Duke off-balance, and he stumbled backward.

Just as quickly, he righted himself and took off after the man before the intruder could reach Andi.

Andi heard the commotion and froze.

What was going on back there?

She took a step toward the kitchen, ready to grab a knife or some other form of weapon.

Before she reached the room, a stranger clothed from

head to toe in black emerged from her hallway.

She froze and sucked in a breath.

Someone had been in her apartment . . .

Why?

She didn't have time to think about that now.

The man barely even glanced at her.

Instead, he ran right toward the front door.

Stop him! an internal voice told her.

Yet she was frozen in place.

He threw the door open and ran outside.

Duke emerged mere seconds later, hot on the man's trail.

He disappeared outside.

Finally, Andi came to her senses.

What if Duke needed help?

She sprang into action and ran to the door.

But the two men had already vanished out of sight.

Her heart thumped in her ears.

Where had they gone?

She darted into the parking lot and glanced around.

But she saw no one still.

Nearby, an engine roared to life.

Someone yelled.

Thoughts racing, Andi considered her options.

She had two choices—run to the left or to the right.

She chose left.

Just as she reached the end of her apartment building, she glanced around the corner and spotted a figure striding back toward her.

chapter
twenty-nine

ANDI HELD HER BREATH.

Then realized it was Duke.

His shoulders were tense as if he were upset.

She rushed to meet him. "Are you okay?"

He nodded. "I'm fine. You? You're not hurt, are you?"

"No, I'm okay. What happened?" She fell into step beside him as they walked back toward her apartment.

They slipped inside, and Duke locked the door.

Then he turned toward her. "That man was hiding in your closet. He jumped on a motorcycle and got away."

"What was he doing in my apartment?"

"That's an excellent question. We should probably check it out." He started down the hallway again.

"Should we call the police?"

"It's your decision. But I'm not sure how much they'll be able to do."

She followed behind him as he strode into her room and to her closet.

He studied it a moment without moving.

"You see anything missing?" he finally asked.

Andi stepped closer and shook her head. "No, I don't. There's not much in here other than clothes and shoes."

"We need to check out the rest of the apartment," he murmured. "Look for anything out of place. Do you have any idea what the man could've been looking for?"

"Other than me?" Andi rubbed her arms. "I have absolutely no idea."

Duke couldn't stop ruminating about finding that man.

If he'd been able to catch the intruder, Duke could have demanded answers.

But that was all over and done with.

There was no changing what had happened.

Still, he didn't like any of this.

They'd searched the rest of Andi's apartment, but they hadn't found anything.

He had no idea why the man had been inside.

Waiting for Andi to return?

It seemed unlikely. These people seemed to know their every move.

Did this relate somehow to Celeste?

Victor?

Someone not even on their radar?

The questions wouldn't stop circling in his mind.

Back in the living room, Andi turned toward him,

clearly having something on her mind. "I think we should FaceTime Charlotte and ask her about her description of her almost abductor. I can't stop thinking about it, and I need some answers."

"You think that's the best approach?" Duke observed Andi, interested to know her thoughts. She was a smart woman, and he knew her brain was always working, calculating and evaluating everything.

"Ideally, we'd talk face-to-face," Andi said. "But considering the fact Charlotte lives at least five hours away, we're going to have to settle for a video call."

"I'm on board with that."

"Perfect." Andi grabbed her phone and found the woman's number.

Duke stood close as she called Charlotte.

Would the woman answer? What if she ghosted them?

Or worse. What if she'd disappeared?

So many crazy things had happened so far in this case that nothing would really surprise him.

DUKE WATCHED AND, a moment later, a chime sounded on the phone and Charlotte's face filled the screen.

She appeared to be in a club. The background was dark—other than the occasional strobing light. The music was loud. People filled the place.

She had her hair swept up on top of her head, wore a blue skintight top, and some kind of sparkling gems had been adhered to her face.

"Sorry for the noise, but when I saw your number, I knew I had to answer," Charlotte rushed. "Did you guys figure out something? You got the picture of the police sketch, right?"

"We did get the picture," Andi started. "Thank you for sending that. Unfortunately, we haven't discovered anything yet."

Charlotte frowned and shifted the camera away from a group behind her as they started to cheer at something unrelated. "That's too bad. I was really hoping that if I told my story, it would help . . ."

"We're all hoping for the same thing." Andi paused just a second before launching into the real reason she'd called. "Charlotte, I have a question for you, and it's going to be a little awkward. But I need to ask it anyway."

"Sure. Anything."

"The description you gave us of the man who almost abducted you . . ." Andi started.

"What about it?" She blinked rapidly, her fake eyelashes thick and unnatural-looking.

Andi hesitated only a moment before launching into her opinion. "I couldn't help but notice that your description sounded an awful lot like Freddie Dylan."

Her eyes widened. "What? What are you talking about?"

"Everything down to the scar on his jaw are similar."

Charlotte's mouth dropped open. "Are you accusing me of making this up?"

"I'm not accusing you of anything." Andi sounded calm, like the ultimate negotiator. "I'm just asking questions."

"I'm not making this up!" Charlotte rushed. "I can't believe you'd even think that."

"I'd be foolish not to ask you about the similarities."

"It sounds an awful lot to me like that's what you're doing! You're accusing me of lying."

"I'm sorry that's your perception."

"Well, you know what they say." Charlotte scowled at

the phone. "No good deed goes unpunished."

Andi's screen went blank.

Charlotte had ended the call.

Andi looked up at Duke and frowned. "That didn't go well."

Maybe not, but Duke wasn't entirely surprised. "Even if Charlotte *did* make all of this up just to get attention, it's not as if she'd admit it."

"I don't know what to think."

"All along, you said there was something about her you didn't trust. You were right."

"Maybe." Andi let out a long sigh. "But I guess we should probably get back now. See what the rest of the team is up to."

"Good idea." Duke placed his hand at the small of her back, realizing just how nicely it fit there.

He remembered again how Ted had gotten remarried. How he'd moved on.

Was that a normal reaction in a situation like this? Was Duke the anomaly who was holding onto something that no longer existed?

He wasn't sure.

That was something Duke would have to think about long and hard.

Back at the hotel, Andi and Duke were supposed to meet with the group in the conference room again.

But as they walked into the lobby, Gibson stepped from down the hallway.

Had he been meeting with Braden?

Andi thought about her encounter with the man, and her shoulders tightened.

She had plenty of sympathy for Heidi but not even an ounce for her husband. Even as a lawyer, she'd never had any compassion for cheaters.

Gibson paused in front of them. "Hey, you two. What's new?"

They exchanged a glance before telling him about the break-in and giving him an update on Charlotte.

Gibson let out a whistle. "Life is never boring with the two of you, is it?"

"It sure isn't," Andi muttered. "Anything new that you're allowed to share about this case?"

Gibson glanced around before stepping closer. "Look, there is something that's not exactly hush-hush. You can't use this for your podcast, though."

Andi held her breath. "Understood."

"We found Heidi's camera in her car and were able to find some images on it. Most of them weren't helpful—nature, the highway, the Dalton Highway sign. But there was one that we thought was interesting."

"What was that?" Duke asked.

"The final photo she took appeared to be taken from her car window. It was of a briefcase. Brown, leather, standard issue."

"A briefcase?" Andi scrunched her forehead. "On the

highway?"

Gibson nodded. "That's right. And there were some nails in her tires."

"Wait . . . so you think someone set her up to break down and find that briefcase?"

Gibson shrugged. "That's the theory right now. If you discover anything that has to do with the briefcase, you let me know."

"Will do," Duke muttered.

But Andi's mind wouldn't stop racing through the image of someone causing a person's tires to pop and then leaving a briefcase near where they might pull over.

Why would someone do that?

Exactly who were they dealing with here?

It was getting late, and they would need to go to bed soon. They had a long drive ahead of them tomorrow and would need their rest for the trip.

Alfonso had already collected the items for his latest delivery. He hadn't told them what was inside the boxes, which were now stacked in the conference room. The team would need to load them in the morning.

For now, Andi knew Mariella had something on her mind.

She also knew the woman was still miffed over their earlier conversation. But Andi had needed to address her suspicions. She didn't regret what she'd said.

"Alpine called to check in." Mariella didn't bother to sit down as she started their meeting.

Instead, she stood near the front of the table to address everyone. Her icy tone confirmed she still had a chip on her shoulder.

Andi casually leaned back in her chair and took a sip of her hot chocolate.

She wasn't going to let Mariella get under her skin.

Mariella turned toward Andi. "He wanted to know if you've had a chance to look over that contract yet."

Great. Sore subject number two.

"I already told you about my thoughts on it." Andi didn't back down, even though she knew she'd only irritate Mariella more. "There are way too many stipulations in it for me to be comfortable. There are also too many gray areas that could be left open to interpretation."

"Why would Alpine want to scam us?" Mariella's eyes narrowed in confusion.

"I'm not saying he wants to scam us." Andi hated the fact she always had to be the bad guy. At least that was how it felt today. Between Mariella and Charlotte, Andi was becoming the queen of confrontation—not a title she'd been seeking. "But it's better to have things spelled out in advance than to take someone to court later."

"I just can't see Alpine ever trying to take advantage of us." Mariella crossed her arms defiantly. "What could he possibly gain from doing that? He has everything so there's nothing he could want from us."

Andi wasn't so sure that was true.

chapter
thirty-one

ANDI EYED HER FRIEND, trying to read her body language and tone.

Did Mariella have a crush on Alpine?

The thought nearly startled Andi. But that was the impression she had based on the way Mariella defended the man.

Mariella was so different than Andi. Truthfully, Andi had a hard time understanding the woman sometimes. That didn't make Mariella a bad person. But Andi needed to know she could trust her, that the woman would look out for the team and not just herself and her own agenda.

"Maybe we should all just take a breather," Simmy murmured, clenching her hands in front of her on the table as she frowned.

Andi cleared her throat, trying to break some of the tension around them. "I'm sorry we're not seeing eye to eye."

Mariella stared at Andi another moment before softening her shoulders and sighing. "Could you add whatever changes you'd like to the contract? Then, if Alpine agrees to them, we'll all sign."

"That sounds reasonable," Andi said.

Mariella offered a quick nod, apprehension still in her gaze. "Great. What about Keith Morrison?"

"What about him?" Andi asked.

Irritation flashed in Mariella's gaze before quickly disappearing. "Did you think any more about being interviewed?"

"That's nonnegotiable for me." Andi shook her head. "I don't want to be interviewed. But *you* can be."

"If we have Keith Morrison's interview and Alpine's resources behind us, then we'd be unstoppable. You need to think about that, Andi." Mariella stared at Andi as if that would drive home her message.

Unstoppable? Andi wasn't so sure about that.

She still had a lot of reservations about all this. The podcast. The investigation. Their ability to all work together.

However, she was never one to back away from a challenge.

Andi intended on seeing this case through until the end.

After that . . . then she'd have to make a judgment call.

Andi knew she should sleep.

She knew tomorrow would be a long day.

It was already late. Even if she was lucky, she'd get only a few hours of sleep.

But she only remained in her room a few minutes before heading out.

She was going to grab some lemonade.

Before she even picked up a cup, she glanced at the bar.

Braden was there again.

With multiple empty glasses in front of him.

A pretty woman sat beside him, hanging on his every word.

Fury rose inside Andi.

His wife was missing, and he kept hitting on women?

Without thinking, she stormed over toward them and took the seat on the other side of the woman.

Braden's eyes lit when he recognized Andi. "You again. Did you miss me?"

Andi ignored him. Instead, she turned toward the woman. "I just thought you should know that his wife is missing, and he's supposed to be in the area searching for her. If he's hitting on you, know it's because he's a major jerk wad who's unfaithful to his missing wife."

The woman gasped as she looked back at Braden.

Then she turned her back on him and stormed away, muttering things under her breath.

Braden turned toward Andi, his gaze tumultuous. "Why did you do that?"

"Because your wife is missing."

"Our marriage has been in trouble for a long time."

"So you cheat on her every chance you get?"

He narrowed his eyes. "You wouldn't understand."

Andi stood. "I understand plenty. I hope if—or when —she's rescued, she leaves you behind just as fast as she leaves her abductor."

"Are you saying I'm just as bad as the man who took her?" His voice rose until others in the room turned toward them.

Andi looked back at him and leveled her gaze. "Yes, that's exactly what I'm saying."

chapter
thirty-two

ANDI FELT as if she'd just gotten to sleep when her alarm began buzzing at 2:30.

She quickly got out of bed, showered, and dressed. Then she packed her things since she wasn't sure exactly when they'd be back to the hotel. It made more sense to bring everything, just in case.

When she stepped into the lobby, the rest of the team was already there looking surprisingly bright-eyed and bushy-tailed—even Mariella.

Had she put her irritation with Andi behind her?

Andi supposed she'd find out soon enough.

Duke met her halfway across the room and handed her a cup of coffee. He looked freshly showered and handsome in his jeans and camel-colored sweater.

"It may not be as good as yours, but I tried to spruce it up," he told her. "I dropped a peppermint in it along with a little bit of cream and half a packet of hot chocolate."

"Peppermint mocha. Just what I wanted." Andi took

a sip, the mixture tasting surprisingly good. "I've taught you well."

His grin was all the reward she needed. Something about it made her forget her problems—if just for a split second.

Simmy held up a large paper bag. "I put together some breakfast for us for on the road, and Alfonso left us some water bottles to bring along."

"It sounds like we are all set then," Andi said. "Now we just need to hope everything fits into the back of our vehicles."

It took several minutes, but they managed to get everything loaded between Duke's SUV and Ranger's truck.

Then Duke got behind the driver's seat. Andi sat beside him, and Mariella and Matthew sat in the back. Ranger and Simmy would drive together in Ranger's truck.

She was surprised Mariella wanted to ride with her. But Duke's SUV had a lot more room than Ranger's smaller truck.

Maybe Mariella had gotten over her irritation toward Andi. Even if that was the case, how were they going to move past the issues standing between them? Was it possible they could come to some type of compromise?

Andi wasn't sure.

However, maybe today would be the day they found some answers—to more than one of the mysteries hanging over them.

In fact, maybe this was the opportunity Andi had been looking for since she came to Alaska.

She hoped that was the case, at least.

"I have a couple of updates," Mariella said as they started down the road. "I already told Simmy and Ranger since they were the first to arrive this morning. Anyway, last night around 1:30 I got a phone call."

"From whom?" Duke asked.

"The same person who tried to call on Friday. The one who mentioned something about a body before being cut off."

Andi's pulse raced. "What did he say this time?"

"He said he thinks he found the body of one of the missing women."

"Where?" Duke's voice contained an urgent edge.

"I don't know. Our connection was horrible, and he kept breaking up. Plus, he was whispering like he feared someone might be nearby and hear him."

"Did you get any other information?" Andi realized she was holding her breath as she waited to learn more. She forced herself to exhale, to keep breathing.

"Unfortunately, no." Mariella rubbed her lips as if covering a frown. "But I'm hoping this guy will try to call again. I did try to call back, but there was no answer."

"And I discovered something also," Matthew started. "I was rereading some articles on the victims last night before going to bed."

Interesting nighttime reading, but Andi had no room to talk. She could see herself doing the same thing.

"And?" she asked.

"In three of the articles, the same park ranger was mentioned. A man named John Hopkins. Weird name, right? Like the hospital."

"That is notable, but I'm not sure that means anything," Duke said.

"Maybe Charlotte was lying to us, and she never actually looked the killer in the eye or saw his badge," Matthew continued. "But someone in law enforcement does make sense. I think we should check this guy out. Even better, Ranger said he knows the guy. He thinks we can meet him while we're up in Coldfoot."

"You have a picture of this guy?" Andi asked.

Mariella hit several things on her phone before she held it up. The image of a balding man filled her screen.

Duke leaned in for a glance and sucked in a breath.

"What?" Andi studied his expression.

"I've seen that guy before. He was in the restaurant last night."

"No way . . ." Andi's voice came out louder than normal.

"It was him. I'm sure of it."

Andi didn't like the sound of that.

"We should definitely still ask him questions and try to feel him out," Duke said.

"It can't hurt to ask questions," Andi murmured.

But as soon as the words left Andi's lips, she realized her statement wasn't true.

Asking questions could lead to a lot of trouble, actually.

In fact, asking questions could get a person killed.

For the first part of the drive, Duke had insisted on listening to a sermon he'd downloaded.

Andi wasn't in a position in argue.

He told everyone in his SUV that he usually went to church on Sundays. Since he couldn't today, he could at least listen to a sermon. Mariella and Matthew had asked him questions about his church and his faith.

Andi stared out the window as Duke answered.

She no longer considered herself religious, but she'd had no choice than to listen. She had to admit that the sermon on "Trusting God Even When Life Crashes Around You" was a good one—and very applicable.

Even though she'd lifted some desperate prayers lately, she still wasn't sure she truly believed there was a good God out there who cared for His people.

If that was true, then Andi would hate to see what an unloving God looked like.

She'd grown up in church, so she knew most of the answers. She knew the explanations about sin and living in a fallen world.

But those things brought her no comfort when her pain went without explanation.

When the sermon finished, Duke listened to some praise and worship music.

They were now a few hours into the trip, and the time had passed relatively quickly.

Andi glanced at the barren road around them, one she'd traveled so many times before.

There was truly nothing else around.

"We're still about an hour from where Heidi was last seen." Matthew's voice pulled her from her thoughts. "Her last known location is the first area we'll hit on the drive."

If Heidi had broken down, she'd have to either wait for a passerby to stop or walk. But setting off on foot in this area would have been dangerous—not to mention a waste of time. This wasn't the kind of road people walked along. There was no shoulder, and the truck traffic would have made walking treacherous.

Someone picking her up was the only thing that made sense.

"Do you know what I find confusing?" Mariella started as she pointed at a gas tanker headed north. "Prudhoe Bay is where we get our oil that becomes gas, right? It doesn't make any sense that gas is being trucked back up to where it came from."

"That's because the oil that's extracted from Prudhoe Bay hasn't been refined," Duke explained. "So after it goes south down the pipeline to the refineries, it has to be brought back up north. The whole process is kind of crazy."

Not quite as crazy as this investigation, but, yes, it was crazy.

"There's just something about this highway . . ." Mariella shook her head. "It's got a personality of its own. I certainly wouldn't want to drive it every day."

"As part of my training when I started as an ice road truck driver, we learned a lot of the facts about this road." Andi clearly remembered that meeting. "Approximately one driver has been killed for every mile on this road—and there are more than four hundred miles. At least, that's what my boss told me."

Mariella frowned. "I don't like the thought of that."

"It's unnerving, to say the least," Andi said. "We haven't even gotten to the worst part. Atigun Pass, especially in the winter, can be quite scary—especially when it's snowing. Thankfully for you, we'll drop you two off before we reach it."

"I don't even know how you did that job." Mariella flicked a lock of hair behind her shoulder. "I would have never lasted in that world."

Andi sometimes wondered how she did it too. Except her dad had been a trucker so she knew the ins and outs of the business.

Still, it was quite a change going from being an attorney making her case in a courtroom to driving a truck on a lonely highway.

Mariella let out a sigh. "This is going to be *such* a long trip, isn't it?"

"For Duke and me, it's going to be at least eleven

hours," Andi said. "That's why we got started early. Be thankful you're not going the entire way."

"Five or six hours is enough for me. What else do we want to talk about as we drive?" Mariella continued, her head still popped forward between the two front seats—as much as her seatbelt would allow.

"There's one thing I think we can do," Andi said. "Let's pay attention to everyone we pass so we can get an idea of who frequents this road."

"Some of them are just cars so it's hard to know who might be inside." Mariella shrugged.

"That's true," Andi said. "But so far, I've seen truckers, I've seen tourists, and I've seen a couple of people who work for the highway transportation system. I also saw a park ranger and state trooper coming by as well."

"A state trooper?" Matthew murmured. "Now that's a possibility we haven't considered . . . what about Gibson?"

Andi's eyebrows flung up. "What about him?"

"Maybe my brother is right," Mariella rushed. "What if Gibson is the one behind this? Didn't he investigate the case?"

"It wasn't Gibson." Duke's voice left no room for argument.

"I think we should consider every possibility," Mariella pressed. "He *is* a connection in this case."

"It's not him." Duke's jaw hardened.

Andi, however, felt a little more open-minded than Duke. "The theory *is* something worth thinking about. Gibson has worked in this area many years. I like the guy. I don't want to think he could be behind this. But likeable guys can sometimes be killers. Just think of Jeffrey Dahmer—polite, soft-spoken, good-looking."

"It wasn't Gibson." Duke's voice hardened even more every time he said the words.

Andi heard the edge in his voice and backed off. But that didn't mean she wasn't going to consider the possibility Mariella was right.

They *should* think about Gibson.

Because they'd be foolish not to consider every possibility.

chapter
thirty-three

I HAD to get ready for work.

I was needed out on the front lines.

I took a quick shower and then glanced in the mirror.

Tattoos covered my arms and torso, remnants from what I called my rebellious phase.

If I had to do it again, I wouldn't have gotten them. But they were there, and they reminded me of my past. They reminded me of all the things I'd done wrong.

I vowed not to be that person again.

I vowed to be stronger.

Life was better back when women knew their places. When social media didn't exist. I couldn't change the world, but I could change my own life.

Which was exactly what I was doing.

I glanced at my watch—an heirloom from my grandfather.

Now, I needed to set out to earn my paycheck—the way it should be.

Anna would stay here and clean.

I hoped to get home in time for a warm meal.

She should have something prepared and waiting, no matter the time I get home.

I'd seen some dirt under my recliner and had almost cleaned it. Then I'd decided to test Anna and see if she noticed the spot.

I'd find out when I returned.

I zipped up my uniform and grabbed my keys.

I would take my snow machine to the end of a two-mile pathway. My garage was at the end but still out of sight from any who might pass by the area.

That was where my vehicle was parked.

It made my house more private with only a path leading to it.

So far, it had worked out wonderfully.

I stepped from my room and pulled on the snowsuit I needed to wear until I reached my proper vehicle.

Anna paused from washing dishes and looked at me.

I crossed the room until I reached her and kissed her cheek.

She went still. Not daring to move.

"I'm off to work, but I'll see you soon. Okay, my love?"

She nodded. "Okay."

With one last glance, I slipped out the door.

If that dirt wasn't gone from beneath my chair when I returned home then she'd need to be punished . . . again.

I was going to need to be harsher. She wasn't learning her lessons quickly enough.

Maybe using the belt was being too kind.

Maybe I should use the whip my grandfather used on me.

I still had it in my closet.

It especially hurt when it hit bare skin.

I'd tried to spare her that.

But time was running out.

chapter
thirty-four

DUKE DROPPED Mariella and Matthew off in Coldfoot with Ranger and Simmy.

While they were there, they would talk to people who knew Kiah Franz, the prostitute who went missing. Depending on how things went, the foursome would either remain there or they'd drive back to the Almost Halfway Trading Post for the night.

The team would stay in touch, which would be tricky considering the spotty phone service in the area.

Duke didn't like the fact Mariella had suggested Gibson as a suspect.

Gibson was a good guy, someone who'd been on Duke's side after Celeste disappeared. In fact, he was one of the only cops who'd taken Duke seriously.

Gibson wouldn't be behind something like this.

Duke also knew there was an amazing lack of suspects. Having just one decent lead might keep their hopes up and keep the team from getting discouraged. But Gibson shouldn't be the one they focused on.

Duke and Andi still had four or five more hours to go, and no time to waste.

He felt a surprising sense of relief when it was just him and Andi in his SUV.

She was only quiet a moment before blurting, "It *could* be Gibson."

How long had she been waiting to say that? Two hours?

It wouldn't surprise him.

Duke shook his head, still not backing down from his stance. "It wasn't him."

"Why are you so convinced of that?" Andi's gaze burned into him.

"Why are you so *not* convinced of that?" he shot back.

"We're looking for common threads, and Gibson is one of them."

He shook his head again, harder and faster this time. "I'm just going by gut instinct. He's not the type who'd do something like that."

Andi clamped her mouth shut and didn't say anything else, even though Duke could clearly see she hadn't changed her mind.

"Do you want to talk about your disagreement with Mariella?" he asked.

Andi practically snorted. "Not really. I stand behind what I said."

"You *did* accuse her of going behind our backs and telling the media about Luna."

Andi opened her mouth to talk but then shut it again. "When you word it that way, it sounds pretty awful."

"Then there's the national interview with Keith Morrison and the contract . . ."

"I thought you'd be on my side," Andi said, defensiveness rising in her voice.

"I am. I don't want to go on national TV, and you have some good points about the contract."

"So why are you bringing this up?"

"Because you called me out when I butted heads with Ranger. And you were right. I thought you might appreciate some perspective also."

"The perspective being that I was too hard on Mariella?" Andi stared at him as she waited for his answer.

"Yes, I think you were. She's young. Naive. Annoyingly optimistic. But I don't think her intentions are wrong."

"I'm not saying they're wrong either."

"I'm just saying maybe you should ease up on her some."

Andi clamped her mouth shut and nodded. "You've given me something to think about."

He and Andi both lapsed into silence for the next couple of hours. But it was a good kind of quiet—not the uncomfortable kind.

The road rolled past, along with the minutes.

Finally, they reached Deadhorse—the industrial town

where all the construction camps were set up—and Prudhoe Bay where the oil fields were located beyond the town.

The whole area looked more like a settlement on Mars than part of the United States. Most of the buildings were modular or prefabricated and built on tundra bog. The tree line had disappeared more than an hour ago, so everything around them was flat and gray. Mostly construction workers and contractors frequented the area.

A thrum of apprehension swept through Duke.

This was what they'd been working toward. Getting onto the oil fields.

Now Duke hoped all this didn't prove to be a royal waste of time . . . but he mostly prayed that Andi stayed safe throughout it all.

Andi felt a rush of nerves sweep through her as she stared at the oil fields.

Coming here had been a gamble. There were no guarantees they'd find out information. If this didn't pan out, they would have wasted their time. The other research they'd needed to do would fall by the wayside—and for no good reason.

Andi hoped desperately this trip would prove to be fruitful.

And that nothing went wrong.

She'd gotten this far before. Gotten through the gates. Then her access had been limited.

This might be her only opportunity to get into this area.

However, she was also keenly aware that if prostitutes were working in this area, they wouldn't be behind this fence in the high security area. They'd most likely be in one of the camps.

They pulled up to the gate, and Duke rolled down his window. "Good afternoon. Our names should be on the list. Duke McAllister and Andi Slade. We're here to see Frederick Dominic."

The guard slowly searched the list.

As they waited, Andi's lungs tightened.

She hoped all this wasn't for nothing. She hoped Alfonso truly had been able to get their names on this list.

The seconds ticked by in slow motion as the guard continued to study the list.

Part of Andi feared he was onto them. That the police would show up and make an arrest.

Not that they were doing anything illegal.

Finally, the guard lowered his clipboard and set it on the desk before turning back to them.

"You're all good," the guard told them. "I'm going to radio Frederick to let him know you're here. Just pull into the space straight ahead and walk into that building. He'll meet you there."

Andi's lungs loosened.

Good. Their first obstacle was complete.

Unfortunately, that wasn't the most challenging one.

They did as the guard told them and pulled into the space. Before they'd even gotten out of the SUV, the door at the front of the building opened, and a man who had to be Alfonso's brother stepped out.

The two looked alike except Frederick didn't appear as eccentric as Alfonso. There was no cane, monocle, or artsy bowtie.

Instead, Frederick wore black Carhartt pants and a thick jacket. He carried himself with an air of leadership, with a hard hat in one hand and a radio clipped to his belt.

Andi rose to full height, noting how chilly it was here. Even though it was May, the temperature lingered near freezing in this area.

"I hear that you're here with a delivery for me." Frederick paused in front of Duke and extended his hand. "Frederick Dominic. I assume you're Duke and Andi."

Andi joined them, and they exchanged handshakes.

"That's us," Duke said.

"Wonderful. I can only imagine what my brother sent up for me this time." His voice warmed with obvious affection for his brother.

"I can't wait to see what it is either." Andi grinned.

"I'll help you unload. Then I heard you'd like a tour of the area."

"If it's not any trouble, we'd love that." Andi kept her voice casual. "I've always been curious about this place. I feel like I've just stepped into another world."

"It's another world alright." Frederick chuckled.

As the sound faded, the man studied her a moment.

Andi felt herself flush under his scrutiny.

Did he recognize her from her stint as an ice road trucker? There weren't very many women in the field. Plus, she knew her white-blonde hair and petite figure made her stand out.

There was a good chance the two of them had encountered each other when she'd made deliveries up here. If that was the case, then he'd certainly have questions—maybe even suspicions.

Maybe he'd even refuse to give that tour.

Andi braced herself as she waited to hear what he had to say.

chapter
thirty-five

DUKE WATCHED Frederick as he studied Andi.

What was the man thinking? Duke had no idea—but the guy definitely had something on his mind. He was making no secrets about that.

As Duke waited for Frederick to say something, worst-case scenarios ran through his mind. Had Victor put Andi's picture on a watchlist up here?

At this point, anything seemed possible.

"You, young lady, are going to be a superstar around here," Frederick finally said, seeming to break out of his daze.

Duke's back stiffened as he waited for the man to continue.

"We tell the guys when they come up here to work that there's a woman behind every tree waiting for them. Bad humor, perhaps. But true."

"Especially since there are no trees up here . . ." Andi said with a knowing nod.

Duke tried to relax as he realized the man was making a joke. But part of him still didn't like the idea that men might be drooling over Andi up here.

Frederick grinned. "Exactly! Anyway, the guys are a little deprived, some people might say. Whenever they see a woman—especially a good-looking one—they like to ogle. I apologize in advance."

"I think I can handle it." Andi nodded slowly.

Duke had no doubt Andi could handle herself around these guys. She'd put them in their places quickly and efficiently.

Frederick turned his gaze from Andi and seemed to snap back to reality. "Anyway, I can't wait to show you around. You're friends with my brother?"

"Acquaintances would probably be more accurate," Duke said.

"Tell me, is he still wearing that monocle?" Frederick held his hand to his eye as if to emulate the eyewear.

"He is," Andi said.

Frederick let out a belly laugh. "He just has that for show, you know? It's all about shock value. Making a statement. He knows how to make an entrance and a splash."

"That sounds like Alfonso," Andi said, sounding as if she wasn't at all surprised at the admission.

They followed him back to the SUV, where Duke and Andi each grabbed a box.

"Things are never boring when he's around. I tell you

what, that hotel he owns and runs . . . it's something else. It couldn't fit him better."

"Yes, it is." Andi propped her box on her hip. "I find it quite entertaining to stay there."

"I think most people do. That's what makes my brother so wonderfully unique." Frederick handed them two visitors badges and then grabbed a box of his own. "Okay, let's get these inside. Then I'm going to open one of these up. It feels a little bit like Christmas Day."

Andi glanced around.

What if the answers she needed waited somewhere inside this fenced-in, high-security area?

Answers about Victor.

Answers about Celeste.

Answers about the Missing Women of Dalton Highway.

This was her one chance to dig deeper, and she couldn't blow it.

However, she didn't have a plan as to what she'd do to figure out any answers. This was one of those situations where she'd have to play it by ear and see what opportunities arose. She'd already added photos of each of the victims to her phone.

She hoped to show the images to people working here and watch their reaction.

Frederick set one of the boxes on a foldout table, sliced

through the tape on the top of the box, and opened it. Then he pulled out a onesie.

He shook it until the clothing unfolded and revealed . . . a dinosaur.

Then he let out a loud belly laugh. "Oh, Alfonso. You always keep me on my toes."

"That's really . . . something," Duke muttered, shaking his head.

Andi suppressed a smile.

What else did you say to obnoxious onesies—dragons, unicorns, faux muscular bodies in skimpy bathing suits?

Frederick chuckled some more before turning back to them. "Okay. I know you guys had a long drive up here. So how about if you stretch your legs and I'll show you around? There are only a couple of buildings I'm allowed to take you in—the rest have been off limits since 9-11."

"Perfect," Andi murmured.

This was what they'd been waiting for.

Duke and Andi glanced at each other before following behind Frederick.

THIS WAS the first time Duke had ever been up to this area, and he had to admit he was fascinated.

He'd always been a curious guy. He liked knowing the history of areas. What kind of jobs people worked. What made people tick and what made different regions unique.

It was one reason he'd thought being a tour guide would be a natural fit for him. Not only would he get to travel the Dalton Highway, but he got to use some of that otherwise useless knowledge and share it with others.

"We have about fifteen hundred people living in the area—more or less depending on what project we have going on. Only about twenty people live here year-round," Frederick said as they walked across the gravel between buildings. "Our crews are from all over, and they usually only work for two weeks at a time, rotating in what we call hitches. The guys—and sometimes girls—work about twelve hours a day while they're here."

"Why only two weeks?" Duke asked.

"Not everyone is cut out to live in the Arctic. It's not terribly bad at this time of the year—unless you include the mosquitoes—but in the winter when the sun doesn't come up and the temperature drops to fifty below, it's brutal. No one in their right mind would want to stay here for an extended amount of time."

"I can only imagine," Andi said.

"And just in case you're an environmentalist in disguise —we get those sometimes—I thought I'd let you know that the US currently has the most stringent environmental controls on oil in the world. If we even spill a teaspoon-sized speck of oil, it's considered an environmental event."

"That's good to know," Andi said.

Frederick paused inside one of the buildings. "I can take you in here. This is the cafeteria for our crew. Would you guys like something to eat before we continue the tour? I know there aren't many places to grab a bite around here outside of the camps."

Duke glanced around. At least twenty people occupied the space right now.

This could be one of their best opportunities to talk to a few employees.

"I could use a meal," he said.

"Perfect. I'm not saying that our food selections here are fantastic. But hopefully you'll find something that suits your fancy."

They went through the line, and Duke got himself some baked chicken, rice, and green beans. Andi got a salad with grilled chicken. Then they sat down at one of the tables. Frederick sat with them, but he didn't quite look ready to relax as he typed on his phone.

Finally, he sighed and stood. "I'm going to let you two enjoy your meal. I have a couple of matters I need to attend to, but I'll be back here in about twenty minutes. Are you okay with that?"

Duke was more than okay with that, but he tried to not seem too eager. "That would be fine."

"Perfect." Frederick stood and took a step back, his gaze still wandering back to his phone as if the messages there were urgent. "Enjoy your meals."

"This is our opportunity to get some answers," Andi murmured after Frederick left.

"How do you propose we do that?"

She glanced around the room. "We ask questions. However, the key is to ask our questions while remaining subtle."

Andi tried to ignore the looks the men in the cafeteria tossed her way. But they were clearly curious about why she and Duke were here.

Maybe they were even desperate because they hadn't seen a woman in a while, just like Frederick had said. She could only imagine the shenanigans—to put it nicely— that took place up here.

"Subtlety is the key," Duke whispered. "However, I really don't know a subtle way to ask those questions."

Andi stabbed another piece of lettuce as she thought it through. "Me neither. I've been going over it in my mind, trying to figure out the best way to do this. The truth is, there's not really any kind of best way here, is there?"

"No, there's not."

Andi stood. "I might as well just give it the old college try."

She felt Duke's eyes on her as she walked away. As she approached a table full of men, she grabbed her phone and pulled up the first image she'd downloaded.

She wasn't sure which victim to start with. Because Celeste may not have been a victim at all. Instead, Andi started with the most recent woman who'd disappeared.

Heidi Billingsworth.

The group of workers eating nearby looked up at her with approval in their gazes as she approached.

Andi sat down, propped her arms on the table, and plastered on a smile.

"Hey, y'all." She kept her voice friendly and warm.

"Hello to you." One of the men—a thirtysomething guy with a ruddy complexion—gave her an approving once-over.

She pretended she didn't notice.

But she quickly scanned the men at the table. Not many of them caught her eye—except for Ruddy Complexion and one other man, who seemed to have an unusual apprehension about her presence at the table.

He sat the farthest away, something she was grateful about. His bushy beard gave him a lumberjack-like appearance.

The guy gave her a bad vibe, though for no discernable reason.

"Listen, Frederick Dominic has been giving me a tour, and this place is simply fascinating," Andi said. "I've always been curious about it, especially when I learned one of my old friends from high school works here. I figured while I was here, it couldn't hurt to ask if she's still working in the area."

"Not many women work up here," Ruddy Complexion said.

"I can tell." Andi held up her phone. "Anybody ever seen her, by chance?"

She showed the picture to each of the five men sitting near her, and they studied it a minute.

Recognition didn't cross any of their faces—even the scary-looking, bad-vibes lumberjack guy.

"No, I'm afraid not," Ruddy Complexion said. "But I could show you a thing or two while you're here."

Subtle.

Andi had told herself that was what she'd be.

This man needed to learn the art of it as well.

She locked her gaze with his. "I'm sure there's nothing you could show me that I haven't already seen."

Greed. Lust. Disregard for others.

The guys around him cackled.

"I wouldn't be so sure about that," Ruddy

Complexion continued, undeterred. "We could use a few good women working up here. It's an awfully lonely place."

Andi locked her gaze with his, keeping her voice sugary sweet with a touch of Texas twang. "I'd rather be sent to a colony on Mars. At least you wouldn't be there."

His friends began to hoot and holler again.

Ruddy Complexion's cheeks turned even ruddier, but he kept his cool. "You don't know what you're missing."

Andi stood, turned her back on him, before looking over her shoulder. "I'm pretty sure I do."

She made her way back over to Duke as the men around Ruddy Complexion continued to give him a hard time.

As she sat down across from Duke, he glanced at her with questions—and maybe a hint of amusement and admiration—in his gaze.

"Those men *definitely* seemed interested," he muttered.

"Interested but not in helping me solve anything. Interested because they probably haven't seen very many single women here."

"It sounds like you put them in their places."

She shrugged nonchalantly. "Maybe."

"So, does this go back to our theory of human trafficking again?" He glanced around. "This would be the perfect place for something like that."

"Maybe, but even if any of these guys are somehow

involved with trafficking, it's not like they're going to fess up to it."

Duke's gaze locked with hers. "How are we going to figure it out?"

Andi frowned as she thought it through. "This place is too big for us to check out each building. There's just no way we can do that. But I didn't see any recognition on those men's faces. I would think if one of them had seen Heidi before, that they would signal some type of familiarity."

"Then you and I are going to have to figure out our next plan of action." Duke shrugged. "And we don't have much time before our tour will be over."

chapter
thirty-seven

FREDERICK SHOULD BE BACK at any moment.

In the meantime, Duke had spotted a bulletin board on the other side of the cafeteria and decided to check it out while Andi finished her salad. He tried to look casual as he approached it and looked over the papers pinned there.

Most of the information displayed wasn't interesting. People looking for rides. Fundraisers. Work code reminders.

Nothing that helped them.

"You must be new here," a deep voice said behind him.

Duke turned and saw a man wearing a yellow safety vest. The guy looked gruff with his overgrown beard and auburn hair.

He'd been at the table when Andi approached, but he'd had a standoffish look about him.

The look in his eyes made Duke cautious. This guy

was untrusting—though Duke hadn't done anything to trigger that.

"Just made a delivery and got a tour," Duke explained.

The man continued to eye him. "I saw your girlfriend asking questions back there."

This guy was definitely on edge.

"You mean Andi? She's just a friend. We've been driving a long time today, so we're stretching our legs some before we hit the road again."

The man grunted.

Did this guy suspect he and Andi were here for other reasons?

"Seems like you're looking for something," the man continued as he planted himself near Duke.

"What could I possibly be looking for up here in Prudhoe Bay? Not black gold—because that's already been found." Duke let out a laugh, trying to play off the conversation. Truth was that this guy was putting his instincts on alert.

"People come up here looking for all kinds of things." The man's gaze darkened. "Take your pick."

Duke took a step back. "I think you're overthinking this, man. I'm just having some dinner before we head back."

"Your friend was showing a picture of a woman around." The man's nostrils flared. "Why?"

Duke tried to take a step back toward Andi, but the man blocked him.

He really didn't want to cause a scene—but he would if he had to.

"She's looking for an old friend."

The man narrowed his eyes. "I doubt that. Women like the one in the picture don't come up here to work."

Duke shifted, getting tired of this conversation. "I'm not even sure why this concerns you."

"I don't like people poking around up here, especially outsiders who have no business in this area."

Duke heard the warning in the man's tone.

They'd definitely rubbed this guy the wrong way.

"Duke!" someone called.

Duke glanced over the man's shoulder and saw Frederick step into the room. He motioned to Duke, indicating for him to join him.

Gladly.

But Duke would have to be careful.

What was this guy afraid of?

And did it have anything to do with this case?

Frederick continued to give Andi and Duke a tour, but Andi only half paid attention. Instead, she observed everything around her and looked for anything that could be a clue.

As they paused near the management offices, she spotted three men walking toward the door.

Two wore business suits, which made them look out of place in the area.

That was when she realized who one of those men was.

Victor Goodman.

Her breath caught.

It couldn't be . . . but it was.

Frederick followed her gaze. "They're some of our investors. They stop in every once in a while to check on things."

"The one in the middle looks like he thinks highly of himself." Andi tried to offer a reason for her reaction and not to show any familiarity.

"Believe me, he does." Frederick let out a bitter laugh. "Now, let me show you where the oil enters the pipeline."

But Andi's gaze remained on Victor.

Last time she'd seen him in Fairbanks, he'd met with some men in his office building. While they were having a late-night meeting, she'd caught a glimpse of the word "Prometheus" on a board as they'd talked.

She still couldn't figure out what Prometheus meant or what Victor was up to.

All she knew was that he'd had at least nine people killed—ten if she included Tom Walsh, a man who'd recently died in an alleged car accident after meeting with Victor in Fairbanks.

"I'm sorry, but I'm having a bit of a bathroom emergency." Andi nodded toward one of the buildings in the distance. "Do you mind if I run inside and use the ladies' room?"

Frederick nodded. "It's right through those doors."

Duke gave her a warning glance as she slipped away from them and headed toward the building. But as soon as they looked away, she bypassed the building and followed behind Victor.

He stepped into another building in the distance.

Remaining near the building, Andi glanced back and saw that Duke and Frederick were still talking.

She hated to do this.

Kind of.

But this was the opportunity she'd been waiting for.

Sucking in a deep breath, she darted toward the other building. She paused at the doorway before twisting the handle.

The door was unlocked.

A moment later, she stepped inside and scanned everything around her.

The area looked like a construction trailer. An unmanned desk sat in front of her with a wall behind it. A room with a window was to her left and a hallway to her right.

The scent of oil and grease filled the air.

Voices drifted down the hallway.

Andi crept closer.

Pausing in the shadows, she peered around the corner. Victor and the two men with him talked in the distance. She strained to make out what they were saying.

"This is what our country needs," Victor said. "It's the answer we're looking for, and I'm willing to invest in making it happen."

She grabbed her phone. Maybe she could record part of this . . . just in case.

Her hands trembled as she pulled up the camera and hit "Record." She could hardly breathe as she continued to listen.

"There's a lot of red tape standing in the way," another man said.

"You can fix that," Victor said.

The man chuckled nervously. "Maybe. The opposition to this project has been overwhelming. You should see the total number of people who've signed an online petition to stop this."

"We need to convince them otherwise. I know some of the best people who work in the media. We can come up with a campaign that will help the public see things our way. Maybe add some intriguing storylines to some movies or TV shows to alter people's perceptions. I have the connections to do that."

"You really think that would work?" one of the men asked.

"I know it would. I've orchestrated something similar before. It's a mind game. All of it is. People don't think twice about the media they consume, even though it restructures the very fabric they're made of. Control the media and control the world."

His words sent a chill through her.

"We still have a long way to go before this will move forward," Victor said. "But some of our biggest opponents . . ."

"Have been met with untimely deaths?" Victor's friend's voice dipped lower. "I noticed."

The men started walking away, the conversation disappearing along with them.

Andi knew she needed to get out of here. Too much time had passed. Frederick was sure to notice she was missing.

She put her phone away and rushed toward the doorway. As she shoved it open, she collided with someone.

A security guard.

She swallowed hard as the man glared down at her.

Had he seen her recording that conversation?

How was she going to get out of this?

DUKE GLANCED OVER.

He'd seen Andi veer off the path to the bathroom.

She was following Victor, wasn't she?

His heart pounded harder at the thought.

What was she thinking? Did she *want* to get herself killed?

He tried to keep his expression placid, to not give Frederick any hints that Andi had snuck away.

But Duke couldn't deny he was worried about her.

She should be back by now. What if she'd run into trouble?

The last thing Duke wanted was for Victor to get his hands on her. The man was already trying awfully hard to do away with her and to make it look accidental.

They had no proof of that, of course. But Duke knew it was true.

Duke had seen Victor meeting with a hitman. That very hitman had tried to run over Andi when she was on the sidewalk. He was surprised the guy hadn't struck again.

But maybe he was waiting for just the right moment.

"Do you think your friend is okay?"

Duke snapped his attention back to Frederick and smiled. "I think so. You know women . . . they can sometimes take a long time in the bathroom."

"Yes, I suppose they can." Frederick stared at the door to the building Andi was supposed to have entered, and he squinted as if concerned.

Duke needed to think of a way to put Frederick at ease before he went to investigate.

He turned toward an oil rig and began asking about how many gallons it could pump per hour.

As Frederick answered, Duke glanced back in the direction Andi had gone.

Still no sign of her.

He would give her two more minutes and then he'd go look for her himself.

Sure, it would blow their cover. And Alfonso may not like them very much and rescind his offer to let them use his hotel again if they made Frederick mad.

But Duke was willing to face the consequences if he had to.

Andi was more important than any investigation.

"What are you doing in here?" The security guard stared at Andi.

She gulped in a deep breath as she formulated what to say. "Oh, good. Maybe you can help me. I got turned around, and I was really confused."

She stepped outside and made sure the door closed behind her, so they didn't draw the attention of Victor and his men. One look at her white-blonde hair, and he'd definitely recognize her.

She'd been on his defense team for a short period.

Until Andi had realized Victor was as guilty as sin.

When she'd confronted him, he'd had his guys set her up. Made it look like she'd drawn some legal documents for her elderly clients that left all their money to her.

The law council had believed him, and Andi had been disbarred.

That was the story in a nutshell, at least.

"This is an authorized-personnel-only area," the guard continued, not the slightest touch of friendliness or understanding in his voice. "How did you even get inside that building?"

"The door was unlocked . . ." Andi shrugged, trying to look innocent instead of like a lawyer who'd seen everything under the sun. "I was looking for a bathroom."

The man eyed her in disbelief.

Then the door behind her flew open as someone exited.

Andi's lungs froze.

She wanted to run. Hide.

But she couldn't.

Not without raising eyebrows and getting entirely too much attention.

Her body tensed as she slowly turned.

Victor Goodman stepped out and stared at her, his two cronies on either side.

The man was six feet tall with dark hair highlighted with silver strands. He had a clean but thick mustache, manicured eyebrows, and a strong sense of superiority.

"If it isn't Andi Slade . . ." Victor stared at her, his eyes colder than the Arctic Ocean. "What brings you up here? I thought you were down in Texas."

But did he?

She swallowed hard before saying, "I decided it was time for a change of scenery. And what about you? Didn't expect to see you up here. I thought the Middle East was more your hunting ground."

His eyes narrowed. "What can I say? I get around." His gaze went to her visitor's badge. "I take it you don't work here. Too bad. I hear they could use some good lawyers up this way."

"I'm enjoying a simpler life right now."

Something flickered in his gaze. "Is that what you call it?"

Andi's throat squeezed until she felt as if she couldn't breathe.

This man was as calculating and narcissistic as they came.

And he didn't let anything stand in his way of getting what he wanted.

Not only that, but he had uncountable minions under him willing to do his dirty work. The power he yielded was downright frightening.

"She's fine," Victor told the guard with a dismissive glance. "I'll take it from here."

The guard nodded and left.

Terror swept through Andi. She could only imagine what Victor might mean by those words.

Her heart pounded in her ears as she waited.

It was just the two of them right now.

The other two men had slipped away also, seeming to sense that Victor wanted some privacy.

Andi and Victor.

Alone.

Danger snapped through the air.

His icy gaze turned on her again. "You're not following me, are you, Ms. Slade?"

"How would I even know you'd be up here?" Her voice sounded sweetly innocent.

"Maybe for the same reason that you decided to become a cleaner in the very building where my office is housed . . ."

Andi's cheeks heated, but she refused to look away or show any fear. "I don't know what you're talking about."

He stepped closer, glaring down at her. "Don't think I'm a fool."

"I don't. In fact, I don't think anyone would ever say that."

He leaned closer, his breath brushing her ear as he whispered, "Whatever you're planning, it's going to end up getting you killed. Mark my words."

His threat hung in the air as Andi wondered what he would do next.

chapter
thirty-nine

"YOU KNOW WHAT?" Duke said. "I think I *will* go check on Andi. It's taking her a long time. I thought the chicken on her salad smelled a little funny . . ."

"What? Really? Then, yes, it's probably a good idea." A frown tugged at Frederick's lips as if he were becoming uncomfortable.

They started toward the building Andi was supposed to be in. As they did, Duke glanced to the side.

He spotted Andi standing outside next to someone.

Victor Goodman.

The two of them were talking—Andi bristled with hands fisted at her side as Victor stood close. Too close.

The blood drained from Duke's face.

This wasn't good.

The way Victor towered over Andi . . . the man was clearly trying to intimidate her.

Then there was Andi, who stared up at the titan and refused to back down.

It was a quality that made Duke feel equally terrified and impressed.

And a quality that could get Andi killed if she wasn't careful.

"Andi!" Duke knew he needed to break this up before it turned ugly.

"What . . . ?" Frederick muttered, dread filling his voice.

Andi and Victor snapped from their stare off and turned toward him.

"We've been looking for you." Duke kept his voice casual as if this wasn't a big deal.

Andi stepped back from Victor and shoved a hair behind her ear. "I got a little turned around."

"Mr. Goodman," Frederick murmured, a new tension in his voice—almost as if he'd become fearful in the presence of someone so powerful. "I hope we're not disturbing you."

Victor's gaze slid back over to Andi, and he shook his head. "Never. I always enjoy meeting new people. You just never know who you're going to run into up here in Prudhoe Bay."

Frederick let out a nervous laugh. "No, you don't, do you? I was just giving them a tour."

"I've never quite understood people's fascination with touring this place. Maybe seeing the Arctic Ocean or meeting some of the Inupiat people up in Barrow—"

"Out of respect for the natives, they now use the name of Utqiagvik," Andi quipped.

Victor narrowed his eyes but didn't say anything.

"And I don't know . . ." She turned and looked around. "I do think people would be interested in this area. After all, this is where the pipeline starts. It's changed life as we've known it for America. Who wouldn't be curious about it?"

Duke's heart continued to thrum in his ears.

What was Andi's play right now? Her words were pointed, and he could only imagine what the discussion between those two must have been.

Andi was gutsy, he'd give her credit for that.

Another part of him was terrified at just how brazen she could be.

He'd figured it was only a matter of time before Andi and Victor would run into each other. However, it couldn't have happened in a worse place.

Out here, it was like another world with another set of rules.

"Well." Victor snapped back into professional mode by rolling his shoulders back and raising his chin. "I guess I should continue with my meeting. But good to see you all."

He nodded to the men around him, who then followed him back toward a different building.

Andi watched them leave, her shoulders still set and defiance in her gaze.

Frederick closed the space between them before asking in a low tone, "You do know who that is, don't you?"

Andi turned back to him. "Victor Goodman. An investor."

"He's only one of the most powerful people in North America, if not the Northern Hemisphere. I'm pretty sure he's planning world dominance."

Duke stared at Frederick, curious about his words and whether or not he was joking. "Why would you say that?"

"Wherever there's money to be made or power to be had, you'll find Victor. He reminds me of Thanos in his quest for total control."

"Thanos, the Marvel villain?" Andi clarified, her forehead wrinkling in confusion.

"Yes, that's the one." Frederick rolled his eyes. "In fact, people around here have given him that nickname. He makes everyone nervous. What Victor wants, Victor gets."

Duke didn't like the sound of that.

His gaze lingered on Andi.

The two of them needed to talk one-on-one.

Soon.

It seemed as if Frederick couldn't wait to get them out of there.

Andi understood. Now that Victor knew she was here, he'd most likely be on guard. Her chances of finding out any more information about him was highly unlikely.

Even though she'd tried to think of more reasons to stay and ask about the missing women, Frederick walked them back to Duke's SUV and watched as they climbed inside—almost as if he wasn't taking any more chances.

That hadn't gone as well as she had hoped. They were leaving without any answers about the missing women.

She glanced across the parking lot and saw a man staring at them.

It was the same guy who'd talked to Duke in the cafeteria. Andi had mentally named him Lumberjack because of his long, bushy beard.

A shiver raced down her spine. She did *not* like the look in his eyes. It was almost . . . dangerous.

"I think they're ready for us to leave," Duke muttered.

"I think you're correct."

Frederick took their visitor badges, told them to tell Alfonso thank you, and then nodded toward the gate.

With another wave to Frederick, they backed out and headed toward the exit. The guard waved them through, and they were back on the highway.

"What was that about back there?" Duke asked.

Andi filled him in on her conversation with Victor.

He let out a long breath when she finished. "I like this guy less and less all the time."

"You don't have to tell me that. Sometimes I wonder if Thanos even has a soul."

"It seems as if he may be coming and going from this area more than we think." He nodded to a plane in the distance. "Not your run-of-the-mill bush pilot plane."

This one was nice. Expensive.

It practically had Victor written all over it.

"It looks as if he's still trying to do those backroom deals," Duke suggested. "So where to next?"

Andi sighed. "I guess now we head back to Coldfoot. See if anybody else at the Almost Halfway Trading Post found out any information."

"I wish we'd found out more here." Duke's jaw tightened. "But maybe we're looking in the wrong direction."

"You might have a point. But that doesn't mean there isn't something going on outside of this oil patch."

They headed down the road, each lost in their own thoughts.

About five miles out of town, Andi glanced behind them.

A truck quickly approached. "That guy is coming up fast."

Duke glanced in his rearview mirror. "He sure is. I'll slow down and get over so he can pass. Otherwise, he is going to be rushing me the whole time."

Duke did as he said and pulled over as far as he could on the road. He didn't fully stop, only slowed.

But the truck behind them didn't take the hint as it kept speeding toward them.

The vehicle was black with tinted windows, and it appeared clean, as if someone had washed it recently. Most of the vehicles around here were covered in dirt from the highway.

As the truck started to pass around them, suddenly the driver slowed.

Andi tried not to think in worst-case scenarios.

But this guy was definitely up to no good.

Then the sickening sound of metal scratching across metal filled the air, and they lurched.

Andi gasped and grabbed the handle beside her.

This guy had sideswiped them.

On purpose.

Her heart beat harder.

The SUV swerved toward the edge of the road, and Andi braced herself for whatever would happen next.

chapter
forty

DUKE FOUGHT to keep his SUV on the road. There was no shoulder, only a steep drop-off from the layers of gravel that had been laid there.

But just as he gained control, the truck rammed him again.

This time Duke careened into the tundra beside him.

He gripped the wheel, fighting to remain on all four tires and not flip.

Finally, he pressed the brakes, and they came to a stop —still upright.

The engine choked and rumbled before cutting off.

Duke muttered under his breath as he watched the truck speed away.

"Are you okay?" Andi rushed, grabbing his arm.

"I think so." He glared after the truck, trying to memorize the license plate. But he could only make out three of the letters. "It looks like we shook something up there in Prudhoe Bay."

"Yes, it would appear we did."

He tried to start his SUV again, but the engine whimpered before dying out.

He muttered more underneath his breath. He would have muttered far worse things before he became a Christian, however.

"Let me see if I can figure out what's wrong." He pulled the latch to pop the hood and opened the door. A blast of chilly air hit him as he climbed out.

Duke lifted the hood and checked the seals and gaskets near the engine bay.

Then he tried starting the engine again.

Nothing.

Finally, Duke let out a sigh and slammed the hood shut.

They weren't going anywhere. Not tonight, at least.

He climbed back inside and glanced at Andi. "Any chance we're close enough to Prudhoe Bay that you have a cell signal?"

She grabbed her phone and glanced at it. "It looks like I might."

"That's good news. Because we're going to need to call someone to pick us up."

An officer with the North Slope Borough met them thirty minutes later.

Andi and Duke gave their statement about what had

happened, and Officer Plankton—a bearded man in his thirties—took notes. Then he called a tow truck driver for them. The driver, however, was at least two hours away helping someone else.

Apparently, tow truck drivers out here were as scarce as a hen's teeth. That was how Officer Plankton described it, at least. This guy had to come up from Coldfoot.

The officer offered to wait with them, but Andi and Duke had told him they'd be fine. When Plankton left, they climbed back into the SUV to pass time until the tow truck arrived.

Andi let out a breath as she turned everything over in her mind.

"Victor could have killed you." Duke's voice cut into the silence. "Both of us."

"Victor? No. He wouldn't do it himself. And certainly not in a place so obvious."

"The way he looked at you . . ." Duke shook his head, his jaw tightening. "He had murder in his eyes."

"Murder and other things. He wants a piece of the pie up here, and I think he'll do whatever it takes to get it."

"Including killing anyone who gets in his way." Duke threw her a look to make it clear she was on that list.

Andi relayed parts of the conversation she overheard. "I actually recorded part of what he was saying."

Duke's eyebrows shot up. "Really?"

"Really." She grabbed her phone and found the video. Then Duke leaned closer when she hit Play.

Unfortunately, it was nearly impossible to make out anyone's face. That meant this couldn't be used in court.

Disappointment bit at her.

But at least it was *something*.

"If Victor knows I overheard this, he probably did send someone to run us off the road," Andi commented.

Duke rubbed his jaw. "I'm not sure. I made that other guy pretty mad also."

"The one who confronted you in the cafeteria?"

"He's the one," Duke said. "He didn't like you asking about those women."

"Maybe he's involved somehow. Or he knows something about what's going on." Andi sighed. "We may not have discovered any information, but we definitely stirred up the hornet's nest."

Duke didn't argue.

How could he?

He had to know her words were true.

chapter
forty-one

FINALLY, a little over two hours later, the tow truck arrived. The vehicle looked surprisingly clean and new.

The driver, a fortysomething man who said very little, didn't waste any time getting them hooked up to the truck. Apparently, he had two other calls waiting for him after this, so he moved efficiently, well-versed in towing vehicles off this road.

Duke and Andi climbed inside the cab. The driver would take them to a repair shop in Deadhorse, where they could talk to a mechanic.

After everything that had happened on this road, Andi should have been fearful of the tow truck driver. Fearful of anyone on this road, she supposed.

But she had Duke with her, and she always felt safe in his presence.

It appeared the two of them would need to stay in Deadhorse overnight. She had no illusions of the SUV being done anytime soon.

"Dangerous road," the driver said, his voice lackluster as if he'd had this conversation one million times before.

The name embroidered on his shirt read "Milton."

"Yes, it is," Duke said. "I've traveled it many times. But this was no accident."

"I gathered that by the scrape I saw on the side of your vehicle. You mind if I ask what happened?"

"Some guy in a black truck came up behind us and made it very clear that we weren't welcome up here," Duke muttered, his gaze darkening.

The man grunted. "Sounds like you stepped on someone's toes."

"Yeah, I guess we did," Andi muttered.

"A bit of advice for you two . . . Don't mess with those people in Prudhoe Bay. They mean business."

"Do you have run-ins with them very often?" Andi's full attention was suddenly on the tow truck driver.

Maybe he could provide some of the information they'd been looking for. After all, he interacted with people on this road daily.

"Dalton Highway can claim the best." He chewed on a toothpick as he spoke. "There's no shortage of business. Most people I encounter are polite and grateful for the help. There are always a few with their knickers in a knot."

"You get that everywhere, I suppose," Andi muttered.

"If you don't mind me asking, what brings you up here?" Milton asked, his eyes on the road.

"We're actually true crime podcasters," Andi said.

"We're looking into some women who have disappeared from this highway over the past four years."

Milton raised his eyebrows before nodding slowly, thoughtfully. "I've heard stories about them. This is the frozen Wild West. Unfortunately, people disappear around here all the time."

"What's your theory about what happened to them?" Andi crossed her arms and settled back to listen to his answer.

He shrugged and stared straight ahead at the road. "My theory is that sometimes people want to disappear. I'm not saying that was the case for all of them. But I imagine some people just like to come up here because it's the opportunity to walk away and start a new life."

Those words replayed over and over again in Andi's mind.

Was that what Celeste had done?

She stole a quick glance at Duke. His expression made it clear that he was wondering the same thing.

Andi couldn't imagine what he might be feeling. Even when she tried, she knew her empathy couldn't even touch all the thoughts going through Duke's head.

But the more she learned, the less she believed Celeste was one of the women who'd gone missing at the hands of an abductor.

However, if that wasn't the case, Andi had no idea why the woman had just walked away and hidden without telling Duke.

Did he have a dark side he had kept hidden from her? She had a hard time believing that.

She'd never felt unsafe with him, and usually her instincts were spot on.

But out here, she felt a million miles away from civilization.

It seemed as if anything could happen out here.

To anyone.

Yes, this *was* the perfect place to disappear.

And it was the perfect hunting ground for a killer.

As she leaned back, her gaze caught something stuffed behind the seat.

A brown briefcase.

A brown briefcase?

Her heart beat harder.

Gibson had mentioned something about a brown briefcase in Heidi Billingsworth's photos.

Was the man they were riding with the killer?

Duke felt Andi nudge him.

He followed her gaze and saw the briefcase.

Blood rushed in his ears.

A briefcase.

Could this guy be the killer?

He glanced at the man, who seemed so unassuming.

Duke would need to handle this with caution.

But before he could say anything, the man seemed to

follow his gaze and instinctively know what he was looking at. "You think it's weird I drive around with a briefcase?"

Duke kept his voice even, knowing how precarious this situation could turn. "Maybe a little."

"It's not mine. Some guy I picked up left it in here. I've been hoping he'll call me so I can get rid of the thing."

Duke and Andi exchanged a loaded glance.

"Some guy?" Andi said. "You don't get people's names?"

"Not if they want to pay with cash, and they're a one and done. I should probably leave it in the garage, but I figure if he calls me, I can drop it off next time I'm in Coldfoot—or wherever this guy ended up."

"Do you remember anything about him?" Duke asked.

Milton scrunched his forehead. "You're awfully curious about that briefcase. What's going on?"

"It's come up in our investigation," Andi said, a touch of hesitation to her voice.

"Wait . . . the investigation with those missing women?" he said. "A briefcase was one of the clues?"

"That's right," Duke said.

Milton let out a long breath. "Well, I'll be . . . I don't know what to say. I just thought I was doing a good deed by holding onto it."

"Can you describe this guy and what he drove?" A mix of excitement and apprehension captured her expression.

Milton let out another breath. "Let's see. He was probably in his thirties. A businessman. Had dark hair, I believe. Didn't say much. He was the quieter type."

"And his vehicle?" Andi continued to push.

"It was a black Mercedes SUV, I think. One of those expensive cars—one that you don't see very often up this way."

"Did he say what he was doing up in this area?" Duke asked.

"Something with the oil fields. Maybe he was on the board for one of the oil companies? If I remember correctly, he didn't like flying. That's why he decided to drive himself back and forth every time he came up here."

Duke and Andi exchanged another look.

"Listen, would you mind if we looked inside that briefcase?" Duke stared at Milton, praying he cooperated.

The man shrugged. "Be my guest. In fact, take the thing. Call the police. Do whatever you need to do. I don't want anything to do with it."

"The cops might want to talk to you," Andi told him.

"I'm the only Milton's Towing out here, so they should know how to contact me."

Duke's heart thrummed harder.

He couldn't wait to see what was inside that briefcase.

chapter
forty-two

AS SOON AS they arrived in Deadhorse, Milton pulled over on the side of the road just before reaching any buildings.

Andi turned toward him, curious about what he was doing—and maybe slightly frightened.

The whole briefcase thing had definitely shaken her up.

He nodded at the briefcase. "Don't you want to open it? I'm second-guessing whether I should leave it with you or take it to the police myself. I don't want anything to do with whatever is going on, but I'm curious now what's in it."

Andi definitely wanted to see what was inside. If this guy changed his mind and decided to go right to the police himself, they could miss their opportunity.

"I can open it." Duke grabbed it and pulled it onto his lap.

Andi could hardly breathe as she waited to see what was inside.

Half of her expected something mundane.

But another part hoped that maybe there were papers or something that would give them a clue about this killer's identity.

Duke pressed the two latches on top, and the case opened.

Andi's eyes were glued to it as she waited for whatever they might find.

Duke gingerly lifted the lid, revealing the contents inside.

She squinted at what she saw there.

A DVD of *The Rosemary Cleaver Show*.

She vaguely remembered seeing the old black-and-white show on TV.

Even back then, she hadn't really liked it. Some people referred to it as the good old days.

But if she ever got married, she preferred to think of it as a partnership, not a hierarchy. And something about the way the husband on the show had treated and talked to his wife never settled well with her.

Her gaze flittered to the next item.

Was that a . . . whip?

Her lungs tightened.

Why would there be a whip in there?

She didn't like to think through the possibilities.

There were also some dried roses, an apron, and

several recipe cards that appeared to be photocopied from handwritten notes.

Creepy.

It was all creepy.

"I don't know what to think," Duke murmured.

"Me neither." Andi couldn't seem to pull her eyes away.

"You think those things belong to the guy behind these abductions?" Milton asked.

"Maybe," Andi said. "We know the cop in charge of the investigation. We can call him—unless you want to call him yourself."

She crossed her fingers, hoping Milton would say no.

The tow truck driver stared at it another moment. "No, you take it. I don't want anything to do with this. But, like I said, the cops should be able to find me easily if they want my statement."

Andi turned to glance at the man a moment, more questions simmering in her mind. "Where did you drop this man off at?"

"Coldfoot."

"And his vehicle?" Duke asked. "Did you drop it off there also to be repaired?"

Milton nodded. "I did. It was just last week. The guy had a bad vibe about him, but I tried to ignore it. I'll do whatever I can to help. I had no idea I was driving around someone like that . . . no idea."

※

Milton dropped off Duke's SUV with a local guy in Deadhorse. The mechanic promised to look at it and get back with them in the morning.

Then Milton gave Duke and Andi a ride to the main camp in town, one that catered to tourists instead of workers. They grabbed their bags—and the briefcase—and paid the man.

Each contractor set up their own camp—modular buildings, usually three stories high—where their workers ate and slept. Most of them had video game rooms, laundry facilities, workout rooms, and other amenities. People who worked directly for the oil company were lucky enough to have a swimming pool and movie theater. That was what Frederick told them.

Once inside, the woman behind the front desk—a sixty-something with dyed black hair piled on top of her head, purple cat eyeglasses, and an assertive gaze—told them there was unfortunately only one room available. The woman's name, according to the tag she wore, was Eleanor, and her voice was scratchy with age.

Duke turned to Andi and saw the exhaustion in her gaze. "You can have it."

She let out a cynical chuckle. "Don't be ridiculous. Then where will you stay?"

He shrugged. "I'll figure something else out."

"The room has two twin beds if that helps," the woman added, her tone dry as she made no secret that she was listening.

"It does help." Andi glanced at the desk clerk a moment before taking a step closer to Duke. "There's nothing else to figure out. There's nowhere else to stay here. We can share the room. There are two beds, and we're both adults."

He stared at her another moment, trying to read her expression. "Are you sure?"

"Absolutely. I trust you. You make any moves, and you'll find out I've got a nasty right hook." She winked at him before pretending to sock him in the jaw.

Her joking put him more at ease.

But Duke knew tension still simmered between them after the time they'd almost kissed several weeks ago. He'd tried to avoid too much alone time with Andi since then. The last thing he needed was for his feelings for the woman to grow.

Andi turned back to the clerk. "We'll take the room."

"I thought you might." She pushed her glasses up higher on her nose before scribbling something in a logbook with a pencil.

Then she grabbed a key behind her, one that dangled from a little plastic diamond with the room number on it and gave them instructions on how to adjust the faucet in the community bathrooms to get the hot water to work. She included a little jingle about liking it hot that she insisted worked wonders every time.

Almost awkwardly, Duke and Andi started toward the dormitory-style accommodations. They could put their stuff in there and then figure everything else out. The good news was, since they were in Deadhorse, they still had cell service. They should be able to check in with the rest of the gang and tell them what happened.

Duke did the honor of unlocking the room and pushing the door open.

He scanned it as they both stepped inside.

The room was small, probably ten by twelve. Just enough square footage for the two twin-sized beds, a small dresser, and a sink. Community bathrooms were down the hall.

Duke looked at Andi and saw a tremble rake through her.

Was she nervous about staying with him? He could still find somewhere else to crash.

"Andi?" he asked softly.

Her gaze snapped up to his. "Sorry. This place is just so . . . isolated. I was imagining being out on that road by myself and getting in an accident or breaking down. I'm sure it would be easy to feel a little helpless and a lot vulnerable."

"It would probably be terrifying, especially if no vehicles came past for a long time. Or if the weather was bad. Or if it was dark. Polar bears are even known to travel through this area at times. This isn't somewhere to be played with."

"No, it's not." She let out a sigh and straightened. "We need to find answers for these women and their families. This has gone on for far too long."

"I agree," Duke told her. "Maybe they had more luck down in Coldfoot."

They sat next to each other on one of the beds, and Andi pulled out her phone. "First, let's call Gibson."

chapter
forty-three

"ANDI! DUKE!" Mariella's fuzzy image filled the screen. "I've been worried about you guys. I mean, I know it's still relatively early. But still . . . are you okay?"

Andi was surprisingly relieved to see the woman—a familiar face.

They'd tried to call Gibson, but he hadn't answered. That meant they needed to keep guard over that briefcase until they could give it to him.

"Actually, we have to stay in Deadhorse tonight," Andi said. "Someone purposefully ran us off the road, and Duke's SUV is currently out of service."

Andi heard someone gasp right before Simmy's face appeared on the screen. "What? That's terrible. Are you okay? Who would want to do that?"

"Someone who didn't like us asking questions," Duke said. "Thankfully, we still had cell service. We were able to call the police, and they sent a tow truck. But we're not getting out of here until tomorrow at the earliest."

"That's got to be frustrating," Simmy said. "But I'm glad it wasn't worse."

"Me too," Mariella said. "How did it go up in Prudhoe Bay?"

They filled them in on what had happened, leaving out some details about Victor. They would get to the briefcase . . . in a minute.

"Do you think that guy who confronted you in the cafeteria could be behind your accident?" Mariella asked.

"Not necessarily. He did seem shady. And shady people usually know other shady people. But we don't have any clear answers right now." Andi shifted the phone. "We did, however, find a briefcase stashed in the tow truck driver's cab."

"What?" All four faces crowded into the screen, and Andi wasn't sure who had even asked the question. Maybe all of them at the same time.

She explained the situation and what was inside, adding the fact they'd tried to call Gibson but had to leave a message.

"This could be a golden egg!" Mariella said. "But how strange. Why an old DVD? A whip and an apron? What kind of game is this guy playing?"

"Good question," Andi murmured. "We'll keep you updated. In the meantime, what about you guys? Did you find out anything?"

"We managed to track down a couple of people here." Ranger entered the screen, pushing the rest of the team away for a minute. "One of Kiah's friends told us she had a client who was bothering her. The day after Kiah told her friend that, she disappeared."

Surprise washed through Andi. She hadn't expected to hear that. "Did her friend have any idea who the client was?"

"No," Simmy said. "Kiah didn't tell her. Plus, she made it clear they did *not* keep records of their clients."

"I suppose they wouldn't want a paper trail . . ." Duke rubbed a hand over his face and let out a breath as if this whole investigation was exhausting him.

Then again, it was also late. They were tired. And they had a lot to think about.

"But there is something interesting." Mariella practically pushed Ranger out of the way. "Kiah's friend said that Kiah had tried to call her once after she'd disappeared. She didn't recognize the number, but when she answered she thought she'd heard Kiah say her name. But the line went dead right after that. She tried to call her back, but there was no answer."

"Interesting . . ." Andi murmured.

"Her friend said she'd wondered if she'd really heard Kiah or if her mind was playing tricks on her. But to be sure, she tried to call that number again a couple of days later, and the phone line was disconnected."

"How long after she disappeared did that phone call happen?" Duke asked.

"Two months," Simmy said.

Wait . . . if that was true, did that mean that whoever was abducting these women wasn't killing them right away? Maybe he was keeping them alive for some reason.

If so, maybe they still had a chance to rescue Heidi Billingsworth.

A touch of hope filled her.

"What about the park ranger, John Hopkins?" Andi's thoughts raced ahead. "Did you catch up with him?"

Ranger's face came back on the screen. "We did. He seemed to know a lot about the women who have disappeared."

"Anything that indicated he might be behind this?" Duke asked.

The possibility seemed less likely now that Milton had mentioned the man he'd picked up most likely worked up in the oil fields and dressed in business attire.

"Not really," Ranger said. "But I did get the impression that Hopkins doesn't have a very high regard for women."

"Why do you say that?" Andi asked.

"He said women who travel this road alone aren't very smart. That life would be better if women went back to being housewives and stopped thinking they could do everything a man could."

Andi and Duke exchanged a glance.

"Just because he's a chauvinist doesn't mean he's a killer," Andi finally said. "Although, that would fit with that DVD in the briefcase."

"You're right." Ranger nodded, the angle he held the phone making his beard look even bigger than usual. "It doesn't mean he's the killer. But I still think it's smart if we keep an eye on him."

"Agreed," Duke said.

"Do you think you'll be able to come down here tomorrow?" Simmy asked before the end of the call.

"That's our plan. As long as the SUV is fixed." Andi glanced at Duke, who nodded in confirmation. "Either way, as soon as the SUV is ready, we'll be on our way. We'll call you when we can to update you on the situation."

"In the meantime, we'll be working on this podcast," Mariella said.

"Sounds good," Duke said. "Hope you all get some sleep."

They ended the call.

Andi almost wished they hadn't.

Now it was too quiet.

Awkwardness stretched through the room as Duke remained beside her.

Andi did the only thing she knew to do.

Escape.

She stood and grabbed her suitcase. "I'm going to hit one of the showers down the hall and get cleaned up."

Duke nodded as he stood and ran a hand through his hair, his eyes shifting. "Good idea."

Andi didn't mention the fact she just needed to be a little farther away from him for a moment.

Instead, she opened the door and started to step out.

As she did, she spotted a figure coming down the hallway and quickly ducked back inside the room.

She scrambled to twist the lock in place. Then she pressed herself against the door, her thoughts racing.

"What's wrong?" Duke asked.

Her gaze met his. "Lumberjack is here."

"Lumberjack?"

"The man who confronted you in the cafeteria. That's what I started calling him in my head. Anyway, he's here, and he's checking out the rooms along the hallway as if he's searching for somebody." She paused to give that a split second to sink in before adding, "Most likely you and me."

Duke took a moment to process what Andi had just said.

Lumberjack, as she had called him, was here.

Searching for someone.

Andi was absolutely right. The man was probably looking for them.

The guy had clearly been upset with Duke earlier, but Duke had tried to brush it off.

Lumberjack must have heard somehow that Duke and Andi had ended up staying the night.

Maybe because Lumberjack had been the one who'd tried to run them off the road? Maybe he'd been monitoring them ever since.

Duke rushed to the door and pressed his hands against it.

Just in case the man tried to push inside.

"Are you sure it was him?" He glanced down at Andi, noting that her face was mere inches from his.

"I'm positive." Her gaze remained unwavering as she stared back up at him.

"And he appeared as if he was looking for somebody?"

She nodded, her eyes wide and her chest rising and falling too quickly. "Most definitely."

The next instant, the door handle rattled.

Duke's heart quickened.

It was him. Lumberjack.

He was trying to get into their room. Maybe to teach them a lesson.

Duke's first instinct was to confront the guy. To give him a piece of his mind.

But in a confined space like this and with Andi so close, that would be a terrible idea.

Plus, out here he had no backup. He was an outsider.

They didn't know who they could trust.

He was going to have to play this by ear.

He glanced at Andi and saw the fear glimmering in her gaze.

She was scared—and rightfully so.

The guy began to bang at the door. "I know you're in there! Open up."

"Duke . . ." Andi whispered.

He put a finger over his lips, indicating they should be quiet. Lumberjack had no way of knowing for sure that Duke and Andi were inside.

Unless someone had told him.

Which was a possibility.

His gut clenched tighter.

Lumberjack pounded on the door again, calling out some obscenities as he did.

The entire door shook.

Was this guy trying to break it down?

Andi pressed her eyes closed.

Duke knew they needed to figure out how to handle the situation before somebody got hurt.

At that thought, something slammed into the door again.

Probably Lumberjack's shoulder if he had to guess.

The door wasn't sturdy enough.

A few more tries, and this door was coming down.

He had no doubt about that.

chapter
forty-four

ANDI COULDN'T BREATHE.

She knew Duke could handle himself. He probably even had a gun with him.

Not that she wanted him to use it.

But they had no one here to turn to.

There was a good chance that others here at the camp would be on Lumberjack's side instead of theirs.

If that guy managed to get inside . . .

She swallowed hard.

She didn't want to think about what could happen.

The door shifted behind her again as the man threw himself into it.

How many more times would he do that before the door broke from the hinges?

Duke continued to press his palms into it to stop the door from moving.

But Andi knew that wouldn't work forever.

The room suddenly felt like a prison.

The man threw himself into the door again.

This time it cracked.

Andi and Duke glanced at each other again.

Then Duke started to reach into his waistband for his gun.

Right before he grabbed it, a new voice sounded outside.

Andi would recognize that scratchy voice anywhere.

It was Eleanor, the woman from behind the front desk.

"What do you think you're doing?" she demanded. "You trying to destroy one of my rooms?"

"I need to talk to the people inside." Lumberjack's deep voice drifted through the wood door.

"And this is the way you want to go about it? Have you lost your ever-loving mind?"

Andi relaxed just slightly.

She liked that woman. Liked how there wasn't even a touch of fear in her voice, even though that man probably outweighed her by a hundred pounds.

"You need to stay out of this," Lumberjack said.

"No, you need to get out of my camp before I throw you out."

"I'm not leaving until I talk to the people in that room."

"Then you're going to be waiting for a long time. Because they're not in there."

A stretch of silence passed.

Wait . . . did Eleanor really think they were gone? Or was she covering for them?

Either way, Andi hoped this worked.

Finally, Lumberjack asked, "They're not?"

"No, they're not. They left about ten minutes ago, and they haven't come back yet."

"Are you sure?"

"Of course I'm sure. I work the front desk, so I see everyone who comes and goes. I'm the innkeeper around here, genius."

Another moment of silence. "You telling me you notice everyone who passes by?"

"I sure noticed them. That guy and his girlfriend stand out. They're both good-looking. Confident. And strangers. They stand out like sore thumbs among you rednecks. I'm telling you . . . they are not here."

Despite the situation, Andi couldn't help but smile. This woman was colorful. Very colorful.

"Where did they go?" Lumberjack asked.

"Now you're going to have to figure that one out for yourself. I'm an innkeeper, not a genie in a bottle."

Andi thought she heard a low growl on the other side of the door.

"I want to see inside this room first so I can know for sure," Lumberjack said. "Open the door, or I'll open it myself."

"What gives you the right to do that?"

"You can't stop me. What are you gonna do? You can

call the police, but by time they get here it will be too late."

It sounded like Lumberjack was determined to get into the room.

Andi glanced up at Duke.

What were they going to do if he managed to get inside?

There was nowhere to go. No windows.

They'd be sitting ducks.

Or Duke would be forced to use his gun, something Andi knew he wouldn't take lightly.

Duke knew he had to act fast.

Quietly, he moved away from the door. He'd gotten a good look at the room earlier, and he knew that the beds were set up on wooden platforms.

He lifted the mattress of the nearest bed. Dust and some candy wrappers stared at him from the darkness beneath it.

This was going to have to work for now.

He motioned for Andi to crawl in the empty space.

She hesitated only a moment before climbing inside.

Duke quickly squeezed in beside her before lowering the mattress back down over them.

They were completely enclosed.

And just in time.

Only a few seconds later, he heard the door open.

"See for yourself," Eleanor said.

Duke could hardly breathe as he lay there. Andi was pressed up against him, her hair tickling his cheek. They were both stiff, not daring to move or make a sound.

It was better this way. Some moments called for fighting. But others called for disappearing.

He didn't need any more trouble while he was up here in Deadhorse. It wouldn't help solve anything.

He just wanted to get his SUV back and get out of town. They'd done what they came here to do, and now it was time to leave.

Duke hoped they got that opportunity.

"Do you believe me now?" Eleanor asked.

The man grunted. "I guess. But they *have* been here."

"Well, of course they have. How else would their suitcases have gotten inside?"

The man grunted again. "You let me know as soon as they come back."

"And if I don't want to?"

Duke held his breath.

He prayed Eleanor wasn't hurt in the middle of all of this.

"You don't want to know what will happen if you don't do as I ask," Lumberjack growled.

More silence stretched, and Duke tried to imagine what was happening out there.

If that man tried to hurt Eleanor, Duke would have no choice but to burst out from under this bed to help.

But that would be a last resort.

Right now, he needed to keep Andi safe.

He waited again, praying with all his might that no one would be injured.

There were already enough victims, enough innocent lives changed forever.

chapter
forty-five

ANDI COULD HARDLY BREATHE AS she waited.

What was that man going to do?

She admired Eleanor's bravery, but she hoped the woman didn't get herself hurt.

"Don't make me angry because you *will* regret it," the man muttered.

Andi felt Duke tense beside her.

He didn't like this conversation any more than she did.

Then there was silence.

Neither of them dared to move and give away their presence.

Andi thought she heard the door click back in place.

Maybe Eleanor and Lumberjack had left.

But maybe not.

They needed to give it a few more minutes just to be safe.

It was only then she realized exactly how close she and Duke were lying next to each other.

Their faces were only inches apart.

She was gripping his arm, and he gripped hers.

He seemed to realize it at the same time she did, and he went stiff also.

Andi couldn't see his eyes. Couldn't tell if he was looking at her.

Yet, at the same time, she seemed to sense his focus.

As if it was on her.

Her throat tightened.

More than anything, she wanted to scoot closer. To find comfort in his arms. To find strength in his presence.

But she couldn't let herself do that.

Resist temptation, Andi told herself. *Resist*.

She finally whispered, "How long should we stay here?"

"I think they're gone. Let me check." Duke shifted, his elbow accidentally ramming her rib cage. "Sorry."

"I'm okay."

The next instant, a sliver of light crept into the space.

Duke had lifted the bed just enough to peek out.

She froze, half expecting the man to be hiding in the room just waiting to pounce on them.

But so far, nothing.

A moment later, Duke pushed the mattress up farther and rose. "He's gone."

Andi let out a breath. But her lungs still felt tight and achy from being in the confined space. She hadn't even realized how claustrophobic she'd felt until she was under there.

Duke stretched out his hand, and she took it, rising to her feet. She stepped into the middle of the room and waited as Duke readjusted the bed.

He stormed toward the door and twisted the lock in place.

Then he walked back over toward Andi.

As he stared down at her and she up at him, her heart pounded so hard she felt certain Duke could see it pulsating under her sweater.

All the warm fuzzy feelings she'd wrestled with while the two of them were trapped in that snug space flooded back.

There was something between them. She could feel it. Something invisible that seemed to tether their hearts together.

But the question was, what would they do about it?

As Duke stared at Andi, an ache captured his heart.

Why was he so attracted to this woman?

It wasn't just her looks. Duke liked everything about her. Her brazenness. Her intelligence. Her kindness.

He gently tugged a piece of fuzz from her hair before sliding a strand behind her ear.

As he did, their gazes caught.

Instead of letting his hand drop back down to his side, he rested it on her cheek and jawline.

Andi stared up at him, those blue eyes wide and imploring.

More than anything, Duke wanted to dip his head lower. To kiss her.

At the moment, all he could think about was how soft her lips would feel. About the fire that would explode between them.

Andi reached for him, her hand resting on his chest.

Could she feel how quickly his heart was thumping?

Was hers beating equally as fast?

"Andi . . ." Duke's voice came out as a hoarse whisper.

She licked her lips as she stared up at him. "Duke . . ."

He moved closer, pulling her against him.

Until Andi stiffened.

She closed her eyes as if she was fighting some type of invisible demon.

Then she stepped back, her expression pinched with agony. "I can't do this."

His throat tightened until he felt as if he couldn't breathe. "Andi . . ."

Her eyes fluttered open and met his, a new determination there. "*We* can't kiss each other. Because when—or if —we kiss, I don't want to look in your eyes afterward and see any type of regret."

What was she talking about? "Andi . . . I wouldn't ever regret kissing you."

Her lips twisted together before she said, "You may

not be thinking about Celeste now. But you will be thinking about her later. Thinking about how you betrayed her, and thinking about how I was the reason. I don't want to be that person."

Duke should have an argument against her statement, but he didn't. He didn't know what to say.

Because, deep down inside, he knew Andi was correct.

Right now, Andi was all he could think about. But once his emotions cleared, that wouldn't be the case anymore. Reality would hit. The complexity of the situation would overcome him.

They stepped back from each other, heaviness filling the space between them.

His heart pounded in his ears.

Regret already filled him, and they hadn't even kissed.

Andi was right.

This holding pattern in his life . . . it was his own personal purgatory.

"I'm . . . I'm sorry," he muttered.

"Don't be sorry. I think it's great how you've waited for Celeste. I know it must be difficult."

He sat down hard on the edge of his bed and leaned forward gripping his temples as a headache came on.

"Sometimes, just when I think I'm ready to move on, I imagine Celeste coming back." His voice cracked and strained under the emotional pressure welling inside him. "Maybe it's egotistical, but I imagine her telling me that the thought of us being together is the only thing that kept her going through the hard days. Then I imagine how she'd feel if she found out I didn't wait for her."

Andi sat beside him and wrapped an arm around his waist in a comforting gesture. "I can only imagine how difficult it is, especially in light of everything that has happened recently."

"I just don't know what to think. Then I hear about Ted getting remarried after two years. Maybe *I'm* the strange one."

"When the time is right, you'll know."

Duke glanced at her, careful to keep his emotions in check. "You really think so?"

Andi nodded. "I do."

Then she stood.

Instantly, he missed her presence. Missed her touch. Missed her sweet scent.

All things he shouldn't be missing.

"We should probably get some rest," Andi said. "We have a long day ahead of us tomorrow."

"I wish I could."

Andi tilted her head as she observed him. "What do you mean?"

"That man who came here . . . he obviously feels threatened. You ask me, that means he knows something."

"Do you think that guy is somehow connected to these missing women?"

"I have no idea. But the fact he came after us like he did makes me suspect he is. I can't see myself ever coming back up here again. So if I want answers, I need to get them now."

Andi's gaze locked with his. "That sounds dangerous."

Duke rose. "That's because it is."

ANDI SHOT TO HER FEET. "I'm going with you."

Duke shook his head in a way that didn't leave room for compromise. "No, that's a terrible idea."

Andi's hands went to her hips, and she leveled her gaze. "So is the idea of you going out there by yourself. At least I can be close by to call backup in case you need it."

Duke stared at her a moment, emotions swirling in his gaze. "Who is that backup going to be? We know no one else out here."

"I don't know. But you don't know what kind of trouble you might run into."

"Maybe. But it's not like I haven't faced trouble before. At least I've been trained for these kinds of things."

She stared at Duke another moment and knew she wouldn't be able to talk him out of this.

"If you go, I go." She raised her chin. "That's all there is to it."

His gaze remained hot on hers as he continued to stare her down.

Finally, Duke nodded. "Fine. You can come. But promise me you'll be careful."

"Of course."

He grabbed his gun from his bag and shoved it in his waistband. Then he pulled on his coat and hat to ward away some of the cold.

Andi did the same, thankful she'd worn some darker-colored clothing—which just happened to be a coincidence. Thankfully, that would work to her advantage.

Duke crept toward the door and motioned for Andi to stay back.

She remained where she was.

With one more glance at her, he unlocked it and peeked out.

He must have seen that the coast was clear because he indicated for Andi to follow him.

She stuck close behind him as they stepped into the quiet hallway.

Still on alert, they made their way into the lobby area where Eleanor sat behind the desk knitting what appeared to be a blanket.

She looked up from over top of her glasses at them before dryly saying, "Brave of you to come out of your room tonight."

They paused near her desk, still on guard.

"Thank you for what you did back there," Duke said.

"Of course. I don't like bullies. Never have. I knew as

soon as I saw that guy come in here that he would be trouble. I don't know what you two did to make him so mad, but I'd keep my eyes wide-open if I were you. Not sure if I'll be able to protect you next time."

"We understand," Andi said. "We'd never want to place you in that position. But we do have a quick question for you."

"Oh, well, go ahead. I'm here all night." Her voice still contained that no-nonsense tone as she continued to knit.

"Do you know that guy's name?" Andi asked.

She shrugged. "Lots of workers come through here. I've seen him a time or two. I don't know his name for sure. Maybe Phil or Philip or Frank. Never paid much attention."

"Is there anything else you could tell us about him?" Duke asked. "We need to find him before he finds us."

"Sounds risky to me, but to each his own. I'm pretty sure that he works for the Blackwater Contracting Camp."

"And exactly how far away is the Blackwater Camp?" Duke asked.

"You're in luck—or in trouble, depending on how you look at it." She nodded behind her. "It's the next camp over."

Duke took a step back. "Thank you."

"If you're going to go out there this time of night, be careful. You know we have grizzlies around here."

Comforting, Andi mused. She hated bears. As in, they terrified her—probably because she'd watched a movie about a bear attack when she was younger and had never gotten over the trauma of it.

They thanked Eleanor again before stepping toward the door.

On the way out, all Andi could think about was if Duke's gun was powerful enough to stop an angry grizzly . . . and an angry Lumberjack.

Duke wasn't comfortable with Andi coming with him. But he knew he couldn't talk her out of it.

He prayed she'd be safe.

What they were doing was risky but necessary.

What if this guy had the answers they needed? The last thing Duke wanted was to get back to Fairbanks and always wonder what would have happened if he'd tried to find out more answers. Besides, he'd never been one to shy away from trouble.

The two of them stepped outside, and the cold air hit them again.

It was surprisingly quiet and surprisingly light still.

He knew the sun didn't set at this time of the year this far north. So he shouldn't be surprised. But for a moment, he'd forgotten.

Duke had been counting on using the cover of darkness to his advantage, but that wouldn't be happening.

"So what's our plan of action, GI Joe?" Andi hurried

to keep up with him, probably taking two steps for every one of his. But she didn't complain.

One more thing to admire about her.

"I need to figure out where exactly this guy is staying at that camp," Duke muttered.

"And when you do? Are you going to barge into his room and demand answers?"

"Of course not. That would be stupid on my part. But maybe I can find out some things about him. That's my hope."

"That's my hope as well."

They walked beside each other as they headed toward the next building, probably six hundred yards away. As they got closer, Duke saw a few people mingling outside, most wearing their construction gear. A truck drove past, not too far away.

So not everything had shut down.

It had probably been an hour since that guy left their camp. Where had he been in the time since then? Gathering reinforcements?

The last thing Duke wanted was to put Andi in a bad situation. That was one more reason why he hesitated to go inside the camp where the guy was staying.

At least out here they had the opportunity to run. They had a fighting chance.

Duke scanned everything around him, looking for a sign as to what he should do next.

His gaze stopped on a black truck in the distance.

A black truck with a scrape on the side of it.

He grabbed Andi's hand and pulled her to a stop.

"Do you see that?" He nodded toward the vehicle.

"That's the guy who ran us off the road." Her voice hardened as she said the words.

As the sound of voices drifted through the air, Andi and Duke slipped behind the dumpster. Using the container as cover, they watched as two men left the other camp.

His heart pounded harder.

It was him.

The man who'd tried to hunt them down.

He was walking toward the black truck.

As the men got closer, Duke and Andi ducked lower.

"Steve . . ." the other man said.

So that was Lumberjack's name.

"Good to see you, man," Steve told the other guy. "We just got some new girls in. We need to spread the word to come to Room 305."

"Did you get some good ones this time?"

"They're all good ones."

The two men exchanged a sickening laugh.

"And you're sure nobody else knows?" the other guy asked.

"You know I pay off Ralph at the front desk," Steve said. "He won't say anything. But this man and woman were snooping around today, and I'm afraid they're with Homeland Security. They had this air about them, you know? And they were asking about some women. I don't want them to blow this operation."

"So, how can we make sure they don't?"

"That's what I'm trying to figure out," Steve continued. "I'm keeping my eyes open for whenever they come back to the camp. When they do . . . I'm going to have a nice long talk with them."

Duke and Andi exchanged a glance.

It was as they feared. There was some type of human trafficking operation going on here.

Was Heidi one of the girls who'd been brought in?

Was this the answer they were looking for?

Was briefcase man somehow tied up in this? Did he run the business side of things?

"I gotta go to the store and pick up a few things," Steve said. "Keep your eyes open for that man and woman. If they leave, follow them. If they come back, let me know."

"You got it."

Steve climbed into his truck and took off. As he did, the other man walked toward the camp where Duke and Andi were staying.

The other guy would clearly be the lookout for tonight.

Duke's thoughts raced as he prepared himself for whatever would happen next.

chapter
forty-seven

"I HAVE AN IDEA," Andi announced as she turned to Duke. Conviction stained her words.

Duke stared at her, questions in his gaze. "Go ahead."

"You and I are going to go to that camp and talk to Ralph. You are going to hold onto my arm and tell him that I'm the last girl. And then we're going to go up to the third floor and see if there really are women being held there."

Duke's entire expression tightened. "I'm not sure that's a good idea."

"It's the only idea. We can't call the police without more evidence. Besides, if these guys catch wind that cops are coming then who knows what they'll do to these women to cover up their crimes. Who knows how many people here are involved in this?"

"So we do that, and let's say we find these women," Duke said. "What then?"

"We help them to safety. Call the cops. Look out for them and hope those guys don't come back."

"It's risky."

"Some risks are worth the payoff, and this is one of them." Her voice held no doubt.

Duke's gaze locked with hers. "Are you sure you're up for this?"

"I'm positive. And if we're going to do this, we need to do it now."

He stared at her another moment, and Andi saw the agony in the choice. He didn't want her to get hurt, and she could appreciate that.

But she wasn't going to back down.

He finally nodded. "Let's go."

They glanced around once more before slinking from behind the dumpster and hurrying toward the camp in the distance.

But before they stepped inside, Duke did as Andi had instructed. He took her arm, acting as if she was being held captive.

Then they stepped inside and approached the man sitting behind a desk.

A man with the nametag Ralph. The man was probably in his fifties, with a large nose and shaggy, dark hair.

"Can I help you?" Ralph glanced up and pushed his glasses higher on his nose. He set down the word search he was working on.

Duke shoved Andi forward. "I was asked to bring her in. Third floor."

She kept her head lowered, not daring to show the defiance in her gaze.

She knew this was just an act, but her heart sped at the intensity of the situation. Duke would never handle her like this except for the fact they were acting and needed to sell this scenario. She didn't fault him for that.

Ralph stared at Duke as if sizing him up. "Never seen you before."

"I'm one of Steve's guys." Duke's voice hardened into a no-nonsense tone.

The man continued to eye them skeptically, and Andi wondered if he was buying any of this.

If Ralph didn't believe Duke's story, then this whole ruse would be over before it even really started.

Suddenly, this seemed like a bad idea.

Duke had no doubt all this guy had to do was to hit a button to call backup, and Duke and Andi would both be in danger.

He waited, trying not show any apprehension.

Finally, the guy nodded slowly and leaned back. "You know where to go?"

Relief swept through Duke. So far, it appeared their plan had worked.

But they weren't out of the woods yet.

"Steve said the third floor," Duke muttered. "Room 305."

"Knock three times. They'll let you in."

Duke nodded before roughly jerking Andi toward a stairway in the distance.

As soon as they slipped inside the stairwell, he loosened his grip and murmured, "Sorry. I hope I didn't hurt you."

"You're fine. If you were too gentle with me, it wouldn't have been believable."

Maybe. But he still didn't like it.

Any of it.

Apprehension threaded through his muscles. This could go wrong in so many ways. He still didn't like the idea of Andi being here.

But she was right. This was the best way to gain information.

Duke only hoped they didn't get caught.

As soon as he confirmed there were women inside, he would call the police.

He could have gotten one of the security guards in Prudhoe Bay to help, but he wasn't sure who he could trust. Talk about being a stranger in a strange land.

He and Andi climbed the stairway.

Duke kept hold of her arm, just in case.

But they didn't pass anyone, which was a blessing.

When they reached the third floor, they walked down the hallway to Room 305.

After a moment of hesitation, Duke knocked three times.

Then he waited to see who opened the door.

chapter
forty-eight

ANDI COULD BARELY BREATHE AS she waited to
see if someone would answer their knock.

Five seconds later, the door opened.

A thirtysomething man with a dirty-blond mustache
and a mullet stood on the other side staring at them with
contempt in his gaze.

"Who are you?" he growled, chomping on a toothpick
at the corner of his mouth.

"I brought you a new girl." Duke shoved Andi
forward.

Andi dipped her head low again, trying to look
oppressed instead of feisty and strong. Everything in her
wanted to fight. To show she wouldn't be tamed. That her
pride couldn't be taken from her.

She forced herself to appear broken instead.

"Steve didn't tell me anybody else was coming,"
Mullet Man grumbled.

"You know Steve." Duke shrugged. "He has a lot on his mind right now."

Mullet Man grunted and continued to look them over.

As he did, Andi kept her head bowed. Only moving her eyes, she glanced up, desperate to see what was on the other side of the doorway.

Two women were inside, sitting on bare mattresses on the floor. Their eyes were glazed and their faces dirty.

They'd been drugged, hadn't they?

Anger burned through Andi.

She had no doubt Duke saw the women too.

Some type of operation was definitely going on here.

"I know a lot of guys who might like getting to know this one a little bit better." Mullet Man reached for Andi, ready to pull her into the room. His voice dipped low with suggestion. "I'll have to give her a little bit of orientation."

His words seemed to trigger something inside Duke.

In a split second, he released Andi and grabbed the man's shirt, slamming him against the wall near the door. Duke pressed his arm into the guy's windpipe as he held the man in place.

As he did, Andi glanced up.

There were more than two women in here.

There were six.

The others were behind a dresser, pressed against the wall as if trying to hide.

No other men.

Not right now.

Andi scanned their faces but didn't see Heidi.

She rushed toward them, desperate to let them know they were the good guys.

"It's okay." Andi paused by the mattresses and glanced at the women. "We're here to help."

She grabbed her phone and dialed the police.

Mullet Man continued to mutter things underneath his breath. But Duke held him in place.

Now they just had to hope no one else came before the police did.

Andi glanced into the hallway and checked for anyone that might be coming.

Her heart beat faster.

A man walked their way.

A man she'd never seen before.

Andi quickly shut the door and locked it.

Still gripping her phone, she realized the police had answered and were waiting for her to speak.

"Please . . . we need help." Her voice trembled, giving away her fear. "Now."

"You don't know what you're talking about, man," Mullet Man muttered, his teeth clenched and only his lips moving.

"Yes, I do," Duke growled as he glared at the man. He kept his fists at his side, willing himself not to give this guy a piece of his mind. "You're keeping these women here against their will."

Andi touched his arm, snapping him from his fury. She whispered, "There's another man coming down the hallway, and the police are on their way."

He nodded, realizing just how hairy this situation could turn. "Help me tie this guy up."

Andi found some zip ties, probably used on the women, and they bound Mullet Man at his wrists. Then they left him in the corner near the door, and Duke pulled out his gun.

As he did, Andi turned to the women, urging them to come out from behind the dresser. "Are you all okay?"

They nodded, tears rolling down their faces. They eased out and joined the other two women on the mattresses. Their fear was heartbreaking.

Hopefully that would end today.

"Am I correct in saying you're all here against your will?" Andi asked.

Again, they nodded.

A couple of them said something in a different language.

If Andi had to guess, at least one of the women was Russian. A couple were Native American. She wasn't sure about the rest.

She only knew they all looked terrified.

"How long did the police say it would be until they get here?" Duke glanced at Andi as he stood near the door.

"They said they were only five minutes away." Andi's

words came out fast and clipped as the intensity of the situation hit her. "I gave them the name of the camp and the room number."

Andi glanced at the door again. That man she'd seen walking this way should be here any time.

If he realized that Duke and Andi were inside, he could call backup to help him. She had no doubt this was a very profitable business, and whoever was getting paid wouldn't want it ruined.

The last thing Andi wanted for was for these women to suffer because of her and Duke's rescue efforts gone wrong.

"How many men are working with you?" Duke turned back to Mullet Man.

"I don't have to tell you nothing." He sneered at Duke.

Duke raised his gun at the man. "I suggest that you do."

The man's eyes widened before hardening with defiance. "We're not doing anything wrong. They're fine. They want to be here."

"Really? You're going to go with that?" Duke continued. "Look at these women. Do they look fine to you?"

The man didn't say anything else.

Just then, a knock sounded at the door.

Three knocks, actually.

Duke swallowed hard.

This was where the rubber met the road, as the saying went.

"Is that another one of your guys?" Duke asked Mullet Man.

"Why don't you answer and see?" He smirked as if anticipating Duke's plan would be turned upside down.

Duke hesitated. If they didn't answer, the man outside would get suspicious. But if they did answer, that could still lead to trouble.

Duke pulled Mullet Man to his feet. "You're going to answer, and you're going to say everything's okay. You're going to tell whoever this is to leave. If you don't, I'm going to pull this trigger."

Mullet Man muttered under his breath but nodded.

Then Duke prepared to open the door, praying for the best.

ANDI HOPED they'd made the right choice.

She hoped she and Duke hadn't just made things worse for these women.

It was more than hoping.

Several times lately, she'd found herself praying.

Despite prayers, she still wasn't exactly sure where she stood with God or where He stood with her.

She *did* know that during these desperate times in life, she liked the thought of a Higher Being looking out for her.

Yet what happened during the times when people thought God was looking out for them, but things still went devastatingly wrong? How did people come to terms with that?

Andi wasn't sure, but this wasn't the time to think about it.

Instead, she prepared herself to act. She placed herself as a barrier between the door and these women.

It wouldn't take much to take her down. She was just over a hundred pounds and barely five feet tall.

But she'd do whatever she could to protect them.

Duke remained behind the door, his gun drawn. He positioned Mullet Man to the side where the door opened. Duke muttered a few more threats before opening the door a crack.

Mullet Man stared at the person on the other side. "It's a bad time."

"Bad time for you maybe." The man let out a chuckle. "I have an appointment."

"You're going to need to come back later."

"What if I don't want to?" The man on the other side of the door raised his voice. "I already paid at the front desk."

"I said you're going to have to come back later." Mullet Man's voice hardened. "It wasn't a question."

"What's in your craw?" the man shot back.

"Nothing. I'm in the middle of something."

A moment of silence passed. "You can't keep them all to yourself."

"It's not like that, man," Mullet Man said. "Now, I gotta go."

"What's going on? Do you want me to call Steve?"

Andi's heart thrummed harder. That guy on the other side of the door knew something was up, didn't he?

This was where everything could go south.

Something clicked on the other side of the door.

Did that guy have a gun?

Would he try to be a cowboy and come to the rescue of his fellow criminal?

Andi braced herself for whatever would come next.

Duke heard the click.

He knew what was about to happen.

That man on the other side of the door had a gun, and he was about to use it.

Duke couldn't let that happen.

He gripped his own weapon.

The last thing he wanted to do was to fire. Hurting other people was never his prerogative. But when push came to shove . . .

His index finger remained poised on the trigger as he braced himself.

Lord, be with us. Please.

Just then, a commotion sounded in the hallway. Then, "Police!"

Footsteps pounded. People tumbled and jostled.

Mullet Man stepped back, his breathing suddenly labored.

He wanted to run, didn't he?

Duke grabbed the guy's arm before he could do anything stupid.

Mullet Man muttered curses at him and spit, making his feelings clear.

Duke opened the door wider and saw the police in the hallway.

A gun lay on the floor.

The cops apprehended the man who'd tried to get inside and then flooded into the room. As they did, Duke placed his own gun on the floor and raised his hands.

Andi followed suit.

Right now, the cops didn't know what side he and Andi were on. Everyone inside was guilty as far as they were concerned.

"These men are involved in human trafficking," Andi said. "And these women are being held here against their will, being forced into involuntary sexual servitude. Anyone who's used these services can be charged with a Class A felony."

"You're the one who called?" One of the officers paused in front of her, a cautious look in his gaze. "You sound like you know the law."

Her cheeks reddened. "Stuff like this just makes me really mad."

"You're the ones that got run off the road earlier." Officer Plankton entered the room and stepped closer.

"We are," Duke said. "We were run off the road by the man in charge of this operation. He suspected we were onto him, and he wanted to silence us. His name is Steve."

"Is that true?" Officer Plankton turned toward Mullet Man.

The man shrugged defiantly, not saying a word.

"Oh, you're going to want to start talking before

anyone else does." Plankton narrowed his eyes. "Especially if you want any kind of deal out of this. We've suspected something like this has been going on for a while. We've just been trying to prove it. What's Steve's last name?"

Mullet Man stared at him another moment before his shoulders slumped. "Jenkins. His name is Steve Jenkins."

"Where is he now?"

Mullet Man frowned and muttered a few more things under his breath before saying, "He ran to the general store to pick up a few things. He should be back any time now."

TWO HOURS LATER, Duke and Andi arrived back at their room.

Steve had been found and apprehended.

The women were being treated and questioned.

It was just as Duke and Andi had suspected. These women had been lured to the area under false pretenses and were being held against their will, sold for sex.

It was a horrible reality. But Duke was thankful at least six women had been helped. He had asked permission from the cops before showing the photos of the missing women to the women who'd been rescued.

None of the rescued women recognized any of the other missing women.

Then Duke had shown the images to Steve.

There wasn't a hint of recognition on his face either.

This was a terrible operation but . . . it wasn't connected with the missing women they were searching for, was it?

Still, all of this wasn't for nothing. Half a dozen women had been rescued.

Every single one of them counted.

But Duke didn't believe this operation was linked with their case.

Andi paused on her side of the room, appearing as if she didn't dare take a step closer.

There were too many mixed emotions going on right now.

"We did something good tonight," she said, her voice soft. "Sure, maybe we still don't have the answers that we're looking for. But just think about the women we did help."

His throat tightened. "I agree. I don't think Steve thought we'd be brave enough to come after him."

"I'm glad we did. I'm glad we didn't look the other way."

Their eyes caught again, and Duke averted his gaze.

It was already well past midnight. They'd hardly slept the night before since they'd left so early to get here. As soon as their adrenaline wore off, they would no doubt crash.

Tomorrow would be another long day.

"We should get some rest," Andi murmured, pushing a lock of hair behind her ear. "Morning will be here in the blink of an eye."

"Yes, it will." Duke's throat ached as he said the words.

But sleeping in tight quarters next to Andi . . . Duke wasn't sure how much rest he'd actually get.

Andi probably got four solid hours of sleep. She rested better knowing some good had been done and the bad guys were now behind bars.

But bright and early, she finally got that shower she'd been wanting and changed clothes. Then she and Duke met in a small restaurant set up at the camp. They grabbed some breakfast sandwiches and coffee.

The mechanic had already left them a message. He'd gotten to work early to check out Duke's SUV. He'd replaced the battery and checked out the rest of the vehicle to make sure it was safe to drive. By the time they finished eating, Duke's SUV should be ready.

Andi and Duke sat at a small table to eat until the mechanic brought the SUV to them. He'd offered to do so, and they hadn't declined. It was one less obstacle they'd have to face today.

"So what's our plan for today?" Andi started as she unwrapped the paper around her sausage and egg biscuit.

"We're meeting back up with the gang in Coldfoot. They decided to stay there overnight instead of driving back down to the trading post. I have a feeling that Simmy was afraid Lloyd would put her back to work if she showed up there."

The Almost Halfway Trading Post was farther south from Coldfoot, a lone stop on the highway. Lloyd was Simmy's boss and pretty much good for nothing except watching other people work and drinking until he was utterly useless.

"Maybe they discovered some more information," Duke offered hopefully.

"Maybe they have." Just as Andi said those words, her phone rang.

She glanced at the screen and saw it was Ranger.

Since no one else sat in the breakfast area, she put the phone on speaker so Duke could also hear the conversation.

"Hey." Ranger's voice sounded gruff and to the point —as per usual. "Are you guys good?"

Duke and Andi exchanged a glance, hours of unspoken conversation floating between them.

"Yeah, we are," Andi finally said. "You guys?"

"We're good. I figured you all were awake. I just got a phone call I wanted to tell you about."

Andi perked up at the promise in his words. "Go ahead."

"Remember I said I left a message with Tatiana's old roommate?"

Tatiana. The waitress in Coldfoot. The first victim.

"Yes, did you hear back from her?" Andi asked.

"As a matter fact, I did. She was quite talkative. I figured you guys would want to know this information as soon as possible."

"What did she say?" Duke leaned closer.

"Believe it or not, she told me that Tatiana actually got married."

Andi and Duke exchanged another glance.

"What?" Andi was uncertain if she'd heard that correctly.

"Yeah, it turns out that Tatiana was heading down the highway and her car broke down. A man pulled over to help her, and the two of them started talking. They hit it off."

"Why haven't we heard about this before?" Duke's voice rose with surprise.

"I'm not sure except that Tatiana kept to herself mostly. She didn't talk to a lot of people. Maybe just her roommate."

"Did the roommate have any idea who this man was?" Andi all but forgot about her biscuit.

"She didn't remember very many details about him, only that he seemed really old-fashioned—from the way he dressed and fixed his hair, to the way he slightly bowed and put his hand over his heart when he saw her. For their first date, they watched some old show from the fifties. Anyway . . . maybe Tatiana isn't a victim after all either."

Andi's head swirled at the revelation.

Tatiana wasn't a victim.

Luna hadn't been a victim.

Charlotte had made up her story.

Celeste may not be a victim either.

Were they totally off-base with this entire investigation?

That was how it felt sometimes.

"I'm beginning to feel like this entire investigation has been a wild goose chase," Andi finally muttered.

"I don't know what's going on," Ranger said. "But Tatianna is probably living out somewhere on a homestead and completely oblivious to the fact that we think she's missing."

"Good to know," Andi murmured before picking up her cup of coffee. A strange sense of disappointment filled her.

How many more dead ends would they have to follow before they actually found the truth?

chapter
fifty-one

DUKE HAD CALLED GIBSON.

He'd told him about the briefcase.

Gibson had said he'd come up to meet them. He sounded like it was urgent he get his hands on the potential evidence.

Good. Duke would feel better if Gibson were up here. Apparently, he was going to try to charter a plane to Coldfoot.

Duke and Andi were quiet for most of the five-hour drive to Coldfoot.

Duke was ready to stretch his legs halfway into the trip, but he kept driving. He was anxious to get back to the group and catch up.

Finally, they arrived around lunchtime and met the rest of the team at Coldhearted Charlie's, the only restaurant in the area. The place smelled like grease and cigarettes, but the food was decent and warm, the staff friendly, and the tables clean.

They planned on discussing their next course of action.

As soon as they sat down, Duke glanced at his phone and saw he'd missed a call from Gibson. Cell service was nonexistent on most of the highway, except for in Deadhorse and Coldfoot.

He would call him back in a moment.

Right now, they all filled each other in on everything that had happened, including the human-trafficking ring Duke and Andi had discovered.

"I'm glad you two took those guys down, even if it wasn't related to this case." Mariella's eyes glimmered with admiration.

"So are we," Andi said. "But our time is running out. I'm supposed to be at work at noon tomorrow, and I know that Simmy also has work."

"I have a tour lined up to leave at three tomorrow, so I need to be back in Fairbanks by then." Duke took a sip of his tea and shrugged.

A moment of silence fell. Running out of time wasn't what they wanted, especially since they couldn't meet again for another month. Sure, they each did their own research in between. But the time set aside for these investigations was the most useful.

Duke glanced at Andi and saw her eyes fixated on something outside.

He followed her gaze and saw someone walk just out of view of the window.

"That's him." Andi rose to her feet, an urgency to her voice.

She darted toward the door.

As she did, Duke took off after her.

What did she know that he didn't?

Andi rushed outside, Duke right behind her.

"Andi?" he called.

But she didn't answer.

Instead, she sprinted toward a man, grabbed his arm, and turned him around to face her.

She meant business.

Duke observed the man a moment. He was probably in his late thirties/early forties. He was tall and going bald but the hair he had left was light-brown. His face was oval, and he reminded Duke somewhat of Prince William.

"You were staying at our hotel in Fairbanks," Andi said. "Now you're here. Don't even bother to tell me that is a coincidence."

Duke raised his eyebrows.

Had this man followed them?

And if so, why?

He waited to find out the answer.

Andi stared at the man, keenly aware the rest of the group had joined her and now faced off with him also.

Was this guy the killer? Was he keeping an eye on them?

Was this another hitman Victor had hired?

She had no idea.

She only knew it wasn't a coincidence he was here.

He raised his hands. "Stand down."

"We'll stand down when we're good and ready to stand down." Andi's hands went to her hips. "Now who are you and what are you doing here?"

"I can explain," the man rushed. "It's not what you think. Braden Billingsworth hired me. I'm a private investigator."

Andi narrowed her eyes. "What?"

"It's true." He nodded. "I'm a private investigator from Anchorage. I've been up here looking into what happened to Heidi and trying to find some answers for the family. That's when I stumbled upon you guys and decided to see if you knew anything that I didn't."

"If that's the case, then why are you just following us instead of asking us questions?" Andi wasn't about to let this go that easily.

"I figured you might not trust me." He lowered his eyelids with defeat. "I know the family has been very private and hasn't exactly been friendly toward you. I didn't know how my presence would go over. I thought the best thing I could do was just to keep my distance and watch."

Andi narrowed her eyes. "In other words, you're trying to steal any information we find." Another realization clicked in her mind. "Then you planned to take the credit for it. Am I right?"

Mariella stepped closer. "Wait . . . are you the one who told people that Luna was really alive and living in Seattle?"

Based on the way red filled his cheeks, he was.

Regret filled Andi.

She'd accused Mariella of spilling that. She'd been wrong to do so.

When she had a chance, she would apologize.

Right now, they needed to finish talking to this guy.

"What's your name?" Duke used his cop voice as he stared the man down, no doubt tapping into the intimidating persona he'd had to use in the military's CID.

"Ernie. Ernie Hall."

Duke took his arm. "You're going inside with us, and we are going to have a long talk."

Ernie nodded, raising his hands again in surrender. "Understood."

Just what was this guy hiding?

chapter
fifty-two

I GOT HOME from work too late last night for dinner.

But a plate had been waiting in the microwave.

I'd checked under my chair.

The dirt was still there, and that didn't make me happy.

Anna would need to pay the price for that.

I'd bring it up like any loving husband would.

When I'd checked on her, she'd been sleeping in our room.

I'd decided to let her rest.

The next morning, I awoke her and instructed her to cook breakfast for me—homemade biscuits, sausage gravy, and fresh-squeezed orange juice.

She did so without complaint.

But the dirt remained on my mind.

I just needed to wait for the right time to bring it up.

In the meantime, I watched her. I knew she could feel my gaze on her. She kept looking back.

After breakfast, she did laundry and mopped the floor. She cleaned each of the windows inside and out.

My house was to be kept spick-and-span.

Everything in its place.

With no exceptions.

Maybe she'd finally accepted her responsibilities.

Nothing would make me happier.

Especially now that I'd discovered people were looking into her disappearance. I'd heard it on the news. I'd heard people in town talking about it.

I knew investigators were getting closer and closer to finding answers.

That wasn't okay.

I had the perfect setup here, and I couldn't let anyone ruin it.

I was making Anna into the perfect wife.

No one's going to find out, I told myself. *You covered your tracks.*

Things had gone seamlessly so far.

You're practically invisible. An upstanding citizen. Someone who likes to help others.

Besides, even if police did suspect me, it was doubtful they'd ever find this place.

This evening, I would go into work again—if I wasn't called in sooner. I hoped to have most of the day to continue training Anna.

Anna took a break from cleaning to make me a sandwich for lunch.

She was coming along nicely.

But she was getting fidgety. As if she were nervous.

What was going through her mind right now?

She called me into the kitchen, and I walked in to see my sandwich on a plate on the table.

I sat down and inspected the sandwich. Toasted bread with thick layers of ham and cheese with some lettuce and a touch of mayo. Not bad.

"Just let me grab you some fresh water," she rushed.

Anna crossed to the other side of the breakfast bar and grabbed a glass.

I started to scold her for not having the water ready before she called me. Then I decided not to. I wanted to see what she would do next. Why she wasn't fully prepared to serve me.

Was she preoccupied with thoughts of her old life?

It didn't matter. The memories would fade with time.

She set the water on the table.

Then I felt her shift her arm.

I felt something change in the air.

Then she lunged at me. Something sharp hit my throat.

"You're going to give me the keys to the snow machine, and you're going to let me leave here. Do you understand?"

This woman thought she could outsmart me.

The nerve of her.

I stiffened as something pricked my neck.

A knife.

The blade barely cut into my skin.

If she thought she would humiliate me this way, she was wrong.

"What are you doing, Anna?" I barely contained the anger in my voice.

"My name isn't Anna."

Maybe she needed clarification to understand. "My Anna passed, but I know her soul lives on. Death cannot keep us apart."

"I am *not* Anna," she repeated.

The blade pricked my skin again. "I need you to put the knife down."

"I will do it. I'll hurt you. I promise I will." Her voice wavered.

She really thought she could disable me, didn't she?

My simmering anger turned to rage.

In one move, I grabbed her arm, jerked the knife away from her, and spun around.

I pounced on her until she hit the wall.

Then I put the knife to her throat.

She let out a gasp as the blade poked her skin, causing a small trickle of blood.

"What do you think you're doing?" I asked her. "Did you really think you would get away with that?"

She let out a whimpering cry. "Please, just let me go. I have a life. People who love me."

"*I* am the only one you need to concentrate on. *I'm* the only one who matters. Don't you understand that?"

"Please . . ." Her voice cracked.

I had no desire to hurt her—not with this knife anyway.

I flung it across the room.

Then my hands encircled her neck.

"You are not at all who I thought you would be." Fury continued to fill me.

"I can be," she whispered, suddenly changing her tune.

"Don't try to convince me of that now. You're too late."

"But I can make you happy." Her raspy voice made it hard to understand a word she said.

It didn't matter. I didn't *believe* a word she said.

"You're lying." I squeezed tighter. This time I didn't care if I hurt her.

Her time with me was up.

She wasn't trainable for a wife after all.

She hadn't even found the dirt under my chair.

"You should've just listened to my directions," I growled.

"I . . . did. I listened to your directions. Except for today. And I'm sorry." She gasped as fear filled her gaze. "I'm sorry that I didn't obey. I just . . . I just miss my old life."

"Sorry is no longer going to cut it."

I released her neck and grabbed her hair instead.

She let out a yelp as I dragged her across the kitchen.

I grabbed the knife from where I'd tossed it on the floor.

Roughly, I gripped her ponytail and began to saw through her hair.

She cried with every slide of the knife.

I didn't even care if I hit her skin.

Not anymore.

When I finished, I flung her hair on the kitchen counter, along with the knife.

I grabbed her remaining hair at the scalp.

She cried out with pain as I began to drag her behind me.

Barefoot, just like I liked it.

I opened the front door. Then I shoved her so hard that she fell down the three concrete steps at the front of my house.

She hit the ground with a satisfying thud.

She looked back up at me with wide, frightened eyes. "What are you doing?"

I only had one thing to tell her. "You're going to miss me."

chapter
fifty-three

ANDI STARED at Ernie Hall as he sat at the head of the table.

He seemed to realize if he made one wrong move, they would all take him down. He sat in the padded metal chair as if he didn't even dare to move.

This guy might be a PI, and he might even be a good one. Andi hadn't formed an opinion on that yet. But he certainly wasn't tough. Maybe that was what made a person a good PI. If they seemed unassuming.

Which this man most definitely was.

"You need to tell us what you know." Duke leveled his gaze with the man, leaving no room for questions. "We should all be on the same side here. We're all trying to find answers, not trying to one-up each other."

Andi's heart lodged in her throat. She understood exactly where he was coming from. Ernie was acting as if this was a game or a competition to see who could find the missing person first and take the credit for it.

But this was no game.

Real lives were on the line.

"Look, I wasn't trying to start any problems." Ernie raised a hand as if pleading with them to understand. "But I was instructed not to tell you anything."

"Why do the Billingsworths not want us to help?" Mariella sounded offended as she asked the question.

"A friend of their daughter went missing, and when a true crime podcaster reported on it, she got the facts wrong," Ernie explained. "She ended up leading the police on a wild goose chase. Ever since then, they think you guys are just wannabe detectives and will get in the way of real investigations. It's not personal. It's just born from experience."

"I get that some people might be like that," Andi said. "But Duke is a professional investigator. Ranger knows this area better than anyone else. Simmy has a pulse on the people coming up and down this highway. Matthew is an expert at all things technology. Mariella is excellent at engaging people on social media and garnering attention to the cases."

Ernie stared at Andi. "And you?"

She swallowed hard, uncertain what to say. "I'm just along for the ride I suppose."

Duke's gaze burned into her.

"I think it would be beneficial for all of us if you simply talked to us," Duke continued. "We've almost gotten killed numerous times trying to find these answers. The least you can do is to tell us what you know."

Ernie remained quiet a moment as if contemplating his options.

Andi felt certain he knew things they didn't. No doubt the police had told the family information that wasn't public. In turn, the family had told Ernie.

"Fine." He sounded defeated. "There are probably a few things I can tell you. We have a couple of theories. First of all, there were grizzly prints found in the tundra near Heidi's car."

"What?" Mariella's voice rose with surprise. "We haven't heard anything about that."

"A bear being involved is just a theory." Ernie narrowed his eyes as if annoyed he had to police the conversation. "It's hard to know if there was a struggle. There was no blood. So those prints might not mean anything. But one of the theories we're working with is that Heidi got a flat tire, and as she was waiting for someone to help her, the bear attacked."

Andi didn't think that was a viable theory, but she stored the idea in the back of her mind.

"Anything else?" Andi asked.

"There were also tire tracks from a big truck in front of her vehicle. We can only assume someone pulled up at some point, possibly to help her. Possibly because they saw an empty car on the side of the road. It's hard to say for certain."

"Could they tell anything by these tire tracks?" Ranger asked.

"Just that it was from a big truck." Ernie shrugged. "The police sent the castings off for analysis."

"So you've got pattern evidence to work with." Andi stored that information away. "Anything else?"

He let out another long breath. "Not really. I wish there was more to share, but there's been so little evidence . . ."

But a more comprehensive picture had formed in Andi's mind.

A picture of a killer who'd purposefully planted some nails on the road. A picture of a killer who waited for a single woman to head down this way.

Maybe he even specifically picked out his victims. Then set up his nails, hoping they'd be in the right place at the right time.

Then he waited. As soon as he disabled the victim's vehicle, he would also pull over pretending to be a Good Samaritan. But instead . . . he snatched the woman.

After that . . . Andi had no idea what this guy would have done with them.

Based on the items in the briefcase, part of her didn't even want to think about it.

The group talked with Ernie several more minutes before they were done.

After he left, they ordered some cloudberry pie and discussed everything they'd learned.

Duke's phone rang, and he saw it was Gibson. He excused himself to answer.

"I'm about to board the plane," Gibson said. "I should be there in an hour."

"Good to know," Duke said, glancing around for any more signs of trouble. "I have the briefcase waiting for you."

"I thought you should know that Heidi Billingsworth's husband, Braden, was arrested this morning."

"What?" Duke wasn't sure he'd heard correctly.

"He was publicly intoxicated and got into a fight at a local bar. As a side note, he's apparently propositioned several women since arriving at Fairbanks. That last part isn't a crime within itself, but it shows his character. Apparently, he's been a serial cheater."

"You think that has something to do with this case?"

"Not necessarily. But we're keeping it in mind."

"Thanks for sharing."

Duke ended the call and stepped back inside. As he did, Mariella's phone rang.

She glanced at the screen, and her eyes widened. "You guys . . . it's the caller who mentioned something about a body."

Ranger straightened. "Put him on speaker."

Mariella nodded, appearing nervous as she hit the Talk button. Before she could even say hello, the man on the other line spoke.

"Can you hear me?" His voice broke up but not as

badly as before. He sounded as if he were a younger man and like maybe he was somewhere remote.

"Right now I can," Mariella said. "You're not breaking up at this very moment."

"Good. Service is horrible out here. Are you the girl with that podcast? The one looking for answers about the women who've disappeared along the highway?"

Mariella glanced around. "I am. Who is this?"

"I'd rather not say. But I have information for you."

"If you won't give me your identity, then how do I know I can trust you?"

"Look, I just can't tell you. It's complicated. But when I was out dog sledding, I came across a body. It could be one of the women you're looking for."

Mariella exchanged a glance with the rest of them.

"Where?" she asked. "Where did you see this body?"

"It's really the middle of nowhere. I can't show you, but I can give you the coordinates."

"Ask him if he told the police." Duke didn't want to scare the guy off by intruding in the conversation, so he kept his voice low.

"Did you call the police?" Mariella asked.

"No. Like I said, it's complicated."

"Can't you uncomplicate it for me?" Mariella asked, impatience creeping into her voice.

He hesitated another moment before answering. "There's a warrant out for my arrest, okay? I'm not a killer though. But they say I smuggled some drugs into the country. I didn't. They don't believe me. Either way, I don't want anything to do with the cops. But I didn't feel right not telling anybody. That's why I've been trying to call you."

"I got it," Mariella said. "Can you send me those coordinates?"

"I'll do it now. But you didn't hear this from me."

Then the line went dead.

chapter
fifty-four

EXCITEMENT THRUMMED THROUGH ANDI.

Could this be the lead they were looking for?

Another part of her, the more pessimistic side, feared this guy wouldn't carry through with his promise. That he wouldn't send those coordinates.

At least the man had a viable explanation as to why he didn't want his identity revealed. Being wanted by the cops would be a good reason not to come forward with information.

But if there really was a body where this guy said there was . . .

"Do you think he's going to do it?" Duke scanned his team's faces.

They all stared at Mariella's phone at the center of the table, waiting for it to buzz again.

"I pray he does," Simmy said. "We've had so many dead ends already. A lot of what we know has been turned upside down. If what he said is true, then this could be the missing piece of evidence we've been looking for."

Andi continued to stare at the phone, willing it to buzz.

Why hadn't he sent the coordinates yet?

They were running out of time. They couldn't stay up here in Coldfoot forever.

Sure, maybe this was another red herring. Maybe it would lead nowhere.

But maybe it wouldn't—another part of her felt like they were so close.

Finally, Mariella's phone buzzed, and Andi flinched at the sound.

Mariella grabbed it. Then her eyes lit with excitement, and she held up her phone. "He sent it. I've got the location!"

"Plug it into the system and see how far away it is," Ranger said.

She quickly did that and then looked it up. "It's only about an hour from here. Should we go?"

Duke stood. "We should. But I'm going to call Gibson again and tell him what we're doing. He's already on his way up here anyway."

"Okay." Andi stood also and dropped some money on the table. "Let's get going and see what we can find out."

❄

As Duke drove, Ranger sat beside him in the front seat and navigated.

Mariella and Matthew sat in the center row, and Simmy and Andi in the back.

Andi tried to search for who might own the property where this supposed body was located. She knew she didn't have long before she would be out of cell service range.

But she did what she could.

Based on what she could see, this wasn't private property.

Instead, it was owned by the Bureau of Land Management.

On the satellite view of the map she looked at, there were two structures within the vicinity. But those were several miles away.

Her heart thrummed inside her. It wasn't that she wanted to find a dead body or that she wanted any of these victims to be dead. But she did want answers, and maybe this was the best next step.

Mariella chattered about something to anyone who would listen.

As she did, Andi tuned her out. She remembered talking to that PI earlier today. Remembered his confession about Luna. Remembered the way she'd accused Mariella unjustly.

That wasn't okay.

"There's something I need to say, and I need to say it

in front of all of you," she said, breaking into Mariella's monologue.

Everyone grew quiet around her.

She cleared her throat before continuing. "Mariella, I apologize for accusing you of being the one who leaked the information to the media about Luna. I shouldn't have been so quick to judge."

A touch of defiance still glimmered in Mariella's gaze. "It wasn't very nice."

"I know. And I apologize for that. I suppose I'm used to seeing the worst sides of human nature at times. That tends to work to my detriment."

"Thank you for your apology," Mariella said. "It did hurt my feelings. But I know we're all in a tense situation right now and learning to navigate how to work together. So you're forgiven."

She said the words properly and without any emotion.

"Thank you," Andi said, uncertain if Mariella really believed what she was saying.

"I would, however, still love for you to consider talking to Keith Morrison and to be a little more open-minded about that contract with Alpine," Mariella added.

Andi would think about that later, but for now she knew there was no avoiding a certain topic anymore.

She let out a deep breath before admitting, "The truth is, I'm a lawyer by trade, but I was disbarred after I made the wrong person mad at me and he set me up. I came to Alaska to get revenge."

Everyone got quiet in the car again.

"Wait . . . are you serious?" A knot of confusion formed on Mariella's brow.

Andi glanced at Mariella in the rearview mirror. "I am."

"I knew you sounded smart," Mariella murmured. "But you were a trucker. Not that truckers can't be smart. But you sounded like a different kind of smart."

"It was the most humiliating experience of my life, and I lost everything. People I thought were my friends no longer wanted to associate with me. That's just one more reason why I find it hard to trust people. Everyone tends to look out for themselves. I watch these TV shows and read books where they have this strong sense of community where everybody loves and accepts each other despite their flaws. I just can't help but think places like that don't really exist."

"I think places like that *could* exist." Mariella's voice contained a mix of uncertainty and hope. "Not the rest of you guys?"

No one said anything for a moment.

Finally, Simmy cleared her throat. "I don't know if places like that really exist or not. Most of the people I've had in my life have let me down also."

No one denied the sentiment, almost as if they could all relate.

The truth remained that it wasn't chance that led them all here. Each of them had come to Alaska for different reasons. Some of those reasons involved things from their backgrounds.

Now, they were together.

Five people who would have probably never associated with each other if they all hadn't been trapped at the trading post two months ago when the bridge went out.

"Well, maybe we can be that community with each other." Mariella shrugged innocently.

Andi wanted to refute her words, but she didn't allow herself to do that.

Because the sentiment was nice.

Maybe communities like that did exist.

Maybe one day she would find one.

Maybe this group could become that very community.

In the meantime, Andi reminded herself not to be part of the problem. She couldn't be one of those people who rejected everyone else and didn't have other people's back.

She needed to be the person she wanted others to be in her own life.

DUKE WAS proud of Andi for telling the group about her past.

He knew talking about it couldn't have been easy for her. It hadn't been easy for him either when he'd admitted to everyone that Celeste was his fiancée.

Being honest with others required vulnerability, and vulnerability cleared a path for being wounded.

It seemed sometimes like a vicious cycle, like a loop that once you were trapped in, you'd never be able to leave.

But it *was* possible to break cycles. Possible to be the person for others that you wanted them to be for you.

It took effort. Patience. The ability to forgive yourself and others. The ability to cut yourself some slack when you messed up—because you would mess up.

Finally, Ranger—still studying the pinned location—directed Duke to pull to the side of the road.

After stopping and putting the SUV into Park, Duke checked the map to see where they needed to go from here. Ranger added his input as well. They were both on the same page.

"This is as far as we go in the SUV." He draped his arm across the back of the seat before turning to address everyone. "It's going to be about a mile or two, but we're going to have to walk the rest of the way."

"Through that?" Mariella nodded at the boreal forest around them. Spruces dotted the landscape, some snow still covering their branches. Snow also remained on the ground, though it was melting.

It was a winter wonderland of sorts.

"Yes, through that. Are you guys up for the task? Because a couple of us could stay in the SUV."

Everyone insisted they wanted to go and climbed out.

He would have worn different clothes and shoes if he'd known they'd be trekking through the snowy woods.

But his jeans, boots, and sweatshirt should work.

Mariella's GPS might lose its signal, but Ranger had looked at it. As a certified survivalist, he should be able to get them to the location.

Duke just prayed this wasn't a trap. The man on the phone had sounded sincere, but they'd already been thrown so many curveballs with this investigation that Duke couldn't be certain of anything.

The temperature today was in the thirties, and the wind was brisk. Based on the violent gray skies overhead, there was a good possibility it could snow again.

The Brooks Mountain Range rose in the distance like a formidable foe daring them to come closer. If they reached those foothills, there was no way they could cross —not without the proper equipment.

However, the sight of their snowcapped peaks was beautiful, a reminder of how small they were in comparison to the vast landscape around them.

"We're almost there," Ranger said as they continued to trek through the forest.

The cold nibbled at their extremities. There was just enough snow to dampen their boots and make the ground feel slick. The woods were just thick enough to conceal anything that wanted to be concealed—human or animal.

"Everyone, keep your eyes open," Duke said. "Even though this guy dropped a pin on the location, it may not be exact."

They spread out in a line as they marched through the trees.

For all they knew, the body that guy had seen out here may not even be one of the missing women. There were hikers who went missing out here also. Hunters. Thrill seekers.

This was a dangerous land many people underestimated.

"Hey guys . . ." Simmy froze and looked down, her eyes widening with horror as she reached for something to hold onto. "I think I found it."

❄

As Andi looked through the grass, she saw the body strewn there.

It appeared to be a woman. The cold had preserved her flesh. She wore a beige dress, one more suited for the summer. Her feet were bare.

"I think that's Angel Washburn, the sixth victim who hasn't been seen in close to three years." Mariella gulped after she said the words.

She turned and threw up.

That was right. It was Angel. Then after Angel, Celeste had disappeared, and then the newest victim, Heidi.

Ranger nodded at the woman, his gaze clouding with righteous anger. "There are bite marks on her legs and arms."

"A bear?" Andi asked.

"Too small to be a bear." Ranger shook his head. "It almost looks like a canine. There are arctic wolves living up here."

"Was this woman killed by nature?" Andi asked. "Or did she wander off the road where she was attacked by wild animals?"

"She's barefoot and wearing a flimsy dress, so I doubt she'd been wandering around out here," Ranger said. "Besides, if she'd been here too long, I'm inclined to think animals would have eaten her. My guess is she was placed here in the winter and has just now begun to thaw. That's why she's intact."

"So . . . whoever abducted her must have kept her alive for almost three years . . ." Andi murmured with a shiver.

What this woman must have gone through . . .

Using his finger, Duke gently turned the woman's head. "It looks as if her hair was tied back in a ponytail, and that it was cut off. A wild animal wouldn't have done that."

A sick feeling formed in Andi's gut. He was right. A wild animal *wouldn't* have done that.

But a person would have.

She glanced around, wondering what answers the landscape might hold.

Duke seemed to share her sentiment.

He rose from his kneeling position and straightened his shoulders. "While we're here, we should look around. See if we can find anything else. Let's spread out."

Were there any other victims out here? Andi wondered.

She didn't voice that aloud.

The thought was . . . well, it was horrific.

Instead, they spread out as Duke instructed. He reminded everyone that there was no cell service out here, so they needed to stay close.

The boreal forest around them made it hard to always see the rest of the team, and Andi formed one of the bookends.

She needed to pay close attention to where she was in relation to the group.

The last thing she needed was to get separated and lost out here.

They continued to scour the forest, walking probably ten or fifteen feet away from each other.

Yet it felt so far away.

Each time she lost sight of the rest of her team, a rush of anxiety coursed through her.

Would this search even lead to any answers?

It was worth trying. Andi knew that.

They continued to walk.

As she reached a small, partially frozen stream, something on a tree branch caught her eye. It might not be anything relevant, but she wanted to check it out before telling the rest of the group.

Carefully, she wandered down the embankment.

She paused by the tree and observed a lavender-colored piece of cloth.

Not the typical color or material a hunter would use.

It had been torn, like the branch had caught it while someone ran by. The fabric was dirty and damp as if it had been here for a while.

Odd.

But was it a clue?

She wasn't certain.

She took a step back when her foot hit something, and she spilled into the snow.

Her hand hit a root or a rock beneath her.

Quickly, she pushed herself up.

Then she squinted.

That wasn't a rock or a branch, was it?

It looked like . . . a bone.

The air left her lungs.

Was that . . . a body?

A human body?

Her head began to spin.

Something—or someone—had been left here.

She wasn't feeling brave enough to uncover any more for a better look.

She needed to get the rest of the team. Show them this.

She looked up, about to call for them.

That was when she realized she couldn't see or hear anyone else.

Fear pulsed through her.

She hadn't wandered that far away, had she?

Just down the embankment.

But she'd been probably twenty feet away when she'd done that. The rest of the team was covering flat land.

Then she'd fallen . . .

Panic tried to seize her.

How could she have let this happen?

She started to call for her team when she heard a roar behind her.

Slowly, hesitantly, she turned.

A grizzly bear stood on his hind feet and stared at her.

Andi opened her mouth to scream, but no sound left her lips.

She tried again.

Still nothing.

Instead, she froze in place.

What was she going to do?

chapter
fifty-six

SUDDENLY, everything Andi knew about grizzlies disappeared from her mind.

Lie on the ground?

Stay still?

Make yourself big?

Instead, she did what instinctually came naturally to her.

She took off in a run.

She hoped the bear wouldn't follow. That the animal was just as scared of her as she was of it.

But as she wound between the trees, she looked behind her.

The bear galloped toward her.

Her heartbeat nearly pounded out of her chest.

She ran as fast as her legs would take her, dodging trees and trying to put distance between the two of them.

But the bear was fast.

Surprisingly fast.

Surprisingly huge.

And most definitely hungry.

All Andi could do was keep moving. Keep weaving in and out of trees.

And keep hoping for the best.

If she got desperate enough, maybe she would even pray.

Duke searched the area around him and then paused.

He looked for the rest of the group and spotted Mariella and Matthew.

Then Simmy and Ranger.

Where had Andi gone?

Only a few minutes ago, she was fifteen feet away from him.

Had she slipped behind a tree?

He knew the woman had a mind of her own. She very well could have ventured off farther than they'd agreed.

There wasn't much around here except the forest.

But it could still be a dangerous place.

Duke stopped and glanced around once more before asking, "Has anyone seen Andi?"

They all glanced around before shaking their heads.

Tension rose up his spine.

"We need to find her." He paused before calling, "Andi!"

No response.

With every passing moment, the bad feeling in his gut grew deeper and stronger.

"Andi?" Duke called again.

The others followed his lead and did the same.

But there was still nothing.

No Andi.

Ranger began to backtrack, his eyes on the ground as he searched for clues—and footprints.

A few minutes later, he called, "Duke! Over here."

He bristled, not liking his friend's tone.

He quickly hurried across the snow.

Ranger nodded toward the ground and pointed at something. "These are bear prints. A grizzly, most likely fresh out of hibernation and hungry. And a big one at that."

"If Andi saw this bear . . ." Duke's voice trailed.

"We should be able to find her tracks and figure out what happened," Ranger said. "But I didn't hear anything. No screams."

Duke supposed that was a good thing. But he still didn't like the apprehension coursing through him.

Duke drew his gun as they followed the bear's prints through the snow.

Ranger paused to observe something, his shoulders tensing.

Whatever it was, Duke knew it wasn't good.

Ranger knelt and brushed away some snow.

When he did, a skull appeared.

Mariella half gasped/half screamed.

Someone had been buried here.

"What is this place?" Matthew muttered. "A graveyard?"

Duke didn't want to say it was. But that was how it seemed.

Ranger rose and pointed to the ground again. "Look at these footprints. They're fresh. They have to be Andi's."

"They seem to match the boots she was wearing and the size of Andi's feet," Duke said. "She must have seen the bear and taken off in a run."

Ranger's gaze met his. "That's not good."

"No, it's not." Duke didn't want to imagine how the rest of that scenario had played out. Grizzlies could run thirty-five to forty miles an hour. Much faster than humans.

Duke's worry grew until the pressure in his chest caused an ache.

The last thing they wanted was to give away their presence, especially if the killer happened to be nearby. But Andi's safety came first right now.

He took the gun from his waistband, held it in the air, and fired.

If there was a bear chasing Andi, maybe the sound would scare it off.

That was what he hoped.

Silence sounded around them except for some birds scattering from the trees.

Duke heard nothing else.

No cry for help. No screams. No footsteps.

Only silence.

He closed his eyes. *Please, Lord, be with Andi. Keep her safe. Please.*

chapter
fifty-seven

ANDI REMAINED frozen behind the tree, gasping in deep breaths.

Finally, she peered over her shoulder.

The bear had taken off running in the opposite direction.

She closed her eyes as relief swept through her.

She'd heard that gunfire.

Had that been Duke or Ranger?

They made the most sense.

That bear had been close. Too close for her comfort.

Did they somehow know the bear was chasing her?

Either way, the gunshot couldn't have come at a better time.

Now she needed to backtrack and find the rest of the group. Tell them about those bones.

After sucking in several more breaths, she forced herself to move from the tree.

Then she turned and glanced in the direction she thought the gunfire had come from.

Was that right?

It was difficult to tell where the sound had come from as it echoed off the surrounding trees.

As she looked around, everything looked the same.

A moment of panic swept through her.

Was she lost?

No. She could follow her footsteps. They should lead her back to the group.

Her racing heart slowed a moment at that realization.

That was what she would do. Find her tracks and follow them.

And hope the bear stayed away.

But as she took the first step, a new sound filled the air.

She froze again.

Was that . . . dogs?

Wild dogs? Or domesticated?

Were there hunters out here?

She remembered those bite marks they'd seen on Angel Washburn.

Bite marks that appeared to be from a canine.

Any of the calmness Andi had felt only seconds earlier disappeared.

Maybe the bear was gone.

But that didn't mean she was out of danger.

❆

Duke glanced around.

Where had Andi gone?

He needed to find her.

Before the bear did.

"We need to figure out where Andi went. Now." Ranger scanned everything around them.

"Can you track her?"

"I'll do my best."

"We need to divide up," Duke continued. "But no one should be alone."

"I'll go with Ranger." Simmy stepped closer to the man.

"Mariella, you go with them too." Duke glanced at Matthew. "You're with me."

Matthew nodded. "Got it."

They took off to search two separate sides of the woods.

As they did, Duke prayed Andi was okay.

They also needed to keep their eyes open for that bear.

He had his gun, and he knew Ranger had a gun. The last thing Duke wanted was to shoot a grizzly. But if it came down to choosing between the life of a human or a bear, he knew what his choice would be.

One thing was certain: too much was on the line right now.

chapter
fifty-eight

ANDI CONTINUED to push herself through the forest.

She wasn't sure where those dogs were.

But they didn't sound nice.

No, they sounded as if they were on a mission. A mission to attack.

Andi hadn't ever been afraid of dogs before. But right now, terror gripped her.

She wound through the trees, trying to find her way back to the rest of the group. But she wasn't even sure she was walking in the right direction.

She'd never understood how people could get lost like they did. But right now, she more than understood.

She paused and caught her breath for a minute.

As she did, she remembered those bones.

That had been a body, hadn't it?

Terror ran like ice through her veins.

Just what had happened in this forest?

She shivered and took another step.

Her foot hit a pile of rocks.

A large pile of rocks, one that had been purposefully placed.

In the shape of a rectangle.

Almost like a grave.

As her gaze traveled from one end of the pile to another, a scream caught in her throat.

A wooden cross stood on the other side.

This *was* a grave.

Just how many dead bodies were out here?

She took a step back when she caught sight of a structure in the distance.

It looked like . . . a house. A red house with a lake beyond it and some dog pens to the side.

Andi paused behind a tree.

The sound of the dogs was fading.

They were moving away from her, she realized.

Maybe they were going after the bear instead.

So who lived in that house?

Was it someone who could help her? Or someone who would hurt her?

She'd looked on that map. No houses had been close to their search area.

How far had she veered off course?

Or maybe this house wasn't on any map.

She glanced at the gray roof.

It was possible that this place blended in with the landscape.

That it had been hidden in plain sight from any satellite taking photos.

She stared at the place for several moments as she contemplated what to do.

Before she could make her decision, something clicked behind her.

Then a deep voice said, "I wouldn't move if I were you."

As Duke and Matthew ran farther into the woods, he paused and held up a finger to indicate Matthew should stop as well.

"What is it?" Matthew whispered.

"You hear that?"

Matthew's eyes scanned back and forth as if trying to pick up on something. Then he shook his head. "Hear what?"

"Dogs," Duke murmured.

"Dogs as in wolves?" His eyes widened with fear.

"Doesn't strike me as wolves. Almost sounds like hunting dogs."

"So there's a hunter out here?"

Duke didn't bother to answer. His response might only upset Matthew more.

His thoughts rushed forward, trying to come to conclusions.

Before Duke could make sense of the barking, sticks cracked nearby.

Snow crunched.

Something shuffled.

Someone was out there.

Or something.

Could it be the bear?

Duke made sure he was in front of Matthew, just in case.

Then something crashed through the brush, headed right toward them.

chapter
fifty-nine

ANDI DIDN'T DARE MOVE.

She was all too aware that something hard and cylindrical pressed into her back.

Most likely a rifle.

Her heart pounded harder until it was all she could hear.

"I don't know how you found me," the man behind her said. "But you're going to wish you didn't."

That voice . . . she'd heard it before.

But where?

She couldn't place it, no matter how desperately she tried.

"I don't know what you're talking about." Andi's voice trembled. "I just got lost out here and—"

"I know who you are," the man muttered. "I knew when I saw you, you were going to be trouble."

Andi went completely still.

This was someone who'd seen her before?

This was the killer's house, wasn't it?

Her heart began to thrum even more rapidly.

She needed to play dumb. To buy time until she could think this through.

Or until someone could find her.

"I didn't mean to trespass." She kept her hands raised in the air. "I promise. I was walking and I saw a bear, and I ran and—"

"Save it." He nudged her with the end of his rifle. "Get inside the house."

Going inside sounded like a terrible idea.

Did the rest of her team even know where to look for her?

What if they didn't find her?

Or what if this man knew Andi had people out here looking for her? What if that spurred him on to kill her quickly?

Andi had too many questions. Too many fears.

She desperately wanted to turn. To see this man's face.

Did she recognize his voice?

She wasn't sure.

All she knew was that the killer frequented the Dalton Highway. That he was possibly an oil worker. A state trooper. A highway maintenance worker.

And this person had likely married Tatiana.

Maybe killed her.

Then he'd begun his rampage.

For four years, he'd gotten away with it.

This needed to end.

But Andi wasn't sure what the cost would be to end it.

Her life?

Possibly.

She stared at the house in front of her.

Was Heidi Billingsworth inside?

If so, could this be Andi's chance to help her?

But Andi would be no help to Heidi if she was dead.

Her thoughts rushed as the man shoved her again.

"Walk!" he muttered.

It looked like Andi didn't have any choice but to do as this man said.

Duke's eyes widened when he saw a woman come into view.

Andi?

He held his breath.

No . . . it wasn't Andi.

It was . . . Heidi Billingsworth?

Duke froze. Was he seeing things?

No, it was most definitely her.

Based on her frantic motions and wide eyes, the woman was terrified.

She wore a pastel-colored dress, one much too lightweight for the weather in this area.

A white, lacy apron was tied at her waist.

And her hair . . . it looked as if it had been butchered.

But she was alive.

He lowered his gun and raised a hand. "It's okay. We can help."

The woman ran into his arms, tugging at him and hiding behind him as she glanced back.

"The dogs . . ." She gasped in a breath. "They'll kill us. We've got to run."

Duke wasn't sure they were going to outrun any dogs.

The canines were getting louder and louder.

"What are we going to do?" Panic laced Matthew's voice.

Duke glanced up at the spruces around them. "Dogs can't climb trees. That's what we're going to do. We're going to climb."

"I don't know if I can." Heidi glanced at him, fear pooling in her eyes. "I'm weak. And cold. I can't feel my feet."

He glanced down and saw she was barefoot. Her feet must be numb from running in the snow.

He locked gazes with her, knowing he didn't have much time to earn her trust. "I'll help you. You can do it." He nodded toward a tree. "This one should work."

He glanced back and saw the dogs racing through the snow. They were close.

Matthew saw them too.

Duke nodded at another tree and then at Matthew. "You go up that one. The branches are low enough."

Matthew scrambled toward it.

Duke helped Heidi climb the spruce as high as she could. As soon as she was about six feet from the ground, Duke found another tree and started climbing.

But it was too late.

The dogs reached him.

They nipped at the edge of his jeans.

At his ankles.

They tugged on his boots.

Heidi screamed as she watched.

Duke kicked them off.

They all appeared to be mutts, mixes of German shepherd, husky, and retriever. There were at least eight of them.

And they were on a mission.

Finally, he traversed up a few more feet and hugged the tree.

Yes, he had his gun. But he didn't think he had enough bullets for all these dogs. He needed to think this through.

Thankfully, the rest of the team was out there also.

Ranger was an excellent survivalist. If he heard the dogs . . . maybe he would come check out the commotion.

Amidst the barking and snarling of the canines, he glanced at Heidi again.

They'd found her in the nick of time. It didn't appear she could keep running much longer in these conditions.

But did that mean . . . that she had been held captive close to this location?

If so, that meant the killer could be nearby.

It also meant that Andi could be out there alone with the killer.

Duke's throat tightened at the realization.

chapter
sixty

ANDI TRIED to control her breathing.

They reached the front door, the gun still at her back.

She still hadn't seen the man's face, and she didn't dare turn to look.

But she'd met this guy before.

Who was he?

Not knowing was driving her crazy.

But her fear superseded her curiosity.

Right now, she just needed to do what the man said.

She'd figure out the details later.

"Open the door," the man demanded.

Andi quickly looked around, trying to observe everything she could.

She didn't see a vehicle or even a driveway. Only a snow machine under a carport on the side of the house.

And the house . . . looked so normal. Red with wooden siding, built up from the tundra with a deck stretching across the front and a lake behind it.

The ideal secret hiding spot.

She opened the door as he instructed and stepped inside.

She balked when she saw the interior.

It looked like something straight out of the 1950s. All the furnishings were retro. The mustard-yellow and pea-green colors were pristine. Even the couch and coffee table were straight from the midcentury.

Everything was well preserved, as if someone had wanted to keep the house as a time capsule.

On a tube TV in the distance, *The Rosemary Cleaver Show* played in black and white, complete with laugh tracks.

The Rosemary Cleaver Show.

Nausea gurgled in her gut.

The scene currently on the screen was of Rosemary's husband turning his wife over his knee and giving her a spanking after she'd disobeyed him and spent too much money.

The sick feeling continued to grow in Andi's gut.

Just who was this guy? What had he done to his victims?

She wished she could steal a glance at him. That she could see his face.

But she didn't dare.

Was Heidi here?

Andi didn't see any signs of life.

Until she glanced at the kitchen counter.

Nausea rose in her.

A brown ponytail, crudely cut, lay there along with a butcher knife.

Brown hair the same color as Heidi's.

Just what had this man done with her?

"You don't have to do this." Andi paused, her voice trembling.

"You shouldn't have come here," the man snarled. "You should have left this alone."

"What good will it do to hold me here now?"

"You know who I am!" The man's voice rose with tension. "I can't have you telling people. I know what they'll think."

"I haven't even seen your face. We could keep it that way. I can just turn and run away, and I wouldn't have to know—"

"Stop talking." His voice hardened, and he shoved the gun harder into her back.

Andi wanted to turn around, but she didn't dare. Not without his permission.

Her gut told her that one wrong move could land her on the floor . . . and eventually in the grave.

"Is anyone with you?" he barked.

"No." Andi's voice cracked as she said the words.

"What were you doing on my property?"

"I was chased by a bear, and I got lost." At least *that* was the truth.

He paused a moment as if contemplating her words.

"Now I have to figure out what I'm going to do with you." The man's voice held warning and frustration. "You are not my Anna."

Anna? Who was Anna?

Tati*ana* . . . she realized.

The air whooshed from her lungs at the realization.

Was this man searching for someone to replace Tatiana? Was that what all of this was about?

Her gut told her yes.

This man had fallen in love with Tatiana.

Had she died? Had he killed her?

Andi wasn't sure. But a better picture formed in her mind.

"This way." He grabbed her arm and pulled her down the hallway toward a bedroom.

Everything in Andi rebelled. But with the gun at her back, she had no choice but to walk.

Why was he leading her into the bedroom?

Worst-case scenarios flooded her mind.

He shoved her through the doorway.

Directly in front of her, a neatly pressed dress hung from the window.

Similar to the dress she'd seen on Angel Washburn.

Her throat tightened.

"Put that on," the man instructed. "In my house, that's what a woman wears. And you will call me Master. Do you understand?"

She nodded. "I understand."

"I understand, *Master*. That's what you'll say. Every time you don't, you'll receive a lashing. Understand?"

Disgust roiled inside her. "I understand, Master."

A shudder rippled through Andi as she stared at the clothing, a pale-blue dress with a fitted bodice and A-line skirt that stopped at the knees.

What kind of delusions was this man living?

And how long would she have to be a part of it?

"Duke . . . what are we going to do?" Matthew clung to the tree, his gaze darting around.

"Just hang tight for a moment." Duke gripped the tree as the dogs snarled beneath them. Blood was in their eyes.

They weren't playing.

"I'd say we don't have any other choice," Matthew muttered.

Heidi let out another cry as the dogs continued to bark at them, making it clear that one wrong move, and they'd be torn apart.

He needed to distract her before panic got the best of her.

"You're Heidi." Duke studied her another moment, beyond how she was dressed.

Blood trickled from her throat. Her eye was black and bruised. Her lips busted.

And was that blood seeping through the back of her dress? In a line as if she'd been . . . whipped.

Her eyes widened. "You know who I am?"

"You have a lot of people searching for you."

"That man abducted me. I thought he was going to kill me . . ."

"How did you get away?"

"He was angry at me. So he shoved me outside. Told me to go. Barefoot. Then he sent his dogs after me." She squeezed the tree harder as tears poured from her eyes.

"It's okay. We're going to think of something."

Duke had so many questions for her.

But not now. Not with the dogs nipping at their heels.

"I'm starting to slide." Heidi's eyes widened with panic.

Duke glanced at her and saw her slipping downward.

She was too weak to hold on.

He was too far away to help.

He remembered the gun at his waistband.

These dogs were just doing what they'd been told.

He hated to hurt them.

But maybe he could fire his gun and alert the others to their location.

However, if this killer lived close by, he would hear it too. That gunfire would give them away.

Maybe Ranger, Simmy, and Mariella would hear the dogs barking.

But if they were that close, they'd be in danger as well.

As the possibilities all rushed through Duke's head, a new sound cut through the air.

Something big and heavy coming through the brush.

When he looked over, he saw a grizzly emerge.
The beast let out a roar, drool coming from its mouth.
It looked angry.
And maybe hungry too.
Neither of which were good signs.

chapter
sixty-one

ANDI STEPPED FROM THE ROOM.

She'd changed into the dress, one much like a house-wife back in the fifties may have worn.

A shudder raced through her.

She had to face this. She had no choice.

She paused at the doorway and ran her hand over the pale-blue skirt.

She glanced down at her feet.

They were now bare.

Nausea rose in her as she thought about what might happen next.

Pull yourself together, Andi. You're smarter than him. You can get out of this.

She cleared her throat before asking, "Can I come out now?"

"Yes, but walk slowly. I still have my gun. I'll see if you can be my Anna."

Another shudder rippled through Andi.

She still hadn't seen his face yet.

Didn't know what she was walking into.

She held her breath as she stepped from the room, one where the other women had most likely been held.

She didn't even want to imagine the horror his prisoners must have felt.

Because she felt a touch of it now.

This time when she stepped out, she saw the face of the man holding her at gunpoint.

She stared at him until realization smacked her in the face.

She *had* met this man before.

The tow truck driver.

The man who'd helped her and Duke up near Prudhoe Bay.

Milton.

It had been . . . him? *He* was the killer?

That whole briefcase thing . . . it had been his all along.

How could she not have seen it? He had the perfect opportunity to help women on the side of the road. And the man seemed so unassuming, not like someone people would fear.

"You got here just in time." He ran a hand across his sweater vest.

His hair had been combed away from his face.

He'd even dressed the part of a man living in the fifties.

"I'm hungry," he continued. "I need you to make me dinner."

More nausea pooled in Andi's gut.

This man wanted to relive some type of scenario from the good old days.

Back when men went to work, and women stayed home to cook and clean.

Apparently while they were barefoot.

Or was the barefoot part just a means of dissuading her from running?

Andi wasn't sure.

By complying, she could buy some time.

"What would you like me to make?" She kept her voice even and sweet, playing along with the man for the moment.

"Meatloaf," he said calmly as if this discussion were entirely normal. "I would like for you to make meatloaf."

"Meatloaf?"

"That's right." His voice hardened. "I have the recipe out already and all the ingredients. But I promise you, if you make one wrong move, I *will* put you in your place. Do you understand?"

Andi heard the warning in his voice.

She knew the consequences.

Her throat tightened as she realized if she didn't obey, she'd probably die.

❄

Duke caught his breath as he watched the bear.

The creature was magnificent, really. If only he could marvel at it now. Marvel at its shiny coat. Its hulking frame. Its purposeful movements.

A musky smell filled the air as the beast lumbered closer.

Heidi let out a little scream, but Duke put his finger over his lips to motion for her to be quiet.

She seemed to have regained a touch of her strength, no doubt from the adrenaline surging through her.

The grizzly could climb trees. The animal could definitely reach them if he wanted.

Duke prayed that wouldn't be the case and that Fuzzy Wuzzy would stay away.

Fuzzy Wuzzy?

The nickname made the animal seem far less formidable.

Humor had always been his coping mechanism in tense situations.

Duke watched as the dogs around them paused.

The hair on their necks stood on end.

Then they growled.

Backed up.

Would the dogs try to fight the bear?

Duke wasn't sure.

Fuzzy Wuzzy rose up to full height and let out a roar.

The next instant, the canines darted back in the direction they'd come from.

Momentary relief flushed through Duke.

Then he realized they still had the bear to deal with.

He stared at the beast as it stood there a moment sniffing with his nose in the air.

Did it smell them?

And, if so, would the bear choose to chase them or the dogs?

Duke braced himself for whatever would happen next.

chapter
sixty-two

ANDI WAS careful with every movement and every word she said.

She'd never been much of a cook.

But somehow, she needed to figure out how to make this meatloaf.

After reading the directions carefully, she heated the oven. Then she began chopping some peppers and onions, all while keeping an eye on the man.

He sat in his recliner, feet propped and a newspaper in his lap. The TV still played *The Rosemary Cleaver Show*.

This man was obsessed with the old show, with life back then.

"You're the one who took all those women." Andi wasn't sure if her approach was right or not.

But there was no need to play games anymore. She'd already told him that she was looking for these missing women.

"I didn't take them." His voice hardened as he stared

at her. "I rescued them. And I brought them back here to give them a good life."

"Against their will." She continued to chop, adding the vegetables to the ground beef she'd placed in a bowl.

"They just needed time to appreciate what I had given them." His eyes narrowed.

He clearly didn't like being questioned.

No doubt his word was the final authority in his mind.

"You were looking for someone to take the place of your wife, Tatiana. What happened to her?" Andi finished chopping and mixed the meat with the breadcrumbs, onions, peppers, and spices.

"I loved my Anna. She was everything I was looking for, and we had such a beautiful life together." His tone and the wistfulness in his gaze made it appear as if he really had loved her.

"Where is she now?"

"She's gone. She took a walk while I was at work. When I came home, wolves had gotten to her." His voice cracked with emotion. "It was too late. There was nothing I could do for her."

Andi's heart pounded into her ears until it was all she could hear. "Did you report her death?"

"There was no need. She was still a Russian citizen. Nobody was going to come looking for her. So I buried her on my property. At least, I tried to. The ground was too frozen. Instead, I covered her with rocks to keep the animals away."

That was the grave she'd found, Andi realized. Tatiana's.

She glanced at the hair on the island again. "Why is there hair on the countertop?"

His gaze darkened. "Before I laid Anna to rest, I cut off her hair so I could always remember how beautiful it was. When I'm feeling blue, I stroke it and pretend like she's still here with me."

"So Tatiana came and lived here of her own free will? But those other women didn't, did they? Where's Heidi?"

"Stop asking questions!" The sadness snapped from his eyes, replaced with anger. "I tried to give them a good life. I provided everything they needed."

"You provided everything they needed except their freedom."

"I'm tired of talking about this!" His hands fisted, and he rose to his feet.

The next instant, he was in front of her.

Terror ripped through Andi when she saw the dark look in his eyes.

Something wasn't right about this man.

Suddenly, he grabbed her head and slammed it into the kitchen counter.

Pain burst at her temples.

He held her there against the cold, hard surface.

He grabbed a butcher knife and poised it over her head.

The blade glinted in the light coming from the window.

Andi gasped, struggling to get away.

It was no use.

His grip was like a vise.

"You should have stopped talking when you had the chance!" Then he raised the knife higher before slamming it toward her.

Duke held his breath as he watched Fuzzy Wuzzy and wondered what the bear would do.

Things could turn really ugly.

Then Fuzzy lowered himself and stopped sniffing the air.

Instead, his nose went to the ground.

He found the track the dogs had left.

Finally, the bear meandered after the canines, leaving them behind.

But Duke didn't dare move or say anything until the grizzly was out of sight.

He turned back to Heidi, questions racing through his mind. "Heidi, do you remember what direction you came from?"

She nodded in the distance. "That way. That's where he lives."

If Duke's instincts were correct, Andi had run right toward the house Heidi had escaped from.

Duke couldn't stay here. He had to help Andi.

Yet he couldn't leave Heidi or Matthew here alone. He

could give Matthew his gun, but then Duke wouldn't have one. He might need it in order to rescue Andi.

Thankfully, just then he heard footsteps.

Ranger, Simmy, and Mariella appeared.

"What's going on?" Ranger rushed toward them, his gaze stopping on Heidi.

Duke hopped from the tree and hurried over toward Heidi, helping her down also. She practically collapsed in his arms. "Ranger, I need you to get her to safety."

"Heidi?" Simmy asked breathlessly, her eyes widening as she soaked in the woman.

Heidi nodded as Ranger took her from Duke and swooped her into his arms. She was practically limp and clearly needed help.

"What are you going to do?" Ranger glanced at Duke, his muscles rigid as he stood there holding the woman.

"I'm afraid Andi ran right into this killer's domain. I need to help her." Urgency pressed on Duke, reminding him he had no time to waste.

"You shouldn't go alone." Ranger's terse gaze met Duke's.

"It's more important that you take Heidi to safety. And tell Gibson where I am. He should be here soon."

Ranger stared at him another moment as if uncertain he should leave.

"Take everyone else with you." Duke nodded to the group around him.

As much as Duke would love some backup, Simmy, Mariella, and Matthew were not those people.

"I want to help." Matthew stepped forward, an earnest but pensive expression on his face.

Duke shook his head. "I appreciate that but no. You're not trained."

"I can do it." Matthew bristled, his shoulders rising as if he was trying to prove how strong he was.

Duke knew Matthew would be too much of a liability.

It was better to go alone than to go with the wrong people.

"Look, after this is all over, I'll teach you some things. But until then, the best you can do is to go with Ranger and make sure Heidi gets the help she needs." He took a step back.

Simmy grabbed his arm. "I'm worried about you."

He drew in a breath, reminding himself that these people simply cared about him. But he couldn't delay this. He needed to move.

"I'll be okay," he assured Simmy. "But I can't talk much longer. I need to find Andi."

Simmy stared at him another moment before nodding. "Go get our girl."

There seemed to be something more to her words. Did Simmy sense the feelings he had for Andi? The feelings he couldn't act on?

Right now, it didn't matter.

Only saving Andi did.

"Go!" Duke said.

With one more glance, they nodded.

Then Ranger began to carry Heidi through the woods toward the SUV.

They'd probably hiked at least a couple of miles.

The journey back wouldn't be easy, and it was getting colder. A few snowflakes even swirled in the air, something not entirely unusual for this time of year in Alaska.

As they walked away, Duke turned in the direction the dogs had run.

And Fuzzy.

He knew he'd face whatever he had to if that was what it took to find Andi.

chapter
sixty-three

ANDI WAITED FOR THE PAIN.

Had the knife's blade hit her brain? Were her pain sensors blocked?

She didn't know.

She only knew this man still held her head against the counter.

That he'd withdrawn the knife.

That he stared at her now with malice in his eyes.

Her heart beat so fast she feared it might suddenly stop, that it had been pushed to the limit.

Then Milton reached down and picked up something.

He held it in front of her face.

She gasped.

Her hair.

He'd cut off her hair.

Outraged tears pressed to her eyes.

Women made their hairstyles a part of their personality and image.

Now her hair had been butchered.

It could have been worse, she reminded herself. He could have cut into her flesh.

But more tears kept coming.

Finally, he released the pressure from her head.

Relief filled her as soon as his hand stopped pressing on her ear.

But her entire head hurt from when he'd slammed it into the counter.

"Stand up!" he ordered.

Slowly, she raised her head.

Then he took Andi's arms and shoved her back toward the food she'd been preparing. "Cook!"

She swallowed hard and picked up the spoon she'd been using to mix everything.

Her hands trembled so badly that she didn't think she'd be able to finish the meatloaf.

But she forced herself to keep mixing.

What had these women endured at this man's hands?

The thought made her sick to her stomach.

Milton stood close, scowling at her, and watching her every move.

As she glanced at the kitchen counter, she caught another glimpse of her butchered hair. The pale blonde locks lay scattered over the green laminate countertop, looking like soldiers lost on a battlefield.

She didn't even want to imagine what she looked like.

She'd never considered herself vain but . . . maybe she was.

A few minutes later, she stuck the meatloaf into the oven and began to clean her mess.

She definitely needed to start the mashed potatoes soon.

In fact, maybe she should have boiled the potatoes as she prepared the ground beef.

Why hadn't she paid more attention?

Probably because she preferred to get takeout. If takeout wasn't available, sandwiches and salads worked. Her career had been more important than cooking. In fact, she'd rebelled against those traditional skills women learned.

She began peeling the potatoes, but her hands trembled so badly that she accidentally took off a layer of skin from her thumb.

She tried not to wince.

That's only an ounce of the pain you'll feel if you make him mad.

She quickly wiped away the blood and reminded herself to be more careful.

Milton finally moved back to his recliner.

Pull yourself together, Andi.

She drew in a deep breath, knowing she had no time to waste.

She needed to keep him talking. But she couldn't push him so much that he became angry with her again.

She drew in another breath. Then another. And another.

She didn't usually have to work up her courage.

But the throbbing pain reminded her to be cautious, reminded her of what was at stake.

"How many women have there been?" she asked as she continued to peel the potatoes.

She would dice them into small cubes so they'd cook faster.

How long would they take to boil, though?

She wasn't sure.

"It's not important." He continued to watch from his recliner. "I'm not the madman you think I am."

"I understand. You just wanted to help."

His shoulders seemed to soften at her words. "That's right. I just wanted to help."

"I'm sorry they weren't more appreciative."

His gazed darkened. "Me too."

"You know, maybe you can find someone else like Tatiana. Someone who will truly love you."

"It's hard to meet many women up this way."

"I guess so. You do live in the middle of nowhere. How do you even get to work?"

"I take my snow machine to a garage I have at the end of the road. It makes more sense, so I don't have to shovel the snow on this driveway."

"Smart thinking," Andi told him.

"It's good money working out here. And I love the tundra. Not everyone is cut out to live in such a solitary place, however."

"I can imagine."

She glanced out the window, hoping to see Duke or Ranger. Anyone that could help.

Instead, she saw something move in the brush.

The dogs, she realized.

Her heart beat harder.

Had this man sent these dogs out to find Heidi?

Milton seemed to hear the animals also and rose from his recliner. He walked toward the door, muttering underneath his breath.

Then he stomped toward her. He reached into a drawer and pulled out some handcuffs. He snapped one to her wrist and the other to the oven door.

"Stay here and don't try anything," he growled.

He opened the kitchen door, and a rush of cold air invaded the space.

The dogs came into view as they approached the house.

Had those dogs found the rest of her team?

What if the canines had hurt her friends?

No, don't think like that, Andi.

But how could she not?

Duke followed the dogs, keeping his eyes wide open in case he encountered that grizzly again.

Everything about this situation was dangerous.

He only hoped Gibson arrived soon—with backup.

Duke simply didn't know what he was walking into.

Each step felt like an eternity passed.

If that man found Andi . . . what would he do with her? Kill her before she could talk? Accuse her of trespassing and take justice into his own hands?

He didn't like any of those scenarios.

Tension embedded itself in Duke's muscles as he continued to follow the dogs' footprints.

Where had Fuzzy Wuzzy gone?

Finally, he noticed the dogs' tracks headed one direction and the bear's tracks the other.

Maybe the bear had gotten distracted by something else.

Hopefully not Andi.

Duke swallowed hard.

He couldn't let his mind go there.

Several steps later, a house came into view.

His heart pounded harder as he stared at the red building with the lake behind it.

That was the killer's house, wasn't it? It was the only thing that made sense.

He darted behind a tree when he saw the door open.

A man he recognized stood there.

Was that . . . the tow truck driver?

No way.

But it made sense. Milton had access to anyone who broke down on the highway.

Why hadn't Duke thought of that before?

He watched as the man stood near the door talking to his dogs.

Then he began to lead them around to the back, probably to where their pens were.

Duke searched the snow, looking for any human footprints.

Had Andi come this way?

The trail leading directly from the door probably belonged to Heidi.

But to the side of the house there was another set.

Two sets of footprints.

A small set and a larger one.

Milton and Andi?

That was Duke's best bet.

He had no time to waste.

Duke needed to get inside and see if Andi was there.

And he needed to do it before Milton got back.

chapter
sixty-four

ANDI TUGGED AT THE HANDCUFF, but it was
no use.

It wouldn't budge.

Fighting despair, she stepped as far as she could to the
left and peered out the window.

That was when she saw movement.

Was that . . . Duke?

Her heart thrashed against her rib cage as she waited.

Then the door opened.

Duke stepped inside.

Her pulse rushed as air flooded from her lungs.

He was here. He'd come for her.

"Andi . . ." He quickly scanned her, a frown tugging at
his lips when he saw her hair, her clothes.

The handcuffs.

This was no time to explain her housewife outfit, or
anything else. "Duke . . . we have to hurry. He'll be back
soon."

He rushed to her side and reached for her handcuffs, tugging at them in vain. "Did he happen to stash a key somewhere?"

Andi shook her head frantically. "I never saw a key. My guess is that he took it with him."

"Do you know where a knife is?" He glanced around.

"That drawer on the left." Andi nodded toward it.

Duke rushed over and grabbed a knife. Then he began to work the tip of it into the handcuff lock.

"Thank you for coming." Andi's voice sounded hoarse as she said the words.

"Of *course* I was going to come," he murmured. "Did you think I wouldn't?"

"I . . ." The truth was, Andi wasn't sure there was anyone in her life who'd come for her. She'd lost everything and everyone—except her dad—when Victor went after her back in Texas.

It had been devastating.

Finally, the handcuff snapped open, and Duke quickly pulled her wrist from the cuff. "Come on. Let's go."

He took her hand and began leading her toward the door.

Before they reached it, Milton stepped back inside, gun raised. "Where do you think you're going?"

Duke pushed Andi behind him as he stared at Milton. "You don't have to do this."

"Of course I do. Now, put your gun down nice and slow. No sudden moves or I'll pull the trigger."

Their best hope right now was that Gibson would show up.

Enough time had passed.

For now, Duke had no choice but to comply.

He nodded as he stared at Milton. "Okay, don't shoot. I'll set it down."

"You shouldn't have come here," Milton sneered.

"You shouldn't have taken Andi." Duke bristled, his eyes on the man's gun.

"I don't take my women. They're provided for me." An air of superiority stretched through his words.

What kind of sicko said something like that?

"What do you mean?" Duke asked.

"My grandmother on her deathbed promised me she'd take care of me even from heaven. That's what she's doing. She's making sure the right woman comes into my path at the right time. Right now, it's her." He nodded at Andi.

"I'm sorry to tell you, but Andi's not up for grabs. And she's certainly not going to stay here to cook and clean for you."

Milton glowered at him. "You're standing in the way of fate. When that happens, things always turn ugly. I'd be careful what you're saying."

"So is it your grandmother's spirit or fate that brought Andi to you?" Duke raised his arm, keeping Andi behind him. "Which is it?"

Milton sneered. "Both."

"So fate is looking out for you. Why isn't fate looking out for Andi? You can't possibly think she wants to be held hostage here, do you?"

"Stop talking!" He raised the gun slightly and pulled the trigger.

Andi screamed and ducked.

The bullet hit the ceiling just above Duke's head, and chunks of plaster rained down.

It had been a warning blast.

"You don't understand," Milton seethed.

"I understand that you're living with delusions. You want life to be like it was back in the times of *The Rosemary Cleaver Show*." Duke nodded toward the TV where the show played in the other room. "That's not realistic. Time passes. Things change. Life isn't like that TV show. You can't make people do things against their will."

"If they would just be more open-minded, they'd see this is a good life."

Andi gripped his arm as Milton crept closer.

"You need to put down that gun, Milton." Duke kept his voice even.

"You're not going to ruin what I started."

"I can't let you finish this." Duke could feel the pressure mounting in the room.

Milton raised his gun, pointing it directly at Duke's chest. "You don't have any choice."

ANDI HELD HER BREATH, bracing herself for gunfire.

Please, God—no! Protect Duke. I'm begging You!

The next instant, Duke grabbed the barrel of the rifle.

As he did, a bullet blasted through the air.

Andi screamed.

No!

Duke and Milton both hit the floor.

Wait . . . they were both alive.

Everything was a blur, but Andi didn't see any blood.

The two men struggled, Duke's hands gripping the gun's barrel.

He was okay.

But for how long?

She glanced around the kitchen.

She needed to find something she could use as a weapon.

Saw the cast-iron frying pan on the stove.

How appropriate.

Quickly, she grabbed it.

Wasting no more time, she raised it above her head.

After only a brief hesitation, she slammed it as hard as she could on Milton's head.

Then she held her breath.

Watched.

Waited.

Milton froze.

A second later, his eyes closed, and he slumped to the floor.

Duke quickly grabbed the man's rifle, slid it across the floor out of reach.

The next moment, he grabbed his own gun.

He stared at Milton another moment before rising to his feet and turning toward Andi. "Are you okay?"

She nodded, even though she was a trembling mess. "Yes . . . I think so. You?"

"I'm fine."

They met in the middle and embraced each other. Duke never let his gaze off Milton—just to be certain.

That had been close.

Too close.

Andi pressed her eyes closed, her heart still racing madly out of control.

"Police! Hands in the air!" The front and side doors suddenly flew open at the same time.

Police flooded the house, led by Gibson.

He saw Milton on the floor and stepped over the man, putting his gun back into his holster.

"You guys okay?" he asked Duke and Andi as he cuffed the man.

Andi nodded, still not letting go of Duke.

As she glanced beyond the police, she saw the rest of the team emerge from the woods.

Ranger. Simmy. Mariella. Matthew.

They were all okay.

Then she saw someone else with them.

Was that . . . Heidi?

Andi blinked, uncertain.

But it was her!

The woman was okay!

Relief swept through her.

Maybe this nightmare was finally over.

Everything that unfolded over the next several hours was a blur—at least, it was to Andi.

Milton had awoken and been cleared by EMTs before he'd been taken to the station and was being questioned.

Heidi was picked up via helicopter to be taken to a hospital in Fairbanks and checked out. Her feet were frost-bitten, and her back had bruises and some lacerations. But otherwise, she seemed to be okay.

Gibson had interviewed Andi about her brief but

frightening ordeal. He'd allowed her to change back into her clothes, and they'd taken the dress as evidence.

The entire house had been searched.

Animal control had come to take possession of the dogs.

Five bodies had been found on the surrounding property.

The team was cleared to leave.

However, leaving wasn't nearly as easy as it sounded.

Instead of hiking out, someone on a UTV had to shuttle them back to Duke's SUV.

The whole time Andi kept reliving what it had been like inside that house. How she'd faced death.

Would Milton have killed her?

Or would he have let her go and let his dogs and nature do his dirty work?

Either way, the thought was horrifying. What had those other women gone through before they died? She didn't want to think about it.

At Duke's SUV, the team climbed in.

They caught up as they drove to Coldfoot.

There, the rest of the gang piled into Ranger's truck to head to the trading post for the evening.

Duke and Andi would ride together alone.

They hadn't discussed any details yet, but Andi guessed some of them would leave for Fairbanks in the morning.

She was just thankful to be alive.

The situation had made her realize how precarious life

could be. How death could be only one last breath away. How the situations she'd entangled herself in were dangerous and possibly even deadly.

As soon as she and Duke were alone, he pulled her into his arms again. Andi nestled her head against his chest, surprised by the comfort she found in him.

She didn't usually allow herself to depend on others.

But she was so thankful Duke had been there.

"Are you okay?" Duke murmured.

"I'm fine." She reached up and touched her hair. "Although I don't know how I'm going to explain this."

"You look good whatever hairstyle you have."

A grin feathered across her lips. She didn't believe his words, but the sentiment was sweet. "Thank you."

His gaze grew serious, and his voice deepened as he said, "I can only imagine what that must have been like. He didn't have you for long but . . ."

"Whatever happens, it's only going to make me stronger. There's no other option." Her throat tightened as she said the words. She meant them. She might get knocked down, but she wasn't going to stay there—not if she could help it.

Duke studied her a moment before grinning. "I like that mindset."

Andi shifted back in her seat and cleared her throat. "Duke, I don't want to dance around this anymore."

"Dance around what?"

"There was only evidence of five women being on the property. None of them were Celeste."

Not only did the locks of hair not match, but Milton had hung a photo over his mantel that he'd taken of himself with Heidi. When the police removed the picture, they'd discovered four other photos behind the current one—one with each woman he'd held captive.

His gaze clouded. "I know."

"I'm . . . I'm sorry."

He shrugged. "No need to be sorry. It's reality, and I need to face it. Celeste most likely wasn't a victim of this man. I think I already knew that, though I was in denial."

"What are you going to do?"

"The only thing I can do. Keep searching for answers. Keep living in this purgatory of sorts."

Andi nodded slowly, pushing a rough-cut lock behind her ear. "I understand."

Their gazes caught one more time until Andi looked away.

Too many thoughts raced through her mind.

Thoughts she didn't want to own up to.

Instead, she glanced out the window. "We should probably get to the trading post."

"Probably." He put his SUV into Drive. "I'm glad you're okay, Andi."

She smiled again. "Me too."

chapter
sixty-six

ANDI ENDED her phone call and slowly lowered her cell, still in shock.

She turned back to the rest of the group around her.

They were all staying at the Almost Halfway Trading Post tonight. It was too late to drive back to Fairbanks. They were too tired, and the police had more questions.

It was probably better this way since they still had things to discuss. Andi didn't like leaving matters unfinished.

"What's wrong?" Duke sat on a couch near the corner fireplace, watching her as he often did. Not in a creepy way. The man was just too observant for his own good sometimes.

The phone call still played on repeat in Andi's head. "I just called to say I would be late for work tomorrow. My boss told me not to come in, that I've been fired."

"What?" Simmy gasped, her hand covering her mouth. "Why would they fire you?"

Andi knew. This was Victor's doing.

But she didn't want to get into all of that right now.

"They said they're downsizing." She knew that was just an excuse, however.

As she stood there, Andi touched the back of her head.

She still missed her hair.

Mariella had trimmed it for her, giving Andi a wedge cut that was shorter in the back and longer in the front.

It looked better, but the missing hair was a sickening reminder of what had happened.

And Andi would rather forget.

Every time she closed her eyes, she was transported back in time. She could feel Milton holding her head on the counter. See the butcher knife being held over her. Feel the fear trembling through her body.

But perhaps remembering would keep her sharp.

"What will you do for work?" Matthew took a sip of the soda he was drinking.

Simmy had insisted on making them all dinner—chicken sandwiches, chips, and a salad. It was all she could pull together at the last minute. But it had been delicious.

"I have no idea. But I'll figure something out." Andi turned to Matthew. "But I might need your help."

He squinted. "Why is that?"

"Someone drained my bank account, so now I'm totally broke and without a job."

"What?" Mariella's voice rose. "When did you find that out?"

"A couple of days ago." Andi shrugged. "We had other more important matters to discuss at the time. But now that I'm out of a job . . ."

"I can definitely help," Matthew said. "I'll just need to get some information from you."

"Maybe we can talk tomorrow," Andi said.

"For sure." Matthew nodded, a new determined look in his gaze.

Andi let out the breath she'd been holding.

Victor would *not* defeat her.

She sat down in a lightly padded chair and stared at everyone around her.

Maybe a subject change should be in order . . .

"Well . . . we did it," Andi murmured. "We solved another case."

"And we could have died in the process," Duke pointed out with a knowing look.

"But we didn't," Mariella added with a touch of optimism as she sat upright in her seat with a perky expression.

"Because of our efforts, Heidi is now safe." Andi looked at each member of the group to drive home her point. "Hopefully, she'll be able to rebuild her life—though I'm not sure if that will be with or without her husband. He's out on bail, but he's a total mess."

"Life for both of them will probably never be the same," Simmy murmured.

"I'm sure the whole experience has changed her," Duke said. "She'll probably need some counseling on top of her medical help."

Mariella shifted. "The good news is that I heard we should be getting that reward money Heidi's family offered for anyone who found her."

"Does this mean we don't need Alpine's support?" Simmy glanced around, searching everyone's expression for answers.

Andi knew this subject would come up. She'd dreaded it since it caused so much tension in the past.

"We could do both." Mariella glanced at Andi, trying to read her expression. "Alpine agreed to the changes you suggested in the contract, Andi. Now that I know you were an attorney, I feel more confident that the modifications are for the best. So Alpine is still on board . . . if the rest of you are."

Slowly, everyone else agreed. Given Andi's current financial state, maybe this could be a win-win. The money might help her pay her bills until she could figure out something else.

"Good." Mariella nodded, a gleam of excitement in her gaze. "I'll let Alpine know. Now, about Keith Morrison . . ."

"I think if you want to do the interview, you should," Simmy said. "But if some people don't want to, there shouldn't be pressure."

Mariella nodded slowly. "Okay. If that's the case, then who's in?"

Only Matthew raised his hand.

Mariella nodded slowly again as if letting that settle. "Okay . . . I guess it's decided. I'll reply to the producer and let him know that only two of us are available. We'll see what he says, and we can take it from there."

Andi was thankful Mariella hadn't made more of an argument. She was also thankful Simmy was the one who'd brought the subject up.

She hadn't realized that even Simmy might not want people to know who she was or where she was.

"There's one thing I don't understand." Matthew turned toward them. "The whole briefcase thing. How did that tie in?"

"It appears Milton singled out his victims." Duke shifted, crossing an ankle over his knee as he leaned back. "He'd figure out where these women were going and then arrange a way to catch them alone—mostly due to popped tires on cars, thanks to the nails he threw down."

"And the briefcase?" Mariella continued.

"I think that was his sick way of getting their attention and letting them know what was ahead."

Andi raised her hand. "Actually, that's partially true. But I remembered something that also fits."

Everyone turned their attention on her.

"One of my neighbors back in Texas was elderly, and he loved watching *The Rosemary Cleaver Show*. I remembered checking on him one time when the show played in the background. In that episode, it was a flashback of how Rosemary met her husband. It all had to do with a briefcase the husband left on the side of the road. Rosemary found it and called after him. That was how they met."

"This guy was twisted . . . maybe the most twisted yet," Matthew murmured with a frown.

"The Ice Fairy Killer was pretty twisted too," Ranger reminded them with a knowing look.

Yes, he had been.

Both of those men were now off the streets.

That was something the Arctic Circle Murder Club should be proud of. They'd helped with those cases.

"What investigation is next?" Simmy looked around hopefully.

"That's an excellent question." Mariella reached into her bag and pulled out some papers. "I made a list of some potential cases. I thought we could all look them over and decide. Do we want to stay in this area? Go to other parts of Alaska? We should be able to travel now—on Alpine's dime."

She passed out the papers, and Andi quickly scanned the list.

This could be interesting . . .

What would they all choose? A murder in a coastal town? A man arrested for a triple homicide in Anchorage? The mysterious death of a local politician in Fairbanks?

All intriguing, for sure.

They talked a while longer until exhaustion seemed to kick in for each of them. One by one, they all said good night.

Until it was only Andi and Duke.

Since the car ride here, more things had popped into her mind.

More subjects she wanted to talk to Duke about.

She moved to the couch and sat beside him—with a comfortable space between them.

"I just wanted to say again . . . I'm sorry that you still don't have any resolution with Celeste." Her voice sounded soft as she said the words.

His grim expression told her everything she needed to know.

He was disappointed too. Maybe more than disappointed.

Maybe devastated.

"It looks like I still have some work to do before I have any of those answers," Duke said. "Maybe that *is* Celeste I've seen around town. Or maybe that woman is a lookalike playing mind games with me. It's hard to say."

Andi reached over and squeezed his hand before quickly withdrawing. "We'll keep searching."

Duke's gaze met hers, the haggardness captured in the depths of his eyes making her throat swell with compassion.

"Thank you," he muttered, his voice hoarse and raspy.

"I'm still not sure who was in my apartment," Andi continued. "It could have been one of Victor's guys."

"It could have been . . . or it could have something to do with the Celeste situation. Maybe more answers will come to light. Hopefully, without the danger next time."

But Andi heard the doubt in his voice.

He didn't think that would be the case any more than Andi did.

"I'm sorry about your job." Duke shifted on the couch, his voice dropping lower with empathy. "I could use you as a tour guide if you're interested. I know you're a safe driver and that you're smart and entertaining."

Intriguing idea.

Also a dangerous proposition.

Could Andi really work that closely with Duke and keep her feelings in check?

She wasn't sure.

"Thank you for the offer," Andi told him. "Can I think about it?"

"Of course." Duke shifted again, something clearly on his mind.

Why was she so drawn to this man? Why did she want more than anything to reach for him? To find comfort in his arms? To throw caution to the wind and press her lips into his?

All bad ideas.

"One last thing . . ." Duke's laser-like gaze met hers. "Back at Milton's house . . . you sounded surprised that I'd come for you."

Andi shrugged again, her cheeks heating. "I . . . I don't know what to say."

"You're a lawyer. You *always* know what to say."

She let out an airy chuckle. "I *was* an attorney. And . . . I guess what I mean is that I don't know the right thing to say."

"The right thing is the honest thing."

She rubbed her palms on her jeans as her thoughts

raced. "The honest thing is . . . I've felt alone for a long time. I keep myself busy so I don't have to think about it."

Duke's gaze locked with hers. "You're not alone, Andi. You have me. Friends stand beside each other through thick and thin."

"I wish that were always true." Nearly every friend Andi had ever let into her circle had let her down.

Maybe that was more a reflection of Andi than it was anyone else. She wasn't sure.

Duke leaned closer. "It will always be true with me."

Andi's cheeks heated again, and her gaze fluttered away before quickly wavering back to meet Duke's. "Thank you. I appreciate that. And I'll be there for you also. Whatever you need."

"I appreciate it."

Their gazes lingered on each other another several seconds.

Finally, Andi cleared her throat and stood.

Resist the devil, and he will flee from you.

Did the same thing work for temptation?

And why was she quoting Scripture now of all times?

"I guess we should hit the hay." She wished her voice didn't sound as strained as it did.

Duke rose also. "Probably a good idea."

For a moment, Andi's mind drifted back to their conversation with Charlotte. Even though her story had been fake, one of the things she'd said slammed back into Andi's mind.

You think it will never happen to you. But it can. And it might.

There were a lot of things in life that people thought they were immune from, that they thought only happened to others.

Losing relationships. Facing trauma. Dealing with false accusations. Rupturing faith.

Once a person realized they were susceptible to tragedy, then the doors seemed to fling wide open. If one tragedy could happen to them, anything could.

Then anxiety and apprehension kicked in.

Anxiety and apprehension that could control a person.

That wasn't the life Andi wanted to live.

She'd become cynical about so many things.

But maybe it was time for a change.

If tragedy could happen to her, then hope could also.

That was the cycle she wanted to be in.

She took a step away before pausing and glancing back at Duke. "Thanks for having my back."

His gaze, loaded with emotion, latched onto hers again. But he kept his distance. "Always."

For some reason, Andi believed him.

~~~

Thank you for reading **Never Happen to You**. If you enjoyed this book, please consider leaving a review.
~~~

Stay tuned for ***The Dead of Night***, coming next!

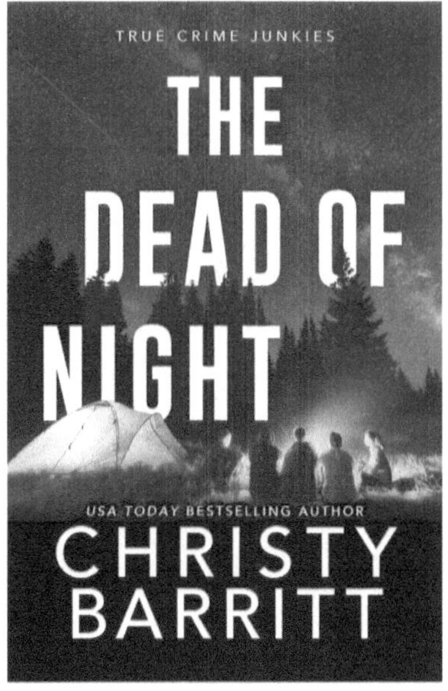

you also might enjoy: fog lake suspense

Edge of Peril

When evil descends like fog on a mountain community, no one feels safe. After hearing about a string of murders in a Smoky Mountain town, journalist Harper Jennings realizes a startling truth. She knows who may be responsible—the same person who tried to kill her three years ago. Now Harper must convince the cops to believe her before the killer strikes again. Sheriff Luke Wilder returned to his hometown, determined to keep the promise he made to his dying father. The sleepy tourist area with a tragic past hadn't seen a murder in decades—until now. Keeping the community safe seems impossible as darkness edges closer, threatening to consume everything in its path. As The Watcher grows desperate, Harper and Luke must work together in order to defeat him. But the peril around them escalates, making it clear the killer will stop at nothing to get what he wants.

Margin of Error

Some secrets have deadly consequences. Brynlee Parker thought her biggest challenge would be hiking to Dead Man's Bluff and fulfilling her dad's last wishes. She never thought she'd witness two men being viciously murdered while on a mountainous trail. Even worse, the deadly predator is now hunting her. Boone Wilder wants nothing to do with Dead Man's Bluff, not after his wife died there. But he can't seem to mind his own business when a mysterious out-of-towner burst into his camp store in a frenzied panic. Something—or someone—deadly is out there. The killer's hunger for blood seems to be growing at a brutal pace. Can Brynlee and Boone figure out who's behind these murders? Or will the hurts and secrets from their past not allow for even a margin of error?

Brink of Danger

Ansley Wilder has always lived life on the wild side, using thrills to numb the pain from her past and escape her mistakes. But a near-death experience two years ago changed everything. When another incident nearly claims her life, she turns her thrill-seeking ways into a fight for survival. Ryan Philips left Fog Lake to chase adventure far from home. Now he's returned as the new fire chief in town, but the slower paced life he seeks is nowhere to be found. Not only is a wildfire blazing out of control, but a malicious killer known as "The Woodsman" is enacting crimes that appear accidental. Plus, there seems to be a strange connection with these incidents and his best friend's little sister, Ansley Wilder. As a killer watches their every move and the forest fire threatens to destroy their scenic town, both Ryan and Ansley hover on the brink of danger. One wrong move could send them tumbling over the edge . . . permanently.

Line of Duty

Jaxon Wilder didn't plan on returning home to Fog Lake, Tennessee, following his tour of duty in Iraq. But after a gut-wrenching failure during his stint in the Army, he now faces a new challenge: his family. Abby Brennan always did her best to be the good girl and to live by the rules. When a wrong decision changes her entire life, she tries to hide from the world. However, a madman known as the Executioner is determined to find her and enact his own brand of justice. When Jaxon and Abby are thrown together in the killer's crosshairs, they're forced to depend on one another to survive. Will Jaxon's sense of duty be enough to help keep Abby safe? Or will deadly secrets lead to the penalty of death?

Legacy of Lies

The justice system failed her family—and so did her hometown. Madison Colson knows deep down that her father—a convicted serial killer—is innocent. But believing it and proving it are two entirely different things. Unable to help her father, Madison has spent most of her adult life overcompensating by helping others. When her aunt dies unexpectantly, duty calls her back to Fog Lake, Tennessee, a beautiful but painful place she'd rather forget. Terrifying events begin to unfold once she arrives, unleashing her worst nightmares. The Good Samaritan Killer—or a copycat—is back, and now Madison Colson is his target. FBI Special Agent Shane Townsend is determined to stop the deadly rampage that has sent the tightknit community into a frenzy. But he needs to earn Madison's trust first. The task feels impossible, especially considering his father is the one who put her dad in prison. With the whole town on edge and pointing fingers, tension escalates out of control. Madison and Shane must sort the facts from the lies—and fight for a legacy of truth—before The Good Samaritan Killer has the final say.

Secrets of Shame

A killer has a promise to keep . . . Attorney Isaac Colson only wants to put his tumultuous past in Fog Lake behind him and return to his life in Memphis. But when an ominous text threatens that he must come back or there will be deadly consequences, he knows he can't take any chances. Rebecca Moreno has only ever loved one man—her high school sweetheart, Isaac Colson. But when his dad went to prison for murder, Rebecca's father forbade them from seeing each other again. Years later, Isaac is back in town and old feelings are stirring. But Rebecca is harboring a secret that could change everything. When The Good Samaritan Killer strikes again, guilt pummels her. She has to tell Isaac the truth. But as events unfold, she has more to lose than ever. Isaac and Rebecca must find answers—their lives depend on it. But everyone seems to have secrets, each that forms an obstacle to finding the truth . . . and to staying alive.

Refuge of Redemption

Home is a place of refuge—unless it's a killer's playground. For years, Bear Colson has been known as the serial killer's son. But now, someone else is behind bars for the crimes his father was accused of committing. Bear wants to believe hope for a brighter future is in sight, but he has reason to suspect more than one killer was involved. Forensic photographer Piper Stephens' career crashed and burned when she trusted the wrong man. Now, after discovering an alarming secret about the infamous Good Samaritan Killer, she sets out to find both answers and redemption. But things go awry when her assistant becomes the next victim. As fear batters Fog Lake residents once again, Bear and Piper join forces to track down the truth. But the killer is determined to remain in the shadows—and he'll destroy anyone who stands in his way.

about the author

USA Today has called Christy Barritt's books "scary, funny, passionate, and quirky."

Christy writes both mystery and romantic suspense novels that are clean with underlying messages of faith. Her books have sold more than four million copies and have won the Daphne du Maurier Award for Excellence in Suspense and Mystery, have been twice nominated for the Romantic Times Reviewers' Choice Award, and have finaled for both a Carol Award and Foreword Magazine's Book of the Year.

She is married to her Prince Charming, a man who thinks she's hilarious—but only when she's not trying to be. Christy is a self-proclaimed klutz, an avid music lover who's known for spontaneously bursting into song, and a road trip aficionado.

When she's not working or spending time with her family, she enjoys singing, playing the guitar, and exploring small, unsuspecting towns where people have no idea how accident-prone she is.

Find Christy online at:
www.christybarritt.com
www.facebook.com/christybarritt
www.twitter.com/cbarritt

Sign up for Christy's newsletter to get information on all of her latest releases here: **www.christybarritt.com/ newsletter-sign-up/**

 facebook.com/AuthorChristyBarritt

 x.com/christybarritt

 instagram.com/cebarritt